To Norma
Best wish

CW01430224

Beyond Belief

Kath Radford (signature)

Kath Radford

"The story in this novel is fictional and does not depict any actual persons or events"

Published in 2009 by New Generation Publishing

First Edition

Prologue

It was a little after six in the morning when the doctor passed through the doors leading to the main body of the Intensive Care Unit. Unseen in the shadows of the inner doorway, he stopped to adjust his tie and smoothed down his neat tailored jacket. His face and demeanour had a quality that gave him an instant air of superiority. His nostrils flared at the layered stench of disinfectant smothered illness. It was as if the miasma of disease penetrated the pores of his skin and he knew the smell would stay with him for the rest of the day.

Taking a moment to savour the familiar surge of adrenalin, his carefully crafted mask of geniality slipped and he sneered. The Doctor wondered what the nurses would think if he let them in on his little secret. Concluding they would probably commend him for his courage, he stepped out of the gloom into the half-light. His silver-tongued voice belied the nervous energy he felt.

'Good morning ladies! I hope you are all well?' he said, cheerfully. He made his way over to the nurses' station, where he deposited his briefcase on the floor. Despite the early hour, the buzz of electronics and ping of alarms coexisted uneasily with the hiss of medical gasses and wheeze of ventilators. A shrill voice sliced through the high-tech clamour.

'Good morning doctor.' Maureen Dent wore a tight bun perched on the top of her head. The sweeping hairstyle accentuated her sharp roman nose giving her an air of snobbishness. Others marvelled at Maureen's ability to remain immaculate, no matter how traumatic the shift. She joined the doctor at the desk and began to relate the latest gossip. Although he maintained his outward face of civility, the doctor didn't listen. Instead, he marvelled at his ability to tolerate a woman who was so obviously his inferior. In fact, he could think of no one that could match him on an intellectual level. In a way, he thought, it was a pity that he was forced to keep up this charade. On the other hand, the challenge of deceit had turned into a game; a game he was very good at.

Eventually he brought the conversation to an abrupt close and left the night sister at the desk to make his way round the unit, where he reviewed the patient charts and made an occasional change to treatment. It was a tedious, but necessary gesture to maintain the subterfuge. After returning to the desk to retrieve his briefcase, he made his way over toward the side-ward. Maureen's high-pitched voice haunted him.

'I'm sure Frank's charts are up to date, if you wanted to get away,' she said.

He ignored her and carried on towards his ultimate destination. Although his pace remained steady, his heart raced and he had to force himself to breathe more slowly.

On entering the room, he was greeted by the soporific shush-thump of the ventilator. The sound reverberated around the walls and reached his ears at the same time as he inhaled the smell of impending death. His nostrils twitched with revulsion. He drew the faded curtains across the large observation windows before turning to examine the small room. The adjustable overhead lights had been switched off, leaving a series of floor level night-lights to radiate an eerie hue across the walls. The only other source of light was an angle-poise lamp, which cast a large yellow triangle over a laminated chart-board. A gold St Christopher pendant dangled from one corner. It glinted as it slowly rotated in the air conditioning. The large sheet of paper, which had been clipped to the board, neatly charted the ebb tide of Frank Hoyle's life.

The doctor put his briefcase on the bedside table and then, for the first time since entering the room, turned to study the man that lay on the bed. A nebulous glow from the angle-poise highlighted Frank Hoyle's head and upper torso. The jaundiced beam cast a sombre shadow over the gaunt, skull-shaped features that showed all the ravages of septicaemia. Silver tufts of cotton wool hair stood erect against the grey white of the pillow. Half closed, unseeing eyes stared into oblivion. Fingered ribs rose and fell to the syncopated beat of the ventilator. He averted his gaze and simultaneously flicked both catches of the briefcase with his thumbs. He eased open the case, rested his hands on the lid and pondered on what had brought him to this point.

He recalled his first subject had been an old woman, but could not remember her name. She had been dying for weeks, her body disintegrating. Her family refused to let him stop treatment, but it had never been their decision to make. He found the act unsurprisingly easy and the effect it had on him unbelievable. It had brought to the surface a force that he had always suspected was within.

A flash of gold from the spinning St Christopher startled him from his reverie. He crossed over to the workstation and removed a pair of latex examination gloves from a box on the shelf. The thin rubber clung to his skin and slapped against his wrists when he released it. After deactivating all the alarms, he returned to the table and removed a pre-filled syringe from an elasticated pocket at the back of his case. He attached a needle and then, out of habit, held the deadly fluid up to the light. His hands trembled imperceptibly as he flicked at the hard plastic casing to remove any air bubbles. Realising the absurdity of his action, he grunted and then made his way over to the head of the bed. Bending over, he whispered into Frank Hoyle's ear.

'I'm doing you a favour old man.'

He rested the syringe on the top of the ventilator, stretched his back and watched the rhythmic rise-and-fall of the silver-haired chest. He interlaced his fingers, cracked his knuckles and flexed his wrists in an attempt to relax the muscles.

The sound of a crash brought him to his senses. Realising he was taking too long, he picked up the syringe, grasped the infusion tubing, punched the needle into the injection port and squeezed the plunger. The syringe gave up the lethal juice reluctantly and he needed both thumbs to force it in. He watched as the viscous fluid trickled down the clear plastic tubing and visualised it mixing with the blood. He followed the deadly concoction's journey as it crept through the circulation towards the heart. There was no connection. No empathy. No emotion, only a spark of power. Light glistened off his adrenaline-beaded forehead; his palms sticky with sweat. He allowed himself a moment to indulge in the feelings of omnipotence and ran his tongue over his top lip, savouring the tang of salt.

After withdrawing the needle, he returned to the workstation and threw the empty syringe into the sharps box. He depressed the foot pedal of the flip-top bin with his highly polished Oxfords. The latex gloves clung to his damp skin and thwacked against the metallic lid with a resounding ping. Annoyed because it was taking so long, he screwed the gloves into a ball and threw them, with force, in with the detritus of care.

After reactivating the alarms, he made one final check of the room, before crossing over to the chart-board. He unravelled the St Christopher from the bulldog clip and twisted the chain round his fingers. Returning to his briefcase, he dangled the pendant over the pocket and watched it rotate. It hadn't brought its owner much luck, he thought as he dropped the medallion into the pocket vacated by the syringe. Lowering the lid, he snapped shut the locks and left without a second glance.

Chapter One

Despite having worked in Intensive Care for many years, the senior sister still struggled to find the right words of comfort. Theatre scrubs hung loose over her slender frame as she knelt before the two elderly ladies. They sat on a sofa that had seen better days.

'I am so sorry,' said Paula Hobson. She gently squeezed Ethel Hoyle's hand. There was nothing striking about the sister's looks, but there was a kindness in her pale blue eyes that warmed the recipient to her compassion. If there was one thing Paula had learnt in her long career, was that it was preferable to say nothing, rather than stumble on with inane platitudes. She glanced up to the grime-encrusted windows where the tepid early-morning winter sun seemed to reflect her lacklustre mood. She allowed her eyes to wander round the shabby Visitors' Room. Tendrils of floral wallpaper dangled from the walls, picked and torn by anxious fingers. A small battered television rested on top of a disused treatment trolley. The TV had been padlocked to the radiator. Its remote control long since lost, the control panel door hung on one hinge. A series of watercolours were reflected in the window. They depicted the Lake District and had been purchased by a grateful relative in an attempt to give a sense of peace and escapism to the room. Paula could see that one of the pictures hung lopsided. She made a mental note to straighten it then immediately forgot.

The cup-laden, ring-stained coffee table gave evidence of a weary vigil. Ethel Hoyle looked frail and dishevelled following a sleepless night. She plucked at a handful of tear-soaked tissues and smiled weakly at the nurse.

'I promised to show you a picture of our Frank,' she said, retrieving her handbag from the floor. Ethel produced an old sepia photograph and smoothed out the creases before handing it over. Her voice was hoarse from crying.

'That was taken on our wedding day,' she said.

Along with the photo, Paula removed a lump of soggy

tissues from the arthritic fingers. She added the tissues to a growing pile in the bin, before turning her attention to the picture, which showed a young couple standing on the steps of an impressive stone-clad building. The young man, forage cap neatly tucked into his epaulette, proudly displayed three stripes on his right forearm. Next to him, pillbox hat on bobbed hair, the pretty girl clutched a small posy of flowers.

Paula automatically stretched out behind her for the box of paper hankies, which were a permanent fixture on the coffee table. One of her anti-static clogs slipped and she grabbed hold of the arm of the sofa. Her finger slipped into a brown-edged cigarette burn that looked as if it had been made by a giant grub. She sighed heavily and made a mental note to check if there was enough money in the charity fund for refurbishment. There was a muffled tap on the door.

'Come in,' she said, raising her voice. Paula turned as the young student popped her head round the door.

'I'm sorry to bother you, Sister.' said Celia Young

'That's okay.'

'Sister Coleman told me to tell you they're ready,' said Celia. 'And Mr Edmonds has been on the phone. He asked me to remind you about the away meeting at eleven.'

Paula's deputy, Nancy Coleman had been overseeing the preparation of Frank Hoyle's body for viewing. Charles Edmonds was their in-line manager who also ran the Operating Theatre Department, which was situated opposite the ICU. Paula thanked the student and then returned her attention to the photograph. Celia quietly closed the door as she left.

'You make a lovely couple,' said Paula, handing the photo back to its owner.

Ethel's face crumbled. 'He used to say we were two sides of the same coin,' she sobbed. 'I don't know what I'm going to do without him.' She took hold of Paula's hand. 'I could never have got through these weeks without your help.'

Paula flushed with embarrassment.

'Can I ask you something?' said Ethel.

'Of course you can.'

The old woman tightened her grip on Paula's fingers. 'I know the doctor said you couldn't do any more for Frank and they wanted to stop his antibiotics and things-' she hesitated. '-but he did say - the doctor - he did say that you wouldn't do anything, didn't he?'

Paula frowned.

'Did they do something to him?'

'I don't understand.'

'Last night, did they do something to Frank?' Ethel said, in desperation. 'Stop his drugs or something?'

Paula looked aghast. 'N-no of course not,' she stuttered. Her knees ached. She shuffled uncomfortably. 'We would never do anything like that. What on earth makes you say such a thing?'

'That sister wouldn't let me sit with him,' Ethel's voice was tinged with anger. We were stuck in here all night - when - when I should have been with Frank.'

'I know and I'm sorry,' said Paula, with genuine sympathy. 'Sister Dent asked me to apologise on her behalf.' Maureen had said no such thing, but Paula felt Ethel deserved the apology. The floor was becoming increasingly uncomfortable and the sister was beginning to worry about the passage of time. She eased her hand from under Ethel's and sat back on her heels.

'Why was it so sudden?' said Ethel's friend Betty, speaking for the first time. 'He's been ill for weeks.'

Paula gave a brief explanation of how pneumonia could lead to multi-organ failure and sudden cardiac arrest. She ended with, 'the only comfort I can offer is that as soon as the nurse realised what was happening, she held his hand.' That wasn't a lie. 'We didn't know Frank, but from what you have told us, he was a kind and loving man.' Paula held out her hand. 'It's time to say goodbye.'

The nurses fell silent as the senior sister ushered the two women across the cavernous room. A smattering of natural light seeped through a series of long narrow windows, which traversed the top of one wall. Streaks of sunlight shimmered off the specially treated gunmetal wall-covering.

The trio entered Frank's room together. Paula eased the door closed behind them. Most of the equipment had been removed, curtains drawn and overhead lights dimmed. Now devoid of precious life signals, the blank-screened monitor faced the wall. The chart-board had been taken away and the angle-poise lamp cast its yellow beam over a carefully positioned spray of dried flowers and a bible, resting on the bedside table.

In the peaceful stillness that is death, Frank Hoyle's cold, mottled body lay between pristine starched-white sheets. Ethel slumped into a chair at the bedside. Betty stood beside her. Paula rested a supportive hand on the widow's shoulder and gently laid Frank's limp hand in Ethel's open palm before leaving the room.

Chapter Two

On returning from escorting the women as far as the hospital foyer, Paula re-entered the unit and glanced up to the clock on the wall. She had done none of the planned admin work and her spirit sank when she realised the time. She joined Nancy at the nurses' station. Her deputy was flicking through the patients records. Four years younger than her boss, in contrast to Paula's naturally fair colouring, titian tints streaked Nancy's spiky hairstyle. Her doubly pierced ears and matching bellybutton stud, along with a little devil tattoo on her right buttock, gave credence to Nancy's reputation as a proponent of the work-hard, play-hard principle. Taking the adjacent swivel chair, Paula ran her fingers through her permanently tousled hair.

'I always feel guilty when the relatives thank me,' she said. Her eyes automatically scanned the central monitor, which nestled in the elbow of the L-shaped desk. The large TV screen reflected the output of the bedside monitors. 'I always feel as though we've failed them somehow.'

'If you're talking about Frank, he never stood a chance,' said Nancy, pushing the files to one side. 'When he was admitted the poor bugger was practically moribund.' She crossed her arms and leant back against the chair. 'You know sometimes I think we can be a little gung ho with some of these old wrinklies.'

'We have to give them a chance.'

'Oh come on. You didn't really think we were going to get anywhere with him, did you?'

'Maybe not, but that doesn't mean to say we shouldn't have tried. How would you feel if it was your dad?'

'I don't think I'd want him to go through all that.'

'I have a feeling Ethel thinks we-'

'What?'

'-let him go,' said Paula. 'In fact she might even think we gave him a push.'

'Why on earth would she think that?'

'Because we wanted to stop treatment, but then promised to leave things until today.' Paula removed a blue bound diary from the cluttered top drawer of the desk and made a note to ring Ethel Hoyle after a couple of weeks to check on her.

'It's not our fault he gave up before we did,' said Nancy.

'That doesn't make her feel any better.'

Nancy muttered something unintelligible and returned her attention to the file. Paula returned the diary to the drawer, popped the pen in her breast pocket and leant back to survey the room.

The open-plan ward had been nicknamed 'The Garage' because of its resemblance to a car maintenance workshop, except that it was broken bodies rather than motor vehicles which occupied the three bays in the main area. Two single side wards, one of which still held the body that awaited relocation to the morgue, made up the complement of five beds. The remaining patients were attached, via lengthy corrugated plastic tubing, to individually-tuned ventilators. A cornucopia of wires and drips snaked over bed covers, coupling the patients to innumerable infusion pumps and syringe drivers that delivered their life-giving drugs and fluids. Horizontal tramlines ran along the walls. They supported the piped oxygen, air and suction. Pings, buzzes and the hiss of gas accompanied the chatter of care, as the nurses bustled around their charges like nurturing mothers. Paula stretched her arms above her head.

'You know that's the second time this month I've come on duty first thing and had a death to deal with before I've even woken up properly.'

'Me to-'

'Sorry.'

'Last week - same time - same place.'

'Really,' said Paula, running her fingers through her hair again in an effort to tame it. 'Don't you think that's a bit odd?'

'What,' Nancy said, laughing. 'Do you think the Bat's been knocking them off?' She had nicknamed Maureen the Bat and wasn't shy of using it.

11

'No of course not,' said Paula. 'I'm just saying it's a bit unusual. That's all.'

Nancy gave up on the report she'd been reading and placed it on the top of the pile. 'Don't you start getting into old Dunc's conspiracy theories,' she said, referring to Paula's long-time boyfriend. 'Anyway, the guy that died on me was a new admission, so he can't count.' She yawned and stretched. 'So, oh great leader, what are you up to today?'

'If I get back from this bloody management "away meeting",' said Paula, making quotation marks with her fingers. 'I'm going to make a start on the audit. I had hoped to do it this morning, but there isn't time now.' She swivelled her chair to face Nancy. 'Actually friend – pal - colleague, you could do me a favour.'

'Oh, yeah,' said Nancy, looking at her suspiciously. 'I'm not going to the meeting for you if that's what you think.' She kicked the foot-plate of the chair and began to spin herself around.

'No, but you could bleep me with an excuse to get out of it.'

'Yeah, right -'

'I'd do it for you.'

'No you wouldn't.'

'Oh come on. At this rate I'm never going to get the audit finished,' said Paula. 'I'll end up having to take it home.'

Nancy was beginning to feel dizzy; she grabbed the edge of the desk to stop the chair from spinning. 'I thought Duncan didn't approve of you taking work home,' she said.

Paula's eyes glazed over as she thought of her partner and recalled their first meeting. It was three years since Duncan Harvey had literally dived into her life. Having decided that she needed something new in her life, she had joined the local scuba-diving club. She fell in love with the beauty and ultimate relaxation of the underwater world. A world so far removed from the rapid pace and trauma of ICU. A world which phones and pagers could not penetrate; a world of tranquillity, where stresses evaporated and problems could be put into perspective. Nothing could be rushed; every slow, smooth movement had dissipated her tension and forced her to relax. She could almost feel herself sitting on the sandy floor of some ocean, watching her exhaled air gently gurgle through the water, like a multitude of balloons floating toward the heavens. She had fallen, just as quickly, for her dive buddy and for a while everything had been more than great. More recently, however they had begun to row over her work. Nancy's voice cut into her thoughts.

'Do you fancy coming to Busters tonight?'

'No thanks it isn't really Duncan's cup of tea.' said Paula. A headache threatened. She pinched the bridge of her nose.

'Who asked Duncan?' said Nancy.

Paula, thinking she'd seen some anomaly on the monitor, leant forward to get a better look. 'No thanks,' she said, as she ran off an electrocardiograph strip from bed three.

'I know something's up with you two,' Nancy said.

Paula didn't reply.

'You can be so irritating sometimes,' said Nancy. 'I wish you'd talk to me.'

Paula continued to focus on the strip of paper. 'I am talking to you,' she said.

'You know what I mean.'

'I'm not going to play gooseberry to you and -' Paula couldn't remember the name of her friend's latest conquest. 'Trevor,' she said, more in hope than knowledge.

'Trevor,' said Nancy. 'I haven't seen him for months.' She twisted her chair and kicked at Paula's clogs. 'I'm going out with the girls tonight and it would do you good to get drunk. Show them that you're a human being. Instead of this -' she struggled to find the right word, 'this little Miss - super-nurse.'

Paula screwed up the paper and threw it into the bin. She stretched out her arm. Nancy, thinking she was about to receive a clip round the ear, ducked. Instead, Paula grabbed the chair and spun it round.

'Less of the cheek, buggerlugs,' she said, with a sly grin. 'I suppose you'll be going to the football on Saturday.'

'Nope, some of us don't get every weekend off to watch their boyfriend play rugger just because they're the boss.' Nancy said, giving a posh accent to the word rugger.

'I do my share of weekends,' said Paula. 'And

anyway, remind me, who does the rota?'

'Okay, I do – but -' said Nancy. The two friends were about to launch into an ongoing debate on the merits of the testosterone-filled games when Paula's bleep interrupted them.

Chapter Three

The away meeting had been as tedious as anticipated. Frank and Ethel Hoyle were now a distant memory as Paula struggled to find space for her Volkswagen Polo in the overcrowded car park. She eventually managed to squeeze the car in-between a BMW and an oversized Mercedes. Taking a moment to catch her breath, her eyes settled on the distant hills, whose proximity to the market town had been a significant factor in her decision to settle in Lyedale.

Her gaze drifted back to the hospital. It ascended out of the sprawling red brick terraces, like a giant concrete pillbox out of a field of rusted clay. She stared at the drab multi-windowed façade behind which extremes of life and death were being played out in a microcosm of society. Paula had been unable to throw off the feeling of unease that had settled in the pit of her stomach. She sighed, ran her fingers through her hair and muttered to herself. 'Oh get a grip, woman.' Having retrieved her handbag from the passenger foot-well, it took a feat of elasticity for her to squeeze her slender frame out of the car and through the narrow gap between the vehicles.

By comparison, if the ICU's visitors' room had been drab, then the staff rest-room was positively wishy-washy. Even though smoking had been banned several years earlier, the pale cream walls oozed a fluorescent nicotine glow. Scratched Formica-topped coffee tables had been interspersed with tan-coloured leatherette chairs, many of which were either torn or had lost webbing or both.

Paula deposited the two mugs of tea she's just made on the nearest table and plonked herself down onto one of the chairs. She threw one packet of sandwiches she'd just bought at the hospital shop into the concave cushion of the adjacent seat and draped her leg over the uncomfortable wooden arm. Before long, she was joined by Nancy and the young student. Nancy moved Paula's legs out of the way, retrieved her sandwich and sat next to her boss. She replaced the mug of tea on the table with her clogged feet.

Paula kicked at them. 'How many times do I have to tell you not to put your clogs on the table?'

Nancy muttered under her breath. 'Yes, Mother.' She let the clogs slip to the floor and returned her socked feet to the table.

'Did I tell you its dad's birthday on Sunday?' she said, to no one in particular. 'My mum's bought a saddle of venison.'

'Do you have to pluck it?' said Celia.

'What?'

'Venison, I've never had any.'

Nancy gulped down a mouthful of tea. The student looked from one sister to the other and back again.

A deep flush spread across Celia's cheeks. 'What,' she said. 'What did I say?'

Before anyone replied, a resonating high-pitched bleep commanded and received instant attention. There was a general shuffling of bodies as several of the room's occupants checked their pockets. The noise was found to emanating from the cardiac arrest bleep clipped to Nancy's waistband. She removed it and raised it for all to hear. A disembodied voice crackled out of the thin black-plastic casing.

'RTA Accident and Emergency - Road Traffic Accident - Trauma Team please respond.'

The switchboard operator repeated the message several times. Nancy jumped up and tried to stuff the sandwich back into its packet at the same time as slipping her feet into her clogs. One of the shoes escaped under the low-set table. 'Oh bugger.'

Paula pushed the table away with her foot, allowing Nancy to retrieve the offending article.

'I'll come with you,' said Paula, standing. She suggested Celia should join them and then added with a mischievous smile. 'And if you behave yourself, I'll tell you how to pluck a deer.'

Nancy took vanguard as they sprinted past the operating theatre and two surgical wards to reach the stairwell. They quickly covered the two flights of stairs to emerge onto the ground floor. The Accident and Emergency department was situated halfway along the main corridor. The trio took the sharp left and burst through the doors. They were met by a melee of body-laden trolleys and walking wounded, several of which looked as though they were dressed in their Sunday best. The two sisters stopped, but the student failed to pull up in time and careered into the casualty sister, who had just come rushing out of a store cupboard. Paula grabbed Celia's arm and pulled her out of the way. She told the student to stay close and then turned to face the flustered casualty sister.

'You called.'

Lisa Gower fell in beside the ICU nurses as they threaded their way through the chaos. 'Thanks for coming,' she said.

'That's okay,' said Paula. 'I'd finished my lunch.'

'I hadn't,' Nancy grumbled.

'We've got a really nasty accident,' said Lisa. She took a deep breath and puffed out her cheeks, before letting go of the air. 'It was a four car pile-up, two people died at the scene and we've admitted five. Of those, three are walking wounded. The other two are in resus. We'd be able to manage normally, but we were already struggling with the fallout from a punch-up at a wedding.'

The comment gave rise to raised eyebrows and although Nancy and Paula were curious for more details, they knew it wasn't the time to ask, especially as they had just reached the resuscitation room.

The two accident patients were laid on gurneys at opposing ends of the three bayed room. Someone had pulled back the curtains of the middle bay and removed the trolley to maximize work space. Lisa handed over the drugs she was carrying to one of the doctors. She grabbed a box of latex gloves from a nearby shelf and yanked out a couple for herself before handing them round. At the same time, she gave the ICU sisters a rundown of the patients' injuries, starting with the middle-aged woman at the far end of the room. Despite an injection of morphine, the injured woman was screaming in pain. Lowering her voice, Lisa concluded, 'She doesn't know her husband's died so watch what you say in front of her.' The others nodded sympathetically and Nancy made her way over to where the casualty nurse was struggling with the woman's

17

clothes.

'This young man,' Lisa said, pointing to the boy lying on a blood-splattered gurney in front of them, 'has a nasty head injury. It's bleeding like buggery and someone's going to end up in a right mess.' She looked at Paula and smiled. Paula grimaced. 'Anyway, he's definitely a candidate for "the garage".'

Paula nodded and listened carefully.

'The paramedic said his Glasgow Coma Scale was fluctuating between three and four,' said Lisa, 'he's been unrousable since admission.'

As Paula listened, she observed the trauma team at work. It was like watching some intricate dance with every individual intimately aware of their purpose as they glided efficiently through one task to another, without impeding their colleagues.

'They think he might have a ruptured spleen and several broken ribs,' said Lisa. 'The CT scanner is on standby and we are waiting for a surgeon and the radiographer. Apparently he's held up in theatre, as are all the anaesthetists.'

'Oh great,' Paula sighed. 'That's all I need.'

Lisa joined Nancy. Paula pulled on her rubber gloves and gestured for Celia to follow. They made their way to the top of the gurney where the paramedic was administering oxygen to the boy. Blood and glass were strewn across the trolley and floor. Paula could feel a shard sticking to her clog. At least, that's what she hoped it was. One nurse was cutting through the boy's blood-soaked, tissue-matted shirt. Another assisted the doctor who was attempting to insert a drip. Before attaching the infusion he took a sample of blood which was rushed off to be cross-matched for a transfusion. Once the drip was secured, they swapped sides and repeated the process on the boy's other arm. As soon as the nurse had finished removing the tattered clothes, she attached heart electrodes to his exposed waxen torso. Raised weals had already begun to appear on his hairless chest and abdomen. She fitted a blood pressure cuff to his arm and an oxygen probe to his finger before turning on the monitors, which immediately began to alarm.

Paula checked the equipment she needed before taking

over from the paramedic, who seemed eager to give up his charge. She swapped the clumsy Ambu-bag for an anaesthetic circuit and turned the oxygen flow-meter to full. Hands fully extended, she hooked her little fingers under the angle of his jaw, clamped the black rubber mask firmly over the boy's nose and mouth and began to gently squeeze the gas-filled bag.

Blood clots knotted his blond hair. There was a thick wad of dressing stuck to the side of his head. She eased it back to see a five inch gash, beginning at his temple and tracking backward over the top of his ear. Fresh blood began to ooze from the wound. It trickled down his ear and behind the splint that was supporting his neck. The blood gathered in a pool on the sheet. Paula pulled a face and replaced the dressing.

His breathing was erratic and she tried to increase the air-entry by squeezing the rubber bag at the same time as he took in a shallow breath, but his lungs felt stiff. She briefly eased the mask away from his face. The swelling had already masked his features and there was a distinct, worrying blue tinge to his lips. She could feel tension creeping into her muscles.

A female voice loudly announced, 'His oxygen saturation is seventy-three and dropping; blood pressure is eighty-over-forty; heart rate one hundred and twenty and he is in a sinus tachycardia.'

Paula felt her stomach muscles contract. She turned to the registrar, who was in the middle of inserting yet another wide-bore cannula into a vein. 'John, he needs intubating,' she said. 'And there isn't any sign of an anaesthetist.'

The doctor glanced up to the monitor and then to Paula. 'Are you okay to do it?' he said.

She'd been trained to insert the breathing tubes and it wouldn't be the first time she'd stood in for the anaesthetist when he'd been stuck in theatre. But usually, the patients were much older and had suffered from a cardiac arrest. This was very different.

'Do I have any choice?' she said.

'No not really.'

She lifted the mask from his face. The boy looked so young, no more than seventeen. Paula inhaled deeply and called on a greater being to give her strength. Sadly, all that happened was that the knot in her stomach became even tighter. She clamped the mask firmly over his nose and mouth.

'Oxygen saturation - sixty-eight and still dropping; blood pressure sixty-five-over-forty-five and still dropping; heart rate one hundred and dropping.'

'I'll give him a relaxant to help you get the tube in,' said John. He nodded to the casualty nurse who rushed off to fetch the drugs. The A&E doctor looked Paula squarely in the eye. 'You know we haven't ruled out a neck injury,' he said. 'So I don't need to tell you to be careful.'

'No pressure then,' she muttered. Celia handed her the stainless-steel laryngoscope along with the plastic breathing tube. She laid them on the bed next to his blood-soaked ear and wiggled her shoulders in an attempt to ease the spasm.

'Sats are sixty-five; pulse seventy-two; we're still on a downward trend.'

'Okay, okay I get the message,' she muttered to herself. She carefully removed the neck splint while the doctor injected the drug, which would paralyse the boy's muscles and prevent him from breathing. It would make it easier for her to insert the tube. The immediate effect however, was that it sent Paula's pulse spiralling upward. She knew that they didn't have long before - Paula tried not to dwell on the thought.

Working quickly, she removed the airway and opened his mouth as wide as she dare. She held the laryngoscope in her left hand and slid the cold curved blade along the side of his tongue, easing it out of the way. Blood and spit had congregated at the back of his throat and she cleared it away with a suction catheter. The sound reminded her of the dentist. She still couldn't visualise the larynx, but dared not extend his neck any further in case she damaged his spinal cord. Sweat misted her eyes and she bent her head to rub them on the sleeve of her scrubs. It didn't work. She had to blink several times to clear them.

'Sats - fifty-eight; blood pressure sixty-over-forty; pulse sixty, he's in a bradycardia.' The voice strained with tension.

'Shit.'

'Are you okay?'

She was aware that everyone was watching her and

could sense the collective holding of breath. The effort of keeping her wrist flexed and the laryngoscope still sent searing pains up her arm. She gritted her teeth. Paula realised that if she squinted, she could just make out the rim of his larynx.

'He's going to go to arrest.'

Chapter Four

She only had one chance. If she missed the larynx and the tube entered the boy's stomach, he would certainly die. Paula could feel the eyes watching her every move. Her teeth were clenched so tightly, she could feel the pulse pounding in her temples. She'd stopped breathing. Her neck tingled with sweat. 'Hang in there kid,' she groaned.

She angled the opaque tube to line up with the opening of the larynx. Slowly and smoothly, she guided it passed the uvula, through the vocal chords and into the main bronchus. Certain that she was in the right place, she slipped the steel blade out of his mouth and levered it on the bed to snap it shut. She attached the breathing circuit to the blue connector and squeezed pure oxygen directly into his lungs. As the gas was forced into his airways, Paula sucked in a breath of her own. She stood straight and stretched her back. The procedure had only taken moments, but it felt like a lifetime. Everyone's attention switched from her to the monitor. For several heart-rending seconds nothing happened, and then:

'Oxygen saturation eighty-eight and rising; pulse ninety-five; blood pressure eighty-nine-over-fifty - and rising.' The tension in the room began to subside, but Paula knew that he wasn't out of the woods. She felt sick and closed her eyes until it passed off. The surgeon arrived and made quick work of inserting a drain to release blood that had collected in the lining of the damaged lung, which brought about an even bigger improvement in the boy's condition. Eventually, Vincent's vital signs were stable enough to transfer him to the operating theatre. It was at that point they were joined by a rather breathless Asian anaesthetist. A creased white coat covered his theatre scrubs. Ravinda Kumar clutched at the stethoscope round his neck to stop it bouncing as he made a beeline to join Paula.

'I came as soon as I could,' said Ravi. He automatically took over the hand ventilation. 'I'm so sorry, Sister.'

The Senior Anaesthetic Registrar was well respected by his colleagues and one of Paula's favourite doctors. She took the opportunity to relieve herself of the heavy lead apron she'd worn while the x-rays were being taken and then gave Ravi a quick rundown of events before making her way over to the sink to get cleaned up. The room looked as though a tornado had passed through it twice and then come back for more. Debris of resuscitation littered every available surface. Fragments of shattered glass glittered like diamonds in the electric lighting. Blood-sticky footprints made spiralling patterns across the floor. Paula grasped the cuff of one of her soiled gloves and peeled it from her fingers, turning it inside out in the process. She repeated the exercise with the other hand before throwing them into the clinical waste. She looked up to see Nancy coming back into the room, having returned from escorting her patient to theatre.

'Did you miss me?' said Nancy.

'Me,' said Paula, scrubbing her hands under the running tap. She looked round before saying, 'no.'

'I've been talking to a very nice policeman.'

'Trust you to suss out the talent,' Paula tutted.

'Excuse me, Sister,' said Nancy. 'For your information, I was obtaining the details of your patient. Although I do admit, I wouldn't mind getting to know Sergeant Palmer a little better.'

'I don't know how you find the time.'

'Practice,' Nancy said, grinning.

'You're incorrigible.'

The deputy crossed over to the middle of the room so that everyone could hear. She proceeded to pull a scrap of crumpled paper from her back pocket, raised her knee and smoothed out the creases. Pointing to the gurney in front of her, she said. 'His name is Vincent Stevens and he is seventeen years old.' She turned the paper over and then back again before continuing. 'He was in a BMW- the cops think it was a TWOC.'

Ravi had been in the process of sounding the patient's chest. He unhooked the earpieces of the stethoscope from his ears and interrupted Nancy. 'Excuse me - what is a TWOC?' he said.

'Taken With-out Consent,' was the chorused reply. None the wiser, the moustachioed doctor frowned.

'It means he nicked it,' explained Nancy and then continued with her narrative. 'Apparently, the car had flipped onto its roof. Young Vincent here had to be cut out of it, but his mate wasn't so lucky. He'd not been wearing a seat belt and went through the windscreen. Not a pretty sight by all accounts.' She turned the paper sideways and referred to a scribbled note down the margin. 'If anybody's interested, the second car was driven by a Mr Jordon, he's the other fatality. It's his wife I've just taken to theatre. She's okay, by the way, and when they've finished patching her up she is going to orthopaedics.'

'Did you find out how it happened?' said Paula.

'Of course,' said Nancy, smugly. 'Apparently Mr and Mrs Jordon were driving along the dual carriageway heading into town. As they neared the junction, the BMW tried to overtake, lost control and crashed into the driver's side of their car.' She shifted her weight from one foot to the other, as if she had cramp. 'Mr Jordon was dead by the time they got him into the ambulance,' she said, twisting her legs. 'There were quite a few walking wounded from other cars that shunted into each other.'

Paula had finished washing her hands and was drying them on a paper towel. 'I wish you'd stand still,' she said. 'You're making me dizzy.' Nancy shrugged, folded the paper and returned it to her back pocket.

'Our little bluebottle friends are under the impression that young Michael Schumacher here was driving the BMW. They are very keen to talk to him,' she said, nodding towards Vincent. 'So, how's he doing?'

'I think it'll be a while before he's up to answering any questions,' said Paula, throwing the wet towel on top of her gloves. 'That's always providing he hasn't scrambled his brains in the process.'

'Did I mention his parents are on their way?' said Nancy.

'No,' Paula looked at her legs and sighed. Blood had dripped from the trolley, soaking the thin cotton of her trousers. She tried to ease the sticky fabric from her thighs, but as soon as she let go the material clung back on to her skin.

'I can't take you anywhere,' said Nancy. Paula screwed up her nose and looked over to Ravi. She sensed the mild-mannered anaesthetist wasn't always sure if their banter was serious or not.

'Is it all right if we leave you to it, Ravi?' she said, tugging at her trousers. 'I need to get out of these things before I meet his family.' Now the emergency was over and it had gone well, Paula was beginning to feel positively light-hearted. It was moments like this that kept her going. It was moments like this that made nursing the best career ever. She gestured to where the student was helping to clean up and said to Ravi. 'Celia can keep you company and you can tell her how to pluck an Indian deer.' The doctor looked bemused.

'Don't worry about it,' chuckled Paula. She became serious again. 'By the way, which consultant is on call?'
'James.'

James Bentley was the youngest of the five consultant anaesthetists, who oversaw the medical needs of the ICU. Dark-haired, dynamic and with heavy Dr Kildare brooding eyes, he was a favourite among the female, and at least one of the male, nurses.

'I met him on the stairs as I was coming down,' said Nancy. 'I can't believe it. He told me Florence has died. That's a bit much. She was fine when I transferred her to the ward.'

Paula felt her stomach go into freefall.

Chapter Five

Vincent Stevens had been in the operating theatre for three long hours before being transferred to the ICU. Nancy and Paula were coming to the end of their shift and Nancy was helping the team sort out the mishmash of tubes and wires, whilst Paula read through the operation notes. She was standing by the nurses' station when the imposing figure of Lennox Telleman strode through the airlock and headed straight for her. Paula was surprised to see the Consultant, but tried not to sound too disappointed when she said, 'I thought James was on call for us today.'

'He was,' Lennox said, crossly. The steely-eyed anaesthetist was squeezed into a set of scrubs that were a size too small. His midriff bulged out of the gap. 'Apparently, he's got something more important to do.'

The fact that Lennox was already in a bad mood did not bode well for an interview with distraught relatives. A smile masked Paula's inaudible groan. The lead consultant might be the best gas man that Lyedale General possessed, and a noted expert in the field of intensive care medicine, but he was not renowned for his communication skills. Paula was sure this was because he was intrinsically a shy man, who found the world outside academia a scary place.

'Are his parents here yet?' he grunted.

'They're in the visitor's room,' she said. 'There's a policeman with them at the moment.'

'So?' he said, turning to leave.

'Actually Lennox, before we go in, ' said Paula 'can I talk to you about something?'

'What?'

'Frank, Frank Hoyle and-'

'He's dead isn't he?'

'Yes, but-'

'But nothing,' he snapped. 'I got a message to say you wanted me to talk to these relatives and that's the only reason I'm here.'

'Okay,' she said, 'but don't you want to change out of your scrubs first.' She looked pointedly at the blood splatters on his trousers.

Lennox ignored the comment and walked off. 'I haven't all day, Paula. Come on,' he said, over his shoulder.

Paula was too tired to argue. She dropped the notes onto the desk and followed him to the visitors' room.

Once again dirty cups littered the coffee table. A police officer was sitting opposite a middle-aged woman. She had taken the place of the elderly ladies on the careworn sofa. The woman's ashen face was a veil of bewilderment as she plucked at a tissue from the ever-present box. The policeman's eyes followed a short stocky man who was pacing the floor.

He muttered 'about time,' when they entered the room. Russell Stevens then took up a position by the window. He peered over the top of a pair of metal-rimmed spectacles and watched Paula closely as she crossed the room to take the seat next to his wife. Lennox closed the door and leant against it.

'Who are you?' he said, addressing the policeman.

The officer stood. 'Detective Sergeant Palmer, sir,' he said. 'Do you mind if I stay?'

The consultant gave what could be interpreted as a nod. Jeff Palmer took out his notebook and returned to his seat. Taking a moment to study him, Paula could see why Nancy fancied the plain-clothed detective. The well proportioned officer was wearing a black leather jacket. He had lively grey eyes and a deep tanned complexion. There was half a minutes silence whilst the consultant studied his feet and cleared his throat. Following a muttered introduction, he briefly looked at the father before averting his eyes.

'I've just anaesthetised your son,' he said. 'Erm, he's had an abdominal laparotomy and splenectomy, he has a flail segment of ribs, so we've had to put him on a ventilator.' Lennox seemed to notice the gap in his scrubs for the first time and gave his trousers a tug. Paula wanted to groan out loud. Instead she stared at the policeman, who seemed to be concentrating on his notepad.

Lennox' eyes became firmly fixed on his own feet. He rattled on at a pace. 'Erm, he'll need to stay on the machine for some time. He also has a contusion to his brain and there's a little swelling. We'll just have to see how things go with that. We'll wait a couple more days and then give him a scan and then-.' He stopped in mid sentence having apparently run out of steam. Paula wondered if she could persuade him to go on a counselling course. Doubting it, she consoled herself by gently placing her hand over Joan Stevens' trembling fingers.

Lennox drew in a deep breath and finished with. 'Well that's about all I can say really.'

'Is he going to be all right?' said Joan Stevens.

'Erm, well obviously - he is rather poorly,' said Lennox. 'Things were a little tricky in there for a while and - erm - with the breathing machine there's always a risk of infection and that sort of thing, but there's no reason to suppose he will get a chest infection – and until we do the scan - and wake him up – we won't know what's going on - up there,' he said, tapping his head.

'Are you are telling me my son hasn't had a brain scan?' said Russell Stevens. His cheeks flared with anger.

'N-no I'm not telling you that,' stuttered Lennox. 'I mean – yes, of course he's had a scan.' He tugged at his trousers. 'But it's too early to show anything of note. His chest is the most important thing at the moment. That's the one that's life threatening – not his head - but everything is under control.' Paula saw his hand grab the door handle behind him and knew what was going to happen next.

'Anyway,' said Lennox. 'I'll get my surgical colleagues to have a chat to you about the operation.' And then before anyone could say anything, he disappeared through the door.

Paula tried to repair the damage, but despite all her reassurances Mr Stevens did not seem terribly impressed. And to make matters worse, Jeff Palmer happened to mention that Vincent was suspected of driving the stolen vehicle. It had not been the most auspicious start to their relationship, thought Paula.

Chapter Six

A chilly draught seeped through the kitchen door. The cat raised his sleepy head to reveal a white slash across his otherwise inky coat. He yawned and his clear amber eyes caught the attention of the only other occupant on the blue-grey, leather sofa. She scratched his neck with her bare toes. Barnum rolled over onto his back and stretched.

Paula had lived in the small Edwardian terraced house for five years. Her parents had helped with the down payment and at the time it had seemed like a good idea to live within five minutes from work. With hindsight however, it seemed less of a blessing. She was exhausted. It had been a day of yo-yoing emotions and before leaving work, she had rung the ward to find out what had happened to Florence. She had been admitted to the unit following major abdominal surgery and had borne a difficult time with a gentle patience. Florence had been well on the road to recovery when they transferred her to the ward and Paula couldn't believe that she had died. There was still a half-full jar of Quality Street on the nurses' station, which had been given by her grateful relatives. According to the ward sister, Florence had been found slumped over her bed. Paula kept telling herself, 'stop being silly - these things happen.' But all the clichés in the world could not stop the sense of unease that was growing in the pit of her stomach. There was nothing she could put her finger on, but instinct told her there was something wrong. She reached for her mug of coffee, only to find that it had gone cold. The papers resting on her knee, slipped to the floor. She swore, swung her legs off the sofa, gathered up the papers and dumped them, along with the mug, onto the coffee table.

Her eyes were automatically drawn towards the front window where the wind-lashed sleet dribbled down the black-backed glass. She crossed over to the bay-window where a gate-leg dining table nestled under the window ledge. One of the table's leaves had been propped up to house Duncan's PC. She drew the curtains to shut out the cold and returned to the open fire where she threw on a log and opened the grate.

Paula made her way into the kitchen and filled the kettle. Whilst waiting for it to boil, she leaned against the small breakfast bar and ran her fingers through her dishevelled hair. The clock over the back door read twenty past six. She sighed. Duncan would be home soon. What with his rugby training and her late shifts, they never seemed to have time together any more. She thought he took her for granted and was unsure of his commitment. Despite having virtually lived together for the past three years, he still hadn't sold his own flat. There were times when Paula felt as though she was just a convenient source of food and sex. She opened the fridge door and groaned. Three eggs and week old salad wasn't going to go very far.

The click of the kettle startled her. She made a fresh coffee and returned to the living room; switched on the television; picked up the computer generated stream of statistics; gently moved the cat and settled back onto the sofa. However, instead of going through the papers, she sat and watched the end of the news, tapping the end of the pencil between her teeth. The front door opened. She bit down and broke the end of the pencil.

Duncan shouted from the hall in an American accent. 'Hi honey, I'm home.' He entered the lounge with briefcase in one hand and ruffling the damp from his hair with the other. He crossed over to the sofa, bent his tall frame over Paula's shoulder and said, 'gis-a-kiss doll.'

Paula shied away.

He looked at the papers on the table, straightened his back and said, 'what are you doing?'

She heard the disapproval in his voice and before Paula could reply he'd returned to the hall and dumped his briefcase amongst the pile of rugby and scuba gear. Duncan Harvey worked for a major car manufacture as a design engineer making automatic gearing. He never brought work home. Paula saw the look on his face as he came back into the room.

'It's the audit report,' she said. 'I have to hand it in by the end of next month.'

Duncan loosened his tie, pushed the reluctant cat from

the sofa and sat next to her.

'I know you have a tough job,' he said, 'but I don't see why you can't leave the paperwork behind.'

'Because I can't exactly bring the patients home,' she said, crossly. In truth, Paula was as angry with herself as much as Duncan. She had sat there for over an hour, but hadn't been able to concentrate and had done nothing. She gathered the remaining papers together and added them to the pile on the dining table before sitting back down.

Duncan's voice softened, 'It's only because I care,' he said, as he lifted her legs onto his lap. 'They never give you a break - if you're not bringing some bloody crap home.' He began to massage her feet. 'They're ringing you up about something. Can't you get Nancy to do more?'

'She does her job. I do mine,' she said, wriggling her toes. 'Ouch yes –there.' She was just beginning to think that they might avoid an argument when the phone rang. Duncan's look said it all. She heaved her legs off his lap, made her way to the sideboard and took the cordless phone from its stand.

'Hello, hello.' Her father's voiced bellowed out of the receiver. 'Is that you Paula?'

'Hi Dad,' she said, returning to the sofa. 'How are things, is mum all right?' Duncan left the room. She watched his retreating back and sighed.

'I can't hear you,' shouted Jack Hobson. 'You have to speak up.'

Paula repeated her greeting.

'We've got an appointment with a specialist,' said her father. 'Jennifer says you have to come with us.'

Jennifer Saunders, Paula's elder sister, lived close to their parents in the village of Haarbeck, twenty miles north of Lyedale. Jennifer worked as a part-time teacher and spent the rest of her time looking after her husband and two children. Paula was the youngest of three. According to her, Jennifer was the living proof of the elder sibling syndrome. Their bachelor brother, Malcolm, lived and worked as an architect in London. He rarely ventured up north to visit his family. There had been a message from Jennifer on Paula's answer phone, but she had forgotten to ring back.

'Jennifer said you have to come,' her father repeated.

'I'll try, Dad,' she said. 'But it depends on if I can get the time off.' Barnum had reclaimed his spot next to his mistress and she was absentmindedly stroking his ears. 'What did your GP say? Did they give you an appointment card?'

'It's on the 19th,' he said, 'at the Infirmary with the n-u-o-lo-gist.' Her father struggled with the medical terminology. The Queen Alexandria's Infirmary was in the city of Ridgewell. It provided various regional specialities.

'Are you sure it's the Infirmary?' said Paula. Her eyes followed Duncan as he passed through the sitting room into the kitchen.

'I'm not stupid Paula,' said her father.

'I know you're not,' said Paula. 'What department did you say it was again?'

'Nur-ology,' he shouted

'I thought that she was supposed to be seeing a psychiatrist,' said Paula. She heard the fridge door open and close and visualised her boyfriend's face when he saw there was nothing to eat.

'We've been there,' said her Dad. 'We have to see this other chap now. Jennifer says you have to come because you'll know what they're on about. I can't hear them. Your mother usually deals with that sort of thing.'

'Well, can't she tell you what he says?'

'Your mother doesn't even know what day it is,' he said, crossly.

'Oh come on, Dad, she's not that bad.'

'How would you know?' he said. 'You never come to see her?'

The remark stung. It was true Paula hadn't seen her parents since Christmas and she felt guilty. She sighed. 'Okay,' she said. 'I'll definitely be there.'

Duncan returned from the kitchen to find her hitting the memory buttons on the phone. 'Is everything all right?' he said.

'No not really,' she said, putting the receiver back to her ear. 'I'm ringing Jennifer.' Her sister answered on the second ring, but despite careful grilling, Paula couldn't gain any more information. In the end, she promised to do her best to get time off and returned the phone to its stand. Duncan had changed out of his suit, but was still looking smart. He lounged with his arm resting across the back of the chair closest to the fire and sipped from a can of lager. A yellow glow flickered across his six o'clock shadow. Paula thought he looked just like George Clooney. It was no wonder Nancy called him Dunk-the-hunk.

'Looks like we're eating out,' he said. 'Do you fancy going for some posh nosh for a change?'

'Why?'

'What, apart from the fridge being empty,' he said, taking a mouthful of the lager. 'I didn't really think we needed a reason. I thought you might like a change from the rugby club, that's all.'

When they entered The Bishops Crook, Paula could see why it was so popular with couples. Intimate secluded tables dressed in a cardinal red and gold décor and subtle lighting, gave the impression of privacy and intimacy. The impressive cordon-bleu menu and price list added to the restaurant's reputation.

Paula's enjoyment of the meal was hampered by concern over her mother and, to some degree, suspicion of Duncan's motives for taking her there. His nervousness did not help and their long stretches of awkward silences were only broken by trivia. Paula played with her food so much the waiter kept returning to ask if everything was all right. At the end of the meal they sat in a strained silence as the waiter placed cups of thick black coffee and a jug of cream on the table. After piling in the sugar, Duncan stirred his for several minutes. Eventually, he leaned back in his chair and looked at her with his cool hazel eyes.

'The lads at the club have had right a go at me,' he said. 'They think I take you for granted.' He paused, waiting for a reaction.

Paula couldn't believe he'd been discussing their relationship with his rugby friends. She was angry.

'I don't mean to,' he said. 'I'll -.'

'It's too late.'

'What -,' he said. 'What do you mean by that?' He sat forward and reached across the table to grab her hand. Paula pulled it away and pushed her chair back from the table, putting even more space between them. She hadn't planned this. For god's sake she still loved him, but it didn't seem to be enough anymore.

'Come on, you don't really mean that,' he said. 'Look I know you're worried about your mother and you're tired and all that, but-'

'I don't need the hassle,' said Paula. 'You make everything twice as hard.'

She could see the hurt cloud his eyes. He withdrew his hand. Paula gathered her handbag from the floor and began to scrabble inside. There had been a time when she had been so sure of their love that she thought it had to last forever. They would spend hours searching through estate agents windows looking at the most expensive properties. They fantasized about how many kids and dogs they were going to have together and what they would be like as an old couple. Paula found a tissue and blew her nose. She looked up and noticed that anger had replaced the hurt.

'You've changed,' he said. 'You used to be up for a laugh, but you never have any time for me now. 'You're always too bloody tired for anything.' He threw the crumpled serviette on the table and motioned to the waiter. Lowering his voice, he hissed. 'That place rules your life and I'm sick of it.' The waiter placed a buckskin bound wallet on the table. Without glancing at the slip, he slid his MasterCard between the red leather bindings and the waiter took it away. Duncan took a deep breath before saying. 'Look Paula, I promise you I'll make more of an effort, but you have to do your bit as well. You have to tell that lot, you've a private life. - Get them to give us some space.' The couple were sat with their heads bowed when the maître d' returned the credit card.

Paula waited until he was out of earshot. 'I don't think I can do it,' she said. She bit her lip. 'I need some time apart.'

'Time for what for God's sake?'

'Can we go now?'

He leant across the table. 'You don't mean that,' he said, pleading with her. 'This was supposed to be a new beginning, not the bloody end. – oh come on Paula, things aren't that bad.'

'I'm not saying it's the end,' she said, leaning

forward. 'I'm just saying I need a bit of space, that's all.'

Other diners were beginning to stare. Duncan scraped his chair on the wooden floor and then virtually threw it under the table before storming out.

He snatched the keys out of her hand as they entered the car park. Paula suspected he was over the limit and tried to persuade him to let her drive, but he became belligerent. In the end, she gave in to him rather than have a scene and climbed into the passenger side. Paula fought back her tears as Duncan sped erratically through deserted streets and had to cling onto the dashboard as the car screeched to a halt outside the house. She presumed he was going to follow her, but as soon as Paula shut the door; he rammed the car into gear and careered away at speed. Paula stood staring after the vanishing tail lights of her VW Polo. She felt the cold seep into her bones.

Chapter Seven

The old gas heater made little inroad into the cold dank atmosphere of the kitchen-cum-living room. Toys, dirty clothes and a half eaten takeaway littered every available space. The young woman, her elfin features etched with years of drug abuse and prostitution, made only a cursory attempt at tidying the one bedroom flat.

There had been little work that week. Marty was worried about paying the rent. Her friend, Jude was supposed to be collecting Marty's five year old daughter, Amber, and Robbie, Jude's six year old son, from school. The two single mothers had met on a drug rehabilitation programme. They had been told their babies would be taken into care if they didn't get themselves off the drugs. The parole officer had taken pity on them and helped find apartments in the same dilapidated block of flats. Being clean however, didn't pay the bills and employers didn't take on people with a record of drug abuse and so the girls returned to their original profession. To keep clean they stayed well away from their old haunts, pimps and bad habits and instead touted for business around Lyedale's more upmarket hotels and conference centres and had managed to build up a small, but regular clientele.

Marty chucked an empty pizza box into a black bag in the corner of the kitchen and rinsed her sticky hands under the tap. She lined a row of fish-fingers onto one side of the grill pan and pushed it under the only element of the cooker that still worked.

A short time later the flat bounced into life as two energetic youngsters charged into the sparsely furnished room. They shouted playfully at each other as they wrestled with the straps of their school bags. Amber's, slight build and china-doll appearance belied her rugged toughness. She was more than a match for Robbie's 'Dennis-the Menace' rough and tumble. Emerging from the kitchen area, Marty placed a plateful of fish-fingers, chips and beans before each child. Someone had shoved a folded beer mat under one leg of the low-set table to keep it steady. Jude knelt between the youngsters. She coated the food in tomato sauce and cut it into small mouthfuls. The kids knelt on the grubby, threadbare carpet and ate with spoons.

As Marty leant on the kitchen unit and watched, she remembered a very different childhood. She vaguely remembered her father and could still feel his love, but he died from cancer when she was a toddler. One of her earliest memories was being made to sit upright at a pristine table and forbidden from moving until her plate was cleared. She would force down each mouthful and then ram her fingers down her throat until she vomited. Marty smiled at her daughter's enjoyment of food.

'Can you take the kids tonight?' she said, to Jude.

Her friend was sitting cross-legged at the end of the table supervising the feast. 'Sorry chuck, I can't,' she said. 'It's the end of the month. I need to get myself a couple of extra punters.'

Their contrasting accents showed the girls different upbringings. Marty started to clear up in the kitchen.

'I hate leaving the kids with Mrs Stott,' she said. 'The stupid cow stinks of booze. She was virtually unconscious last time I went to pick them up. There's bloody great holes all over the carpet where she's dropped fags. One of these days she's going to burn the place down - with us in it.' Marty was attempting to scrub the burnt breadcrumbs from the already heavily blackened grill pan.

'I hate her as much as you do, chuck, but beggars can't be choosers,' said Jude. 'And you and me are definitely beggars. We'd never get anyone else as cheap as Stotty. At least we can trust her not to sprag to the cops.'

Jude scrapped beans off Amber's t-shirt with the spoon and then made it zoom around the youngster's head before diving into her mouth. Robbie shovelled his food unaided. Marty sighed in resignation.

'I've had Hot Rod on the phone,' she said. 'He'll be here in an hour.'

Jude lowered her voice and spoke over the kid's heads. 'I thought you were going to tell that weirdo to piss off.'

'I know I did,' said Marty. 'But I'm getting desperate.' She gave up trying to clean the pan and clattered it back under the grill. 'He isn't that bad. It was just a couple of bruises that's all. At least he said he was sorry. And he pays double,' said Marty, trying to convince herself as much as her friend. She dried her hands on the wet tea-towel and made her way into the bedroom where she grabbed a pile of dirty clothes from a stool and pushed them, out of sight, under the bed. She sat in front of a cracked mirror that was perched on top of a skip rescued chest of drawers and began to put on her make-up.

Knees touching, thumbs in mouths, comfort blankets scrunched between grubby fingers, Amber and Robbie sat cross-legged in front of the television. Jude found a station showing cartoons. The auburn rooted, bottle blonde crossed over to the bedroom and stood in the doorway.

'It wasn't just a couple of bruises.'

'I'll put my foot down this time,' said Marty. She smothered her lips in bright red lipstick, pressed them together and then opened them with a smack.

'O yeah, like he's going to listen to you,' said Jude. 'Don't be so bloody stupid Marty, the money's not worth it.' She glanced over her shoulder at the giggling kids and added in a whisper. 'What's Amber going do if you get yourself stiffed.'

'Don't be so melodramatic,' said Marty. 'He likes a bit of rough that's all. It's all part of the job isn't it?' She tried to sound confident, but in reality HR terrified her. A lot of customers used aliases. Marty supposed it made them feel less guilty for doing the dirty on their wives, if they could pretend it wasn't them. When he told her that he wanted to be called Hot Rod, she wanted to laugh; she had wanted to call him PP for Pretentious Prick.

Jude took the kids downstairs to Mrs Stott's apartment. As soon as Marty was alone again, she felt the flat closing in on her, but she didn't have to wait long before the shrill buzz of the doorbell broke the silence and made her jump. Her stomach churned. She took several deep breaths and tried to smooth un-ironed creases from her short tight skirt. She opened the door to a tall, well dressed man. He was leaning against the door frame, exuding testosterone and sweat in equal amounts.

'Hello, Marty.'

HR reminded her of her step-father. Her mother had remarried shortly after the death of her dad and then gave birth to a boy. He had been the only good thing in her miserable childhood. At the age of twelve, she told her mother that she didn't like the way her step-dad touched her. She was banned from ever mentioning the subject again. With no one else to turn to, the young Marty had withdrawn even further into herself. By the age of thirteen she'd turned to drugs and before long found she could no longer do without the only thing that made her life bearable, oblivion. On her sixteenth birthday, she returned home from school, picked up a couple of plastic carrier-bags and an old shovel and left the house. She went to the local park and collected as much dog dirt as she could find, spread the excrement between the sheets of her parent's bed and neatly replaced the quilt. Marty took the only link to her real father, a cross-eyed teddy bear. Leaving her brother had been her only regret. As far as Marty knew, her parents had never reported her missing nor made any effort to find her.

'I hope you're not going to leave me standing on the doorstep,' said HR.

He smiled, but it wasn't in pleasure. There was something in his steely grey eyes that scared Marty and his measured icy control put fear in her throat. She stood to one side to allow him to pass.

'So my dear, how about a wee bit of fellatio to begin with this evening?' he said. His angular face creased into a smirk and he looked down his nose, as if he'd just trodden in something nasty.

Marty knew he was trying to humiliate her. 'Whatever you fancy, HR,' she said. She might be a prostitute, but that didn't mean to say she was stupid. She smiled back.

The client followed her into the bedroom.

'I hope you've cleaned your teeth,' he said. He removed his clothes with precise, controlled movements. Neatly folding each garment, he laid them in a neat pile on the chair at the bottom of the bed. He removed his wrist watch and glanced at the time before carefully placing it on top of the stack.

An hour later the world pulsated in Marty's ears. Bile regurgitated from her stomach, burning her mouth. She leaned over the bed and vomited. Still retching, she held onto her throat with one hand and pushed herself into a sitting position. She leant heavily on the bedside chair and struggled to her feet. Through dizzy eyes, she watched as a bundle of twenty pound notes scattered over the floor, a few landed in the vomit. The room spun and she flopped back on to the bed. It was a few minutes before she could try again.

Eventually Marty managed to stagger to the kitchen area. She swilled out a dirty coffee mug and filled it with water. Swallowing was difficult. She leant over the sink and watched the blood drip from her nose. The droplets made a melodic ping as they splattered on the steel basin. The bright red liquid formed into small rivulets before trickling down the drain. She retched again. Maybe next time he would kill her, but at least this month's rent was paid, even if she did have to scrape the vomit off it.

Chapter Eight

The silver BMW was drenched in the beam from the powerful halogen security light, attached under the eaves of the house. The drive glistened with frost. He drummed his fingers on top of the steering wheel while waiting for the garage's automatic doors to open. The featureless modern detached house seemed to reflect his featureless sterile marriage.

Easing the car into the double garage, he pulled up beside a small Fiat Panda. It looked as though it hadn't been driven for some time. He stiffly pulled himself out of the car and recovered his briefcase from the boot. Grasping the collar of his thick mohair coat, he made his way into the cold night air. A red-rose stained glass motif greeted him as he inserted his key into the front door that opened easily to his push. He could hear his wife's high pitched affected vowels compete with serenade in G coming from the kitchen.

'Is that you, darling?' she shouted. A plump middle-aged woman entered the hall. She was wiping her hands on a kitchen towel. 'They've kept you late again you poor old thing,' she said, air-kissing his cheek.

He scraped the wintry grime from his shoes and thought she must be the only woman in the world who still wore a frilly pinafore and listened to James Last.

'You look all in, dear,' she said. 'Dinner's nearly ready. Can I get you a whisky?'

He grunted his assent, but she had already turned her back on him and returned to the kitchen. The doctor opened the cloakroom door and shook his coat before hanging it on a brass coat-rack. It had been divided into his and her ends. He checked his appearance in the full length mirror and ran his fingers through peppered grey hair.

He crossed the hall and entered his study where a mahogany, green-leather topped table dominated the room. One wall supported a floor to ceiling bookcase, which was crammed with systematically arranged medical books and journals. A high-backed leather chair and a filing cabinet were the only other furniture in the small room. A single casement window looked out onto a large landscaped back garden, kept tidy by a local gardening firm. The highly polished table supported a computer, a green-shaded table lamp and a framed photograph. Not even a paperclip sullied the immaculate surface. The doctor switched on the lamp, removed his jacket and carefully hung it over the back of the chair. He placed his briefcase on the desk, flicked both catches simultaneously and opened the case. He had just removed a document when there was a sharp tap on the door. When his wife entered, he slipped the paper under the briefcase. Ice-cubes tinkled against the tumbler as she placed it on a paper coaster she'd brought with her.

'Will you be long, dear?'

'Twenty minutes.'

'I'll put the veg on then,' she said. An old Yorkshire terrier shuffled through the open door and began to snuffle his way around the unfamiliar room.

'I've told you before,' he shouted. 'Keep that bloody animal out of here.'

His wife shooed the dog in front of her and left her husband alone with his thoughts. The doctor took a generous sip of whiskey. He picked up the silver-framed black and white photograph of a middle-aged woman and young boy. They were in a small back garden. The woman was pushing the boy on a home- made swing that hung from an aging tree. Resplendent in a starched shirt, tie and short creased trousers, the boy clung tightly onto the ropes. Mother and son were laughing. The doctor could not remember why they were laughing, but knew it was not a frequent occurrence.

Victorian values had dominated the early fifty's household. He remembered being made to spit polish his shoes every evening before bedtime. It was a habit he still held to today, except he no longer used spit. Missing from the picture, his father had been a postman who spent his pay packet and free time in the local pub. His mother had wanted him to be better than the other kids in their street. He had preferred her company to that of anyone else and would do anything to please her, but always felt it was never enough. The doctor wondered if she had lived, whether things would have turned out different.

At a time when he was in the grip of adolescent hormones, she'd withdrawn into a world of pain and fear as she succumbed to breast cancer. As a teenager he had become fascinated by the effects of opiates and the psychology and physiology of death. He made sure he was present whenever the GP gave an injection of morphine. He closely observed the highs of analgesic euphoria and the lows of all consuming pain as the drug wore off. The doctor recalled the day when, on returning home from school, he had seen the relief in her cold flaccid face and had been glad she was dead. After the funeral he went for a bike ride and stayed away for two days. It was probably then he resolved on a career in medicine. The young man had not found his chosen subject easy and he had to spend every available minute studying which left little time to socialise. Having always preferred his own company, he had to work on the appearance of respectability.

The doctor swirled the half melted ice-cubes and watched them crack against the sides of the glass. He wondered if his mother would be proud of her son's achievements or would she still want more. He looked at his watch. Ten minutes had already passed. His wife would be calling him for dinner soon. He took a swig of whisky, replaced the picture and retrieved the document from under his briefcase. Putting the case on the floor, he ran his hand over the paper to smooth out the wrinkles. It was a photocopy of Frank Hoyle's personal data. He took a key from the desk drawer, crossed to the filing cabinet and lifted out the contents of the bottom draw before returning to the desk. He put the ragged green box, which once held a pair of long since discarded children's shoes, to one side and added the sheet of paper to a lever-arch file. He closed the file and swapped it for the box. Pushing his chair back, he retrieved the briefcase from the floor and removed the St Christopher. Discarding the case, he held the chain in front of him and became mesmerised by the spinning gold. The doctor thought himself a true man of science and did not believe in a God, but had become fascinated by the convergence of the conscious and subconscious mind; the thoughts and dreams of the psyche as it passed over the threshold into oblivion; the power of life that

43

death could bring. He let the chain trickle through his fingers. It dropped into the middle of the box that contained the remnants of his victim's psyches. He picked up the shoebox and shook the assortment of rings, glasses, photos and bric-a-brac. It had twisted into a knotted mass. He made an effort to untangle the chains until it dawned on him that he could no longer remember who they belonged to. He became frustrated and threw the tangled mass back into the box. It was just a load of tat anyway. His wife's grating voice made him jump.

Even though their two children had left home, the couple kept up the pretence of family meal-times. They sat opposite each other at a large Georgian style dining table and ate in the undemanding silence of those who have lived together for many years. He had never loved his wife and she had few redeeming features, but he had always appreciated her cooking. She pointed to a mark on his sleeve with her knife.

'Did you know that you have some blood on your cuff?' she said.

He laid his fork, tines down, on the plate and twisted round his sleeve. A crimson streak of smeared blood stood out against the stark white of his shirt. He scowled and he pushed his chair away from the table.

'It doesn't matter,' she said. 'Don't let your food get cold. I can put it in the wash later.'

'I'd rather do it now,' he said, and then feeling the need to justify himself, he added. 'I had to see a post op patient before I left.'

'Your fault is that you're too conscientious, dear,' she said, to his back as he left the room.

The doctor threw his clothes into the laundry basket before stepping into the on-suite bathroom. He set the water to hot and scrubbed his hands and genitalia. Turning his face upward, he let the power of the water wash over him and vowed never to use the prostitute again.

Chapter Nine

A computer table vied for space with a traditional wooden desk in the cramped office. They were squashed into one corner and a large, grey-metallic cupboard and two filing cabinets had been crammed into the remaining space. Paula dug her heels into the carpet and glided her chair over to the desk. Numeracy and statistics had never been her favourite subjects and she'd spent most of the morning trying to make sense of garbled statistics, churned out by the audit programme on the computer. If she hadn't met Charles Edmonds that morning, and he hadn't asked how far she had got with the audit, she probably wouldn't be sitting there now. She'd lied to her in-manager, telling him that she was well on the way to finishing the report. Alan Charlton had said he would keep an eye on the unit for her so she'd spent the whole morning shut in the office.

Bleary eyed, Paula stared at the cork notice board that was choked with duty rotas, theatre lists and copious post-it notes and memos. She hadn't heard from Duncan for days, nor had she tried to contact him. Despite taking a couple of Paracetamol her headache was getting worse. She looked down to the mass of papers in front of her and the hairs on the back of her neck tingled. A shiver jolted her out of her reverie. Paula heard the changing room door bang. She rushed out of the office to see Nancy standing in front of the changing room door staring at it. Paula held onto the doorframe and shouted up the corridor.

'Nance, I need to talk to you.'

Nancy made her way along the corridor. 'I've just dropped my pen down the loo,' she said, looking rather perturbed.

'Never mind that,' said Paula. 'Get in here.'

'Oh great,' said Nancy. 'I can't even get through the bloody doors now - what happened to good morning Nancy – how are you today?' The deputy followed Paula into the office. 'What's up with you - did Dunc-the-hunk kick you out of bed?'

Paula scowled. 'I'm sorry,' she said, 'but this is important and I'm in a hurry.' The appointment with her mother's neurologist was scheduled for that afternoon and Paula didn't want to be late.

'It may be nothing to you, but that was my favourite pen,' said Nancy. She stood in the middle of the office and rifled though her pockets looking for another. Unable to find one, she turned to the cabinet and removed a black biro from a box full of the same. 'Are you all right? You look knackered.'

Paula was due to meet her parents at three and glanced at her watch. She considered leaving the conversation to another day, but decided to get it over with. She told Nancy to shut the door and sat down on her chair. 'I'm a half day,' she said. 'I have to be somewhere this afternoon and I don't want to be late.' Paula didn't want to complicate matters by telling Nancy about her mother.

'Has something happened in the unit?' said Nancy. 'I saw Nicky running along the corridor.'

'She's probably on her way to the lab,' said Paula. 'You know what Nicky's like; she can never do anything at a normal pace.' She started to look for something among the mess of papers. 'This has nothing to do with patients well not directly anyway.'

'Okay, so what's so important that you have to drag me in screaming?'

'I think we've got a problem.'

'Your calculators bust,' said Nancy. She kicked at the cabinet door in an attempt to shut it. The metal shuddered, but the door remained open.

'I'm trying to be serious,' said Paula.

'I'm sorry.' Nancy crossed her arms and leant against the door to stop it creaking.

'Look, I know this might sound stupid,' said Paula. 'But - '

'Oh great one, nothing you could ever say to me could be classed as stupid.'

'Pack it in,' said Paula. She took in a deep breath and blew out her cheeks before letting it go. 'I'm being serious.'

'Okay.' Nancy held up her hands in submission.

'You know the other morning,' said Paula. 'When I told you I was sick of coming on shift to a death?'

'Erm, no not really,' said Nancy.

'Well I did,' said Paula. Her headache was getting worse. She nipped the bridge of her nose in an attempt to ease it. 'And I think there's a pattern -'

'I hate to mention this, Sister,' interrupted Nancy, 'but we are an Intensive Care Unit and we do occasionally lose one or two of our clients.'

Paula was becoming irritated by her friend's flippancy. 'For God's sake Nancy,' she said. 'I think somebody's interfering with them.'

'Interfering with whom?' said Nancy.

Paula wondered if her deputy was being dim on purpose. She was beginning to lose her temper. 'The patients, of course,' she snapped.

'This is a wind-up, right?' Nancy said, laughing. She pushed herself off the filling cabinet and crossed over to the window.

Nancy's reaction wasn't exactly what Paula had been expecting. She stared at her deputy.

'You are joking?' said Nancy. She began twiddling the pen. 'Don't you think we'd notice if something was going on? You can't sneeze in there without someone shouting gesundheit.'

Paula sighed. 'Look, I know it sounds ridiculous,' she said, 'but I'm sure something's wrong.' She began to riffle through the papers until she found what she was looking for. 'The figures show over the past four years our mortality rates have ranged from nineteen to twenty-four per cent – that's pretty much in line with the national average -yes.'

'Okay.'

'Up until this year,' said Paula. 'I've done the audit manually so at first, I thought maybe I'd done something wrong. I even dragged that poor runt down from IT and made him go through the computer programme again.' She ran her fingers through her hair. 'Nancy, I'm sure that the figures are right.'

'And,' Nancy prompted.

'Over the past six months the death rate's been

steadily rising,' she said. 'It's gone from twenty-one up to twenty-three per cent.'

Nancy raised her eyebrows. 'So,' she said.

'Fifty per cent of our deaths have happened during the night shift or early morning,' said Paula. 'Look, it might not sound much, but it doesn't feel right.' Nancy made no comment and Paula realised she hadn't made a convincing argument. 'I thought it was a bit fishy. That's all.'

'This really is a wind-up isn't it?' repeated Nancy. 'I mean, it's normal to have peaks and troughs throughout the year. It's probably only a phase we're going through. You know like we get a run of ruptured aneurysms or accidents or whatever.'

Paula bit her lip.

'Oh come on, Paula,' said Nancy. She flipped the pen into the air. 'You cannot be serious. You're not telling me someone's killing the patients, are you?' she didn't wait for an answer. 'Apart from the fact that sort of thing just doesn't happen here; there is no way anybody could get into the unit without being noticed.'

Paula felt her stomach churn at the thought of what she was suggesting. She stared at her deputy.

'Unless you think it's one of us,' said Nancy. She looked at Paula and her jaw dropped. 'Oh my God, you do - you're in cuckoo land.' She shook her head. 'Come on, Paula seriously no one would or could get away with it.'

Paula turned back to the pile of papers and removed another document. 'Don't you think I've been through all that with myself?' she said, holding it out. 'I'm sure it isn't a glitch or a run of bad luck or anything else for that matter.'

Nancy took the paper from her and looked at the graph.

'There,' said Paula, pointing to the top table of a series. 'In the first half of last year there was a slight rise.' She closed her eyes for a moment, willing the headache to go away. 'I grant you it doesn't seem particularly significant, but since then, it's been on a steady upward trend.' She prodded the paper with her finger. 'If you look at the bottom graph, you'll see most of the deaths occur early morning, usually around the time night-staff end their shift.'

'You've got to be kidding me,' said Nancy. 'You're talking in a six month period about one maybe two per cent above the national average.' She shook her head. 'The death rate usually goes up in winter - and – and everyone knows you're more likely to die during the night.' She shook her head again, but more slowly this time. 'Paula, put it down to a bad year - but for God's sake don't throw accusations about.'

'I'm not accusing anyone,' said Paula, crossly.

'That's not how it sounds,' said Nancy. 'Jeez, boss, you really need to start putting more water in your whiskey.'

Paula snatched back the paper, saying. 'That's a fallacy.'

'What is?'

'More people die during the night.'

'Whatever,' Nancy said. 'But you can't jump to bizarre conclusions like that on such flimsy evidence. Have you considered it might be because you've changed from manual to computer analysis?'

'Of course I did,' said Paula. 'But that wouldn't explain the trend?'

'Look,' said Nancy. 'Even if something is wrong and I don't believe for one moment there is.' She put the pen behind her ear and signed quotation marks with her fingers. 'It's a hell of a jump to say somebody is "interfering" with the patients. Whatever you mean by that - It has to be a coincidence.'

'I can feel it.'

'You've been a bit stressed out lately,' said Nancy, taking hold of the pen again. 'Maybe you need to get away for a while. Go for a dirty weekend with Duncan.'

Paula had said nothing about their separation. She looked at her watch, realised she was going to be late for the appointment and started to collect her things together.

'What are you doing?'

'Going for my half day,' said Paula.

'Erm, hang on a minute,' said Nancy. 'You can't drop a bombshell like that and then just pack up and go home.' She crossed over to block Paula's exit. 'Have you told anybody else about this? Have you decided what're you going to do?'

'No of course I haven't told anybody,' said Paula. She pulled her handbag from the bottom drawer of the desk.

49

'They'd either laugh or think I've lost the plot. I actually wanted to run it by you first. Now I'm beginning to wish I hadn't.' She stood, pushed her chair under the table and then faced her deputy. 'Nance, I can't think of anybody who would want to harm our patients. I also know that there isn't much in the way of evidence, but I do know something is wrong.' She flung her bag over her shoulder. 'And I'm going to keep digging until I find out what or who it is.'

'Okay,' said Nancy, moving out of her way.

Tears had begun to well in Paula's eyes. 'This conversation stays between you and me,' she said, rubbing her nose.

'Fair enough,' said Nancy. She tried to lighten the conversation and get a smile from her friend by adding. 'Do you think my pen's got as far as the river yet?'

Chapter Ten

Paula desperately needed to get out of the room and had volunteered to make a cup of tea. All thoughts of work and the argument with Nancy had gone from her mind. She was sitting in the kitchen, head in hands, at the small drop-leaf table, trying to grapple with the enormity of what they'd been told. Of course Paula had always known that one day something like this might happen, but she hadn't been prepared. The specialist's words spun round her head. She thought back to the times she'd broken bad news to relatives. Now she knew now how they felt.

Paula made herself move and found a packet of ginger biscuits. She put them on the tray and took a handful of tea bags out of a canister marked 'Tea'. Realising she hadn't put the kettle on, Paula held it under the tap and stared out of the window at her mother's flower beds. The water overflowed into the sink and she had to empty half of it out before being able to put the kettle back on its stand. She took a bottle of milk from the fridge-freezer and sniffed it. A long forgotten conversation came flooding back. It wasn't long after her parents had moved into the bungalow. She'd been sitting at the table with her mother admiring the newly refurbished kitchen. Jack Hobson insisted frozen food was tasteless and had banned a freezer from the house. Paula could hear conversation echo round the room.

'After all these years, how did you persuade dad to get a freezer,' she'd said.

Her mother had smiled conspiratorially.

'I didn't.'

'What do you use it for then?'

'Oh, the usual,' said Grace, 'meat, veg etc.'

'How do you manage to get away with it?'

'What your father doesn't know,' said Grace 'won't taste any different.'

'What?'

'I told him,' said Grace. 'If we got a small fridge-freezer he could have all the ice-cream he wants.'

'How do you get away with the rest?'

'I take the meat out the night before and he's none the wiser,' said Grace. 'He still compliments me on my cooking.'

Paula could hear their laughter and caught her breath as the echo drifted away. The kettle boiled. She splashed water over her face before making the tea.

The late afternoon sun reached out across the spacious lounge. Paula squinted as she entered the room. Jack Hobson was sitting on the sofa holding his wife's hand. Tears glistened in his rheumy grey eyes.

'You took your time,' he said.

'Sorry,' said Paula. She put the tray on the table in front of her parents. Grace, oblivious to the tension in the room, stared at the television. Biting her lip to stop herself from crying, Paula knelt on the floor to pour the tea.

'You'd better go and ring our Jennifer,' her father said, brusquely. 'Tell her to come round.'

'There's nothing she can do, Dad,' said Paula. She moved the table out of the way so that she could crouch in front of mother. 'Anyway, the kids will be home from school soon.'

Amy and Dan were aged eleven and fourteen, respectively. The cup in Grace's hand teetered precariously. Paula cupped her hands under her mother's to steady it.

'Hello you,' said Grace.

'I love you,' said Paula. A tear forced its way into the corner of her eye. She brushed it away with her free hand. Grace's attention returned to the television. The programme she was watching was a medical drama. A group of handsome young medics surrounded a patient. One of the actors was performing cardiac massage with bent elbows. Normally, Paula would have laughed and made fun of the programme. 'We'll be all right when our Jennifer gets here,' said her father. The remark stung.

Paula pushed herself up on the arm of the sofa and gave her mother a kiss on the cheek, before going into the hall to call her sister. She pulled out and then straddled the small stool from the telephone table. Jennifer's phone seemed to ring forever before it was answered.

'Hello.' The woman on the other end sounded harassed.

'It's Paula.'

'Oh you're back then,' said Jennifer. 'How did it go?'

The lump in her throat made talking difficult. 'Dad wants you to come.' said Paula.

'What did the doctors say?'

'I'll tell you when you get here.'

There was a pause before Jennifer replied. 'Is she dying?' she said, in the brusque manner she'd inherited from their father.

'No,' said Paula. 'I mean - Yes – look, Jen I'll tell you everything when you get here.'

'Give me ten minutes,' said Jennifer. 'I'll ask Joyce next door to keep an eye on the kids.'

Paula took the time to phone their brother. Closer in age, the younger siblings had a history of bickering. She eventually managed to reach Malcolm at work. Their conversation was brief and she ended up slamming the receiver down. She sat in the dimly lit hall and fought back her tears. Her mother's address book rested next to the telephone. Paula caressed the elegant flowing lines of her writing and thought of all the senile old ladies she'd nursed. She couldn't bear the thought of her mother turning into a shell of humanity, to be lost in a world without grace or dignity.

The back door banged. Paula replaced the book and made her way into the kitchen. Jennifer was standing in the middle of the room removing a pair of bright pink and blue woollen gloves. The sisters were the same height, but that was the only similarity between them. Nine years older, Jennifer had the fuller figure of a contented mother. She proceeded to unwind several layers of a multi-coloured scarf from around her neck.

'Nice scarf,' said Paula.

'Amy knitted it,' said Jennifer. 'And if I went out without it, my life wouldn't be worth living.' She flicked the kettle switch. 'Want one?' she asked pulling out a couple of mugs from a cupboard.

'Yeah okay,' said Paula. 'I left mine in the sitting room.'

'Well?'

'She's got Alzheimer's.' Paula ripped a couple of pieces of kitchen towel from a roll and then sat at the table.

'I knew it had to be something like that.'

'You don't sound terribly upset?'

'Of course I am,' said Jennifer. 'But it's not exactly unexpected. I look after them don't forget. You're so tied up in your work you don't listen to what people are telling you.'

'That's not fair.'

'Maybe, but it's the truth.' Jennifer leaned over the table and patted her sister's hand. 'Look it doesn't matter,' she said. 'Have you called Malcolm yet?'

Paula nodded and rubbed her eyes with the heels of her hands.

'What did he have to say?'

'Not a lot,' said Paula. 'He said to let him know if we need a signature,'

'For what -' Jennifer said.

'To put her in a home,'

'You're joking?'

'No, I'm not joking,' said Paula. She blew her nose on the paper towel. 'I got the feeling it wasn't good PR for the up and coming business executive, to have a parent with senile dementia.'

'I don't suppose he said anything about coming up.'

'Nope,' said Paula. She screwed up the kitchen towel and threw it toward the bin. It missed. 'I'm afraid I slammed the phone down.'

Jennifer got up, recovered the crunched up paper, put it in the swing bin and then refreshed her mug with tea. 'Do you want a top up?' she asked.

'No thanks.'

'Jen?' only Paula and their mother could get away with shortening Jennifer's name.

'Yes.'

'The consultant said she's deteriorating rapidly,' said Paula. 'He thinks it won't be long before.' She couldn't finish the sentence.

'Did he say how long?'

'He was pretty vague,' said Paula. 'She's only sixty-two. It's so unfair. What has she done to deserve this?' she sobbed.

Jennifer embraced her sister. 'We can do this,' she said.

Chapter Eleven

Celia opened the office door to see her boss scrambling around the floor. Paula scooped up a pile of papers and deposited them on the desk.

'What can I do for you?' she said.

'There is a policeman at the front door asking for you,' said Celia.

Paula was stiff from sitting cross legged and needed the aid of the chair to help her get up. 'Okay,' she said.

The policeman was standing just inside the outer doors. Paula recognised the tall, plain clothes officer and greeted him.

'It's Sergeant Palmer. Isn't it?' she said.

'Hi,' he said. 'Erm I'm sorry - I was expecting someone else.'

Paula thought he looked disappointed. 'Are you looking for someone in particular?'

'Sorry,' he repeated, flustered. 'It's just that when the nurse said she'd get the Sister, I thought she meant Sister Coleman.' Paula suspected Nancy had been flirting with him.

'I've spoken with her on the phone,' he continued. 'And I just happened to be passing and wonder if she - you - could give me an update on Vincent.

Normally, Paula would have made fun of his embarrassment, but her sense of humour had begun to flounder. In an effort to be more amicable, she held out her hand and said. 'Come in, Sergeant.'

'Call me Jeff,' he said. His large hand enveloped hers.

Paula led him along the corridor to the empty staffroom. Declining her offer of a drink, he threw his coat onto a seat and sat in the one next to it. Paula sat opposite.

'We're waiting for his chest to improve before we can wean him off the breathing machine,' said Paula.

'So, what about this head injury his dad keeps going on about?'

'We're pretty sure it's just contusions.'

'Con - what?'

'Bruising,' she said, in way of explanation. 'Have you got any further with the investigation?'

'The BMW was stolen the day before,' he said. 'We're still not sure how many lads were in it, but at least one was seen running away from the scene.'

'You do know,' said Paula, 'that Vincent couldn't possibly have been the driver?'

Jeff frowned.

'Most of his injuries are on the left side,' she said. 'The mark made by his seat belt traverses from left to right.'

'You see that's the bizarre thing about this,' said Jeff, shaking his head. 'Joy riders don't normally wear seat belts. We've managed to identify the lad that died, but have nothing on any others. We need to find the guy that ran away and Vince is our only hope. That's why I'm so keen to speak to him.'

'Sorry we can't help,' said Paula. 'Even if we woke him up I doubt he'd remember anything.'

'How long do you reckon?'

'Another week at least' she said. 'His parents are waiting to see the Consultant again. To be honest, they're a bit of a pain. I know they're worried, but his father gripes on about anything and everything. I wouldn't care, but neither of them will hold his hand when they go in to see him. We keep telling them, but they sit in silence for ten minutes and then go home. I'm sure he doesn't even know they're there.' Paula realised she was beginning to rant. She rubbed her eyes with the heels of her hands and ran her fingers through her hair. Since visiting her parents, she'd found it difficult to concentrate.

'I thought you said he was unconscious?' said Jeff.

'He is,' said Paula, 'but hearing is the last thing to go.' She wondered if she should confide in the detective, but then told herself the police were probably the last people she needed to talk to. She was beginning to wish he'd go away.

'Look, Paula,' he said. 'I'm not very good at this blood and guts stuff, but would you mind if I have a look at his injuries? It might be helpful, when - if - we catch this other lad if I can tell him what he's done to his mate.'

She couldn't think of any reason to deny the request and so escorted him into the unit. Jeff smiled at the two nurses who were sat watching the monitor at the desk, they beamed back.

Paula peeped over the top of one of the white Formica screens that surrounded Vincent's bed. 'Nice to see you back in the land of the living, George' Paula said, to the ginger haired male nurse who was standing by the head of the bed.

George Hughes grinned cheekily at his manager. 'It's nice to be back,' he said. 'Mind I'm still trying to pay off the loan on my bike so if there's any more nights, I'm your man.'

The backs of Paula's legs were beginning to ache from standing on her toes. She climbed up onto the cross bar. 'Doesn't working here put you off?' she said.

'You still drive a car, don't you?' countered George.

'Touché,' she said. Nodding toward Jeff, she added 'The sergeant wants to have a quick look at our patient's injuries, if that's okay with you?'

'Sure.'

Using the privacy-screen as a scooter, Paula pushed it open with her foot and then closed it behind Jeff.

The naked body of the young accident victim lay between starched white sheets. Wires stretched from a triangle of three nipple-like electrodes stuck onto his chest. Multiple glass cuts and bruises were etched into his swollen features, which were unrecognisable against the photograph pinned to the chart board.

The policeman looked uncomfortable. Paula thought to herself. 'He asked for it.' She nodded to George, who pulled the sheet back and exposed Vincent's rainbow-coloured abdomen. Impact bruises covered his left side and two parallel wheals stretched diagonally from his left shoulder to right hip. A twelve-inch laparotomy incision bisected the wheals. It looked as though somebody had been playing a macabre game of noughts and crosses.

Jeff screwed up his face. 'I think that might be a little too much for me,' he said.

'Are his parents still here?' said Paula.

'They're waiting to see Alan,' said George. 'I don't know why they bother coming in to see him. They spend all their time moaning at the docs'

'Good morning,' said Alan Charlton, cheerfully. 'I understand our errant parents have requested yet another chat.'

Jeff emerged from behind the screen. He looked positively scruffy in comparison to the smartly dressed consultant. 'Excuse me sir I'm Detective Sergeant Palmer. Would you mind if I sit in with you,' he asked politely.

'Fine by me, Sergeant,' said Alan, turning to leave.

Paula was surprised to see Joan Stevens smoking. The ash tray was half full and a window had been opened. A cold chill charged the air. Russell Stevens stood up as they entered.

'Good morning,' said Alan, smiling pleasantly. 'Please take a seat.' Paula wondered if the father would have been as much trouble if it had been Alan who had spoken to them on that first occasion, instead of Lennox. 'I've been given to understand you'd like to talk to me about Vince's treatment?' he said.

'His name is Vincent not Vince,' said Russell Stevens. 'How many times do you people need to be told these things.'

Alan's smile wavered. 'Quite,' he said and then added, 'I'm pleased to say Vi-n-cent,' he stressed each syllable, 'is showing signs of improvement.'

Stevens cut in. 'I want my son transferred to the Queen Alexandria's Hospital,' he said. 'I've made enquiries. He should have been taken straight to a Neurosurgical Unit.'

Paula was impressed by Alan's composure. Lennox and James had both cracked in less than five minutes.

'Look, Mr Stevens,' said Alan. 'There are absolutely no indications for Vincent to be transferred anywhere.' The consultant leaned forward. 'Neurosurgeons are very busy people. You'd be hard pressed to find one who'd be willing to take over his care.'

'I won't have my son festering in some piddling general hospital.'

Alan crossed his arms and took a deep breath. 'Your son has had two CT scans,' he said. 'And although there was some initial swelling on his brain, we treated it appropriately. He is showing all the positive signs we could hope for, but until his chest has improved we cannot wake him up. You are going to have to learn to be patient sir.'

'Are you refusing to transfer my son?'

'I see no reason to put him though the trauma of a transfer,' said Alan. 'So yes I suppose I am.'

'You do realise,' said Mr Stevens. 'I am a solicitor and I will resort to the law, if the need arises.'

'I'm afraid that doesn't change anything,' said Alan.

Jeff stared at Paula who wanted to be anywhere, but there. She made an effort to help her beleaguered consultant.

'We are in constant touch with the neurosurgeon,' she said. 'He has seen V -' she nearly shortened his name again. 'Vincent's scan results and has been advising us on the appropriate treatments.' Paula didn't like the man, but she did have sympathy for him. She was angry at her mother's GP. Even though it wouldn't have made any difference, she thought he should have referred her to the neurologist sooner.

In the end Mr Stevens relented, on the condition that Paula arranged for him to speak to the neurosurgeon on the phone. She promised to arrange the call as soon as possible.

'Bloody man,' said Alan, as they headed back to the unit.

'If it makes you feel any better,' said Paula. 'He's the same with everyone. There's only Brian that hasn't been on the receiving end and that's only because he does a runner as soon as he sees them coming.'

'I'll ban him if he keeps it up.'

'Oh, doctor,' she said, laughing. 'You know anger is a natural reaction in these circumstances.'

'Sister,' said Alan. 'There is nothing natural about that man. He is the most obnoxious person I've ever met.'

Chapter Twelve

It was a couple of minutes before seven pm. The two friends walked, side by side, along theatre corridor. At that time of night the place was eerily quiet. The warmth filtered through their outdoor clothing and they began to peel off the top layers. At Paula request, Nancy had set up a meeting with the junior Sisters.

'Are you really sure you want to do this?' said Nancy.

'Yes, I am sure.'

Nancy grabbed Paula's arm and pulled her up. 'I've been going back over some of the old audits,' she said, standing in front of Paula. 'A few years ago the death rate went up to twenty-nine per cent. That's way above the national average and you didn't think anything was going on then.'

Paula pushed her hands into the pocket of her jeans. 'This is different,' she said.

'And this other thing,' said Nancy. 'About them all dying in the early hours, is rubbish. There's been- what - two - three at the most. You're making a mountain out of a molehill.' She grabbed hold of Paula's arm. 'I don't want you to go in there and -'

'What? Look like a fool?' Paula finished the sentence for her. Her jacket slipped to the floor. She bent over, picked it up and leant against the wall. 'Nancy, I know the stats aren't conclusive and maybe I am being paranoid,' she said. 'But that's why I'm doing this and what if I'm right?'

'Okay, okay, I get the message,' said Nancy. 'Let's presume you're right - what if it is one of the Sisters?'

'I'd rather risk tipping off the culprit than do nothing,' said Paula. 'You never know. It might be enough to put a stop to it. I'd be happy with that.' She flung her jacket over her shoulder and pushed herself off the wall. 'Nancy, I need your support on this.'

Her deputy shrugged. They were about to continue on their way when Philip Birch appeared from the direction of the ICU.

'Where's the fire?' said Nancy.

'What,' Philip said, as he reached them. 'Oh, yes, sorry, have to go.' The young consultant was well known for his absentmindedness as well as one or two, more unfortunate personal habits, for which he was subjected to a lot of mickey-taking behind his back. Paula shouted after him as he hurried off.

'I thought you were on holiday this week.'

Philip stopped, turned and walked back towards them. He seemed flustered. 'Erm, I - I'm doing some research for the pain relief clinic. Yes – have a nice night,' he muttered and then resumed his journey.

'Now that's what I call dedication,' said Nancy.

'If he's been doing work for pain relief,' said Paula, 'why was he coming from the direction of the unit?'

'Why not,' Nancy muttered to herself.

The pair continued in silence. Speculation had been rife for the reason of the hastily arranged meeting and all six junior Sisters were waiting for them in the seminar room. Eight large desks had been jammed together to create a large rectangle in the middle of the room. A flip chart stood at the far end of the extended table. Paula made her way over to it and threw her coat and bag over the back of the nearest chair. Nancy followed and pulled out a seat, placing it close to the chart board. She sat with her legs stretched out in front.

Paula felt her throat tighten. Doubts began to flash through her brain. What if Nancy was right and this was a bad move? She took a deep breath and then coughed nervously.

'Hi,' said Paula. All eyes were focused on her, except for Nancy who concentrated her attention on a scuff mark on the floor. 'Firstly, I want to thank you for giving up your time tonight. I'll try not to keep you too long.' Paula's mind went blank. She grabbed her bag and searched for her marker pen to give her time. Nancy had pushed her chair back and it was balancing on two legs.

'Let me start by stressing how confidential this is,' said Paula, aware of her deputy's posture. 'Anything that is said in this room stays between these four walls. Do you understand?' She looked around for acknowledgement, before turning to the flip chart. She wrote down the figure without referring to any notes. When finished, she stood to one side and ran her fingers through her hair.

'I believe we might have a serious problem in the unit,' said Paula. There were a few sharp intakes of breath. She definitely had their attention now. She pointed to the chart. 'These are our mortality rates for the last couple years. As you can see our yearly average is usually around the twenty-three per cent mark, which is appropriate for a unit of our size. In the first nine months of last year we were slightly above average -'

A noise made several people start. Paula turned toward the noise. Nancy's chair had slipped back onto its four legs with a clatter. She looked sheepish and mouthed 'sorry'. Paula ignored her and continued with her presentation. At one point, she chanced a glance round the table. Puzzled looks were reflected on every face, bar one. Nancy looked decidedly bored. Paula continued. 'I know the numbers aren't terribly significant at the moment, but if you look at the trend.' She felt as if she was begging them to believe her. 'If it continues as it is, by the end of the year our death rate will be way above the national average.' She stopped. The startled looks had been replaced with stunned horror. Nancy leaned forward.

'We're only in February,' she said. 'Surely there's still plenty of time for things to even out. It could be the quality of the patients we've been getting recently. You know yourself; Ted Brown has a habit of sending no hopers.' She began to bite her fingernails.

Paula glared at her. She muttered to herself, 'thanks for your support,' out loud she said. 'Yes, you could be right -' but she struggled to find an argument. She sighed. Maybe Nancy was right. Maybe this was just a way of forgetting her personal problems. The youngest sister came to her rescue.

'What do you think it is then?' said Beatty Pearce.

'Well it could be that Nancy's right,' said Paula. 'And it's just a blip, but I think there are too many coincidences.'

'Paula,' said Kath Hammond. She was one of the more experienced Sisters. 'Surely you're not implying that someone is responsible for this?'

'Something in my gut,' said Paula 'is telling me that these aren't random coincidences.' She tried to sound more confident than she felt. 'I still need to go through the patients notes, but yes I do think we have to consider that possibility.'

A few nervous laughs rolled across the table. She had to raise her voice to be heard above the muttering. 'Let me give you an example,' said Paula. She gave them a rundown of her conversation with Ethel Hoyle. 'I know he was going to die, but there was no reason for him to go like that and -' She knew it didn't sound terribly convincing.

'So what you're saying,' one of them said, 'is that he was dying - and then - he died.'

'No you don't understand,' she said. 'It's the time of day that's unusual.' Paula realised that she was losing them. She hung on to the back of her chair. 'Listen to me. Three out of the last four deaths occurred between the hours of six and eight in the morning.'

Maureen Dent's face flushed with anger. She was sat at the furthest point from Paula, who didn't see her reaction.

'What have the consultants said about it?' said Kath.

Paula threw her pen on the table. 'I haven't told them yet,' she said. 'I need to gather some evidence before I can take this any further.' Her knuckles glowed white on the chair. 'I need you lot to keep your eyes open for me. So far I haven't been able to find any correlation between the deaths and any member of staff.' There was a mass intake of breath. She continued. 'I don't suspect anybody, but we do need to find out what's happening.'

'You mean if,' Nancy muttered under her breath.

'I know this is difficult to get your head round,' she said, 'but even if you don't believe me. I need you to be vigilant.' Paula had still failed to notice the Bat's discomfort.

'How dare you.' spat Maureen. Her neck had turned the colour of a mottled lobster. 'Don't you think I would notice if someone was messing about on my shift?'

Paula raised her hands defensively. 'I wasn't accusing you Maureen,' she said.' In fact, I'm not accusing anyone.' With the intention of appeasing Maureen, she said. 'You weren't even on duty when two of the deaths occurred.' But that only seemed to antagonise her even more. The night sister grabbed her coat and stormed out.

'Oops,' said Nancy.

Paula sighed. The last thing she needed was the Bat in a petulant strop. The others began to pepper Paula with questions and it soon became obvious they were sceptical about her unease. She did however, manage to elicit their cooperation.

'Before you go,' she said. 'Can I just say - if you notice anything – anything at all suspicious - you can ring me at any time and can I remind you, what I have said must stay within these four walls.'

The sister made a noisy exit. Nancy hung back. She sat on the table, kicking her heels.

'Thanks for your support,' said Paula, sarcastically.

'How did you expect them to react?' said Nancy. 'You can't expect them to believe someone is killing off the patients.' She folded her arms. 'So, what are you going to do now?'

'If I can't even persuade my own staff,' said Paula. She ripped the paper from the flip chart and folded it up. 'I'm not likely to have much luck with the consultants or management.'

Nancy sucked in air through clenched teeth and jumped off the table. 'She's not my favourite person,' she said. 'But politically - it might have been better if you'd had a quiet word with the Bat separately.'

She was probably right, Paula thought, but wasn't in the mood to admit it. She crammed the folded paper into her bag. Nancy began to put on her jacket.

'Are you all right?' she said. 'I've heard a rumour that you and Duncan have split.' Nancy waited a moment for a reply. None forthcoming, she pushed harder. 'It's not true is it? Not you and Dunc-the-hunk.' She grabbed Paula's arm and made her look at her. 'For God's sake woman, talk to me.'

Paula was still angry with Nancy and shook her off.

'The word is,' said Nancy. 'Duncan is really cut up about it. I thought I was your friend, but you always clam up whenever something's wrong. Why won't you talk to me about these things?'

'Is that why you wouldn't back me up tonight,' said Paula, 'Because I don't tell you my problems?'

'No, of course it isn't,' said Nancy. 'Don't you get

tetchy with me; I'm only trying to help.'

'Didn't look that way to me,' said Paula.

'Please yourself.' Nancy turned to leave.

Paula slumped into one of the hard plastic chairs. 'I told him I needed some space,' she said. What energy she had left, suddenly evaporated. She bowed her head and ran both hands through her hair and massaged her neck. 'So what does he do? He bombards my answer machine with messages.'

Nancy pulled out a chair and straddled it. 'Why do you need space?' she said.

Paula shrugged. A salty tear trickled down her cheek. She wiped it away with the back of her hand. 'My mother has been diagnosed with Alzheimer's,' she said.

'Oh, no,' said Nancy. 'Why didn't you tell me this before? No wonder you're so stressed out.'

Paula searched in her bag for a tissue. 'I'm not stressed out,' she said. 'I'd be all right if-.' She was going to say *if you supported me,* but thought the better of it.

'Your mother's really nice,' said Nancy. 'Not her, I can't believe it. Your dad must be devastated.'

'Jennifer's there for him,' said Paula. 'I'm useless. I can't bear the thought.'

'Surely she's too young to get Alzheimer's?'

'Sixty-two,' said Paula, wiping a tear from her cheek. 'Malcolm hasn't bothered to come up. He's devastated because she'll probably end up in a psychiatric hospital, but then I can't say anything. I've only been home once since I took them to see the neurologist.'

'Does Dunc know about this?'

'No he doesn't,' said Paula 'and I don't want him finding out either.' She gave Nancy a warning stare. 'This has nothing to do with what's happened between him and me.'

'Do you know something, Paula,' said Nancy.

'What?'

'You can be so annoying sometimes.' She pushed her chair under the table. 'You have this misguided belief,' she said. 'That you don't need anybody - you have to take everything on yourself. Well let me tell you, missy - I am here for you, but I can't help if you won't talk to me.' She took her car keys out of her pocket. 'I'm with you on this - thing,' she said, gesturing at the flip-chart. 'And I'm sorry if I seem negative, but what you are saying - is so mind bogglingly unbelievable - it's hard to get your head round something like that, but I'll try and square things with the Bat for you.'

Paula made her way towards the door. Nancy followed.

'By the way,' she said. 'Talking of Frank Hoyle, did anyone tell you that his wife's been on the phone? She asked if we've found his St Christopher.'

Chapter Thirteen

A sprinkling of white flecks trickled from the snow-laden clouds. It was several days since the sisters' meeting, but Maureen Dent still seethed at the slight on her professionalism. She had just finished the night shift and was putting the key into her car's ignition when she saw the doctor heading across the car park in the direction of the hospital. Maureen climbed out and ran to intercept him. She shouted his name across the tarmac.

'Am I glad to see you,' she said, pulling up beside him.

'Sorry?'

The cold caught her breath. 'I've been trying to catch up with you.' She panted thin clouds of water vapour. 'I half expected you to call in.'

'I'm sorry, Maureen -.' He continued walking.

'I was just wondering,' she said, quickly. 'If you think Paula's lost the plot this time? - I told management they were making a big mistake when they gave her that promotion. - She was never up to the job.'

'I'm late for a meeting,' he said, increasing his pace.

Maureen stopped and shouted after him. 'You do know that she is going round telling everybody someone is killing the patients?'

A chill slithered down his spine and made him shiver. The doctor retraced his steps until he stood directly in front of her. 'What did you say?'

Maureen's neck turned crimson. 'She even had the temerity to accuse me,' she spat.

Grabbing her arm roughly, he repeated the question. 'What did you just say?'

'You mean she hasn't told you about it?' said Maureen. 'That is so typical of her. You'd be the first person I would tell. Not that I'd make up such a ridiculous allegation in the first place.'

'Slow down, Maureen,' he said. 'What on earth, are

you are on about?'

'That woman has absolutely no idea how to run an ICU,' she ranted. 'She's the most ineffectual manager I've ever come across.'

The doctor stared at the breath steaming from her mouth.

'At least they'll have to sort her out now,' she babbled. 'I can't believe she had the audacity to insinuate it was me.'

He cut in to her tirade. 'Maureen, I have absolutely no idea what you are talking about.'

She took a deep breath and started again. 'I was summoned to a Sisters meeting,' she said. 'Where Paula proceeded to accuse me of killing patients.' She took another deep breath and let it out slowly, before continuing at a more moderated pace. 'Of course, no one believes her. They're all saying it's because her boyfriend's dumped her.' She shook her head. 'I've told you before, she can't cope under pressure.'

An icy knot squeezed his solar plexus. Outwardly, he smiled. 'What made her say something so ridiculous?'

'She muttered something about the audit,' Maureen said, with a snigger. 'As if I wouldn't know if something like that was happening on my shift.'

'I thought you said,' he said. 'That she accused you.'

'It's the same thing really.' She stared at him. Flakes of snow had settled on his thick wavy hair. 'You're looking a bit pale. Are you okay?' she said.

His mind was well ahead of his voice. 'Yes, yes, of course I am,' he said. 'It's cold that's all.' He rubbed his hands to give credence to the comment. 'It's not like Paula to be so irrational though. Did she give you any reasons for this - outburst?'

Now Maureen had his full attention, she seemed much more composed. She hugged herself against the cold. 'No. I think Nancy's trying to get her under control,' she said, 'but I'm not sure she's had much success.' The tip of her reddened nose had begun to run. She sniffed. 'You won't let on I said anything to you, will you?' she said.

'Of course not,' he said. The doctor looked over her head to where his car was parked and then added. 'Thanks for letting me know, Maureen. I am sorry, but I really do have to dash. I'll try and catch up with you later.' he said, dismissively.

She didn't notice that the doctor headed, not in his initial direction towards the hospital, but back towards his car.

*

The doctor's wife had settled herself comfortably on the chintz sofa in the lounge. Despite the hour, she had closed the curtains and pulled the glass topped coffee table within easy reach. On it were a box of scented tissues, a half empty box of Belgian chocolates and a large gin and tonic. The small, plump dog was ensconced on his mistress's lap. He watched her, while she watched, not for the first time, a video of Brief Encounter. A long thin drool of saliva dangled from the dog's mouth. The woman straightened the red bow on his forehead and allowed him take one of the chocolates from her fingers, before wiping his muzzle. She let the tissue drop onto a pile on the floor. So immersed in the tear-soaked romance, the woman didn't hear the front door bang. The dog's ears flattened against his head when the doctor opened the lounge door and stood in silhouette.

The sight filled him with revulsion. 'What are you doing?' he said.

She fumbled for the remote control. Billy jumped from her knee and scrambled away from a mistimed kick into the kitchen.

'It's the middle of the afternoon,' he said. 'No wonder you're so fat.'

'I thought you had a list this afternoon,' she said, plumping up the cushions.

'Surgeon's on holiday.' His temper hadn't improved any since his talk with the night sister. 'I'm going to my study and I don't want to be disturbed,' he said, slamming the door behind him. The doctor called into the kitchen, filled a glass with his ten year old malt whiskey and added a handful of ice. As he crossed the hall, he heard the television go back on. He entered his study, crossed over to the windowsill and slotted a CD of Tristan and Isolde into the music centre. Sitting back on the soft leather chair, he closed his eyes and allowed the powerful music sweep over him, but even the vigour of

Wagner could not stop his mind from wandering. At work, he'd made a few discreet enquiries about Paula and had discovered that there was some truth in what the interfering busy-body had told him. Rumours of her allegations abounded, but the general opinion was that no one was taking her seriously and having dropped the bombshell, she now seemed to have disappeared.

He took a generous gulp of whiskey and tried to dismiss Paula from his mind. The doctor pondered on the reason why he'd married a woman he had never loved. Following the death of his mother, he and his father had agreed to go their separate ways. Money was scarce and he ended up taking on a series of degrading jobs and living in cheap digs to fund his medical training, which meant he had little time or inclination for a social life. He knew that women were attracted to him, but could not connect with them on either an emotional or intellectual level. For him, sex was a method to gain erotic pleasure and relieve tension. At one time, he considered if he might be homosexual. In an endeavour to find out, the doctor performed a series of experiments, one of which was to select a range of pictures of both men and woman that he found pleasing. Taking male and female in turn, he would masturbate then compared the strength of his sexual satisfaction. He concluded that, in all probability, he was actually heterosexual, but did not rule out more experimentation with a male on male relationship. However he never got round to it.

At the time he couldn't afford a car and so had to take the bus to the university. A young woman came to his attention. She wasn't particularly attractive, but was easy on his eye. Every day she would stare at him. He stared back. Lacking any other form of entertainment, he eventually decided to ask her out. He was flattered by her infatuation and as she had the ability to fully satisfy his sexual needs, he allowed the relationship to continue. It became a habit and when she fell pregnant, marrying seemed the easiest option. It also occurred to him that being married would enhance his position as a doctor. After the birth of their second child, she lost interest in sex and he lost interest in her.

The CD finished. He could still hear the dog's piercing

yap through closed doors and so replaced Wagner with Bach and finished off the glass of whiskey. Picking up his briefcase from the floor, his fingers hovered over the catches as his thoughts strayed back to Paula Hobson and how she could have found out. Could he have got sloppy? He doubted it. He always made sure he covered his tracks well.

The doctor opened the case and removed several glass ampoules of Potassium Chloride from the elasticated pocket. The majority of his stock was safely locked in his filing cabinet at work, but he liked to keep a reserve at home. He placed all but one of the ampoules into a box in the drawer. Rolling the glass in his fingers, he gazed at the crystal clear liquid. It glistened in the light from his lamp. He thought, in an ideal world, Morphine would have been his drug of choice, however it could be detected after death and the stock was carefully monitored. Occasionally, he would use Insulin, but this was harder to obtain and so Potassium Chloride had become his drug of choice. He carefully laid the ampoule on top of the others.

Chapter Fourteen

Paula felt winter's icy breath on her cheeks as she walked up the path to her parent's bungalow. She let herself in and wiped her feet on the doormat.

'It's only me, Dad,' she shouted

Her father shuffled into the hall in his slippers. 'I'm glad to see you made the effort,' he said, sharply. 'Shut the door, you're letting all the cold air in.'

Paula did as she was told.

'I thought you'd forgotten,' he said.

The remark stung. She dropped the sports bag containing her overnight things next to the telephone seat and threw her coat on top. It had been a long time since she'd stayed overnight and she no longer kept any of her things at the bungalow. 'I said I would,' said Paula.

'You said you'd be here at nine,' her father scolded. 'It's nearly ten. Our Jennifer's never late.'

She spoke softly so her father couldn't hear. 'No, of course not,' she said. 'Jennifer would never be late.' As soon as the words were out of her mouth, she felt guilty. Paula thought her father looked as though he'd shrunk. She kissed him on the cheek and gave him a hug. 'I'm sorry. I couldn't get away any sooner,' she said. 'How is she?'

'She's asleep now,' he said. 'But she's been unsettled all day.'

'Where is she?' said Paula. The sitting room felt hot and stuffy after the cold.

'In the sun-room,' he said.

'Isn't it bit cold for her in there?'

'I can't stop her.'

He sounded tired and deflated. They reached the door to the small annex, which had been built long before conservatories had become popular.

'You are stopping, aren't you?' he said.

'Of course I am.'

Paula opened the door to find her mother slumped on the

reclining chair. Grace Hobson's chin nestled on her chest. A fine dribble of saliva had formed a small puddle in the deep notch of her throat. Grace was six years younger than her husband, but now looked considerably older. Despite Jack's best efforts, she looked a mess. Crumbs of food clung like Velcro to her cashmere jumper, which hung loose over the gaunt frame. Her skirt had ridden up, exposing thin varicose legs. The sight broke Paula's heart.

'I'll put the kettle on,' said her father. He disappeared in the direction of the kitchen.

Paula found some tissues and wiped away the saliva. She sat on the adjacent chair and felt wretched. The French-doors looked out onto the back garden, her father's pride and joy. Paula remembered sitting in the same chair a lifetime ago. It was before she met Duncan. She had been in the process of moving out of the hospital flats into her house and had taken a few days out to stay with her parents. Her father was sick of being hen-pecked and had taken himself off to the golf club. Grace had bought some Mars bars; Paula had made a jug of Pimm's, complete with cucumber. They'd sliced the chocolate into thin portions and had flung the patio doors open to enjoy the warm afternoon sunshine. They'd gigged like naughty schoolgirls and then her mother had become serious.

'Now that you're a high flying nurse, Paula' she'd said. 'Will you promise me something?'

'What?'

'Do you remember Marion Prothero?'

'Yes.'

'She told me her husband's got dementia.'

'Oh, I am sorry.'

'Promise me,' said Grace. 'That if I ever get like that. You'll slip something into my tea. I could cope with anything except losing my sanity.'

At the time, Paula had laughed. Now, she was beginning to wonder if her mother had had some sort of premonition. She rubbed her face and ran her fingers through her hair. The only way she was going to get through the night without breaking down, was to pretend her mother was one of her patients. After sharing a cup of tea with her father, she woke Grace and cajoled her into the shower. Her mother's body had halved its weight in a matter of months. Wrinkled skin hung loose over the frail, skeletal frame. Breasts that once suckled and nurtured children now drooped like deflated balloons. By the time they had finished, Paula could hear her father snoring in the spare bedroom. She was to sleep with Grace to keep an eye on her. Paula managed to get Grace into the bedroom where she flopped onto the bed, giggling. At least she hadn't lost her sense of humour, thought Paula.

'You have absolutely no idea how much I love you,' she said.

'You're silly,' said Grace, 'silly Jennifer, silly, silly.'

'I'm Paula.'

Her mother started to become agitated and pushed Paula away.

'No, no, no I have to,' she said, standing up. Grace looked around for a moment and then began to shuffle round the room, opening drawers and cupboards, pulling out the contents before moving on. Paula followed, unceremoniously shoving everything back. Grace wandered in to one room after the other and then back in again. She seemed to be searching for some unknown object, but couldn't tell Paula what it was. Paula found articles of clothing secreted in bizarre places. A rolled up evening dress, shoved under the mattress of the top bunk in the box room, where the grandchildren occasionally slept; bags of flour in the back of the wardrobes; a shoe pushed down the back of a chair. Its mate was in a kitchen cupboard. Paula gathered them up and dumped them in the kitchen. It was after midnight before she convinced her mother to get into bed. Grace looked up to her pleadingly.

'I don't want to die, Jennifer,' she said. 'I don't want to die.'

Paula gasped with horror. 'You're not going to,' she said.

Grace grabbed Paula's arm and twisted it in a Chinese burn. Paula struggled to loosen the vice like grip. She tried to hug her terrified mother.

'I'm here for you,' she croaked. 'I promise I won't let anything happen to you.' Despite her efforts, Grace became more and more agitated. She got back out of bed and began her search again. Paula burst into tears. It was like Groundhog Day. She couldn't believe her father managed to put up with it night after night. It was two in the morning, before Grace eventually fell into a deep stupor. Paula covered her with the duvet then climbed, still fully clothed, into the adjacent bed. Every nerve ached and her head pounded. Unable to sleep, she sobbed quietly into the pillow. After an hour, she gathered up the duvet and pillow and took herself into the box room.

The following morning, Grace was in exactly the same position. Paula found her father eating his breakfast. A pot of tea brewed on the hob. She could see anger in his face.

'I thought you were supposed to be looking after your mother?' he said. 'What sort of nurse are you?'

'I'm sorry, Dad,' she said. She poured herself a cup of the strong brew. 'I didn't realise she was that bad.'

'Humph.' Jack Hobson took a slice of toast from the rack and began to plaster it in butter.

'Is she like that every night?'

'Mostly,' he said. 'Why do you think I told you not to leave her?'

'I'm sorry,' said Paula.

'Can't you get time off work?'

'No, but I'll talk to Jennifer,' she said. 'We'll work something out.'

Chapter Fifteen

Robbie and Amber were playing tag around the waiting room, whilst Jude thumbed through the outdated, tattered magazines. On returning from picking the kids up from school, she had found Marty semi-conscious on the bedroom floor. Jude had called an ambulance then asked Mrs Stott to look after the kids, but the old hag refused to give up her bingo night.

It was over an hour before a nurse came looking for them. They entered the cubicle to find, Marty dressed in a gown with hospital property written in multicoloured swirls. No matter how hard Marty tried, she couldn't get comfortable on the hard trolley. Her head ached and her body felt like it had been through a car press. Amber and Robbie tried to climb onto the trolley. Jude grabbed the pair by the scruff of their necks and dragged them off.

'I thought you'd had it,' she said, to Marty.

Marty opened her one good eye and tried to grin. She gingerly prodded at her face and said. 'At least he hit me on the other side this time.'

'Yeah, well it's time you went to the cops,' said Jude. She turned, pulled the kids away from the sink and turned off the gushing taps.

'It's not worth it,' said Marty, fingering her teeth to see if any were loose. 'Ouch.'

'The bastard's a psychopath.'

Marty told her friend to be quiet. Amber clambered onto the trolley to get a better view.

'You aw-right mummy?' she said.

'Yes thanks,' said Marty. 'Get down cupcake, or you'll tip mummy out and then we'll both have a bad head.' She held onto her daughter's hand whilst Jude lowered her to the floor. 'Have you been a good girl?'

A nurse passed the open doorway. Robbie ran after her, he was closely followed by Amber. Marty pulled herself up and the gown slipped from her shoulders. Readjusting it made her wince.

'I'm okay,' she said. 'It's only a broken cheekbone and a cracked rib. I'll be fine in a couple of weeks.' She lowered her voice. 'I tell you what; his conscience must be getting the better of him. This time he left a grand.'

'Yeah and how much do you get when you're dead?'

'Just think Jude, a thousand pounds,' said Marty. She attempted to smile, but it hurt and turned to a grimace. 'It's a bloody fortune. We can pay the rent. Go places. Get the kids some nice gear.'

'If I were you, said Jude. 'I wouldn't let the bastard near me.' She added as she smoothed down her short, clinging skirt. 'What did the doc say?'

'I can go home,' said Marty. 'I have to take it easy for a couple of days.' She stroked her cheek with the back of her hand. 'It's just as well. Looking like this, I'm not likely to get much work am I.' She tugged on the side rail. Chuck my things over.'

Jude helped her lower the rail, before picking up the pile of bloodied clothes from the chair. She pulled a face as she handed them over. They emerged from the cubicle to find Amber and Robbie running up the corridor, closely followed by the nurse.

'We're not a nursery, you know,' said the nurse, but she ruffled Robbie's hair and laughed when he kissed her hand. Taking a leaflet from her pocket, she handed it to Marty, saying. 'Head injury instructions, basically it tells you come back if you feel sick, dizzy or drowsy and you'll need someone to keep an eye on you tonight?' She looked at Jude, who pulled a face.

Amber wrapped her arms round her mother's legs. 'I look after mammy,' she said 'You're my mammy, I look after you?'

'Yes, cupcake,' said Marty.

'I'll stay with you,' said Jude, trying to get hold of her son who was swinging off the bottom of the nurse's uniform.

Marty, suddenly did an about turn and disappeared into the cubicle.

'Where you going?' said Jude.

'Nowhere,' said Marty. 'I thought I'd forgotten something, that's all.' She came back out clutching onto her ribs.

'You look bloody awful.'

'I'm fine.'

The nurse had insisted they get a taxi home. The two children squashed on the back seat in-between the adults. To the irritation of the driver, they competed to see who could kick the back of the seats the hardest.

'What was that about?' said Jude. 'You looked like you'd seen a ghost.'

'Did you see the man and woman?' Marty said, quietly over the top of Amber. Jude shook her head. 'It was my mother and her shitty husband.'

*

Paula was stood in the middle of the cramped, overfilled storeroom. A large wooden drug cabinet filled the whole of one wall. It contained an inner cabinet, which contained yet another much smaller cabinet that held the stock of controlled drugs.

Paula felt claustrophobic. She stood zombie-like in front of the open doors, unable to remember why she'd gone in there in the first place. It was over a week since she had stayed over at her parents' and she'd spent the rest of her days off trying to get help for them, but had had little success. She'd only spoken to her father once since returning to work.

Paula stared at the set of keys in her hand. Choosing the one with the red tag, she carefully inserted it into the lock of the inner cabinet and turned the key. The metal door creaked. She ran her fingers over the dozen or so boxes within and then removed a box of Morphine. She opened the flap and took one of the fragile glass ampoules from its plastic casing. She twisted the ampoule in her fingers. The fluid sparkled in the electric light. Paula had always thought the system of checks and counter checks for controlled drugs to be full proof, but she'd realised it wasn't.

Her sleepless nights of the past week had been filled with plans and schemes to help her mother and she had come to the decision that she had to get hold of some drugs. Paula had worked out that all she needed to do was to pocket a few empty ampoules of morphine, along with their tops. The drug was used frequently so it wouldn't take her long to get what she needed. As soon as she had sufficient, she would swap the empty phials for full ones then pretend to drop the box on the floor and get someone to check them with her. They would write off the smashed vials as an accidental breakage. It was simple.

She replaced the ampoule into the box, locked the doors and ran her fingers through her hair. 'Sorry mum,' she said, out loud. Someone entered the room and came up behind her.

'Oh, Celia,' said Paula. 'You made me jump.'

'Sorry, Sister,' said the student. 'I need to get a bag of dextrose.'

Paula handed over the bunch of keys. Celia frowned and held them in her open palm.

'Erm,' said Celia. 'I'm not allowed to hold the keys.'

Paula snatched them back and left the room.

Chapter Sixteen

The doctor stood before the row of stainless sinks in the theatre scrub room and scoured at his hands. Last night he'd told his wife, he'd caught his knuckles changing a bottle on the anaesthetic machine. This morning, one of the orderlies had asked him if he'd been in a fight. He told him that he'd slipped on the ice and grazed them on the garden wall. His wife might have believed him, but the orderly hadn't.

With all the rumours abounding about Paula's accusations, he'd intended to put a hold on his ministrations. But when he found the ICU staff resuscitating a non-starter, he had to do something. They were wasting time, effort and his money. The guy was going to die anyway and it probably didn't need his intervention, but when he saw the nurse straddled over the body, looking as though she was performing some bizarre act of copulation, he'd felt the excitement in his groin. Killing in front of an audience increased the risks. It also increased the challenge and ultimate reward. It had been almost too easy. He was like a puppeteer, pulling the strings in a production of his own making. He'd offered to help and asked the nurse for an adrenalin injection then swapped it for the syringe of potassium in his pocket. The rush had been better than anything he'd experienced before. The power was almost overwhelming. He was surprised that no one noticed. Then he remembered illusion was his greatest talent.

The incident with the prostitute had been regrettable. Although he found it distasteful, violence had become compulsory and cathartic. Some primeval instinct seemed to take over his body and it needed an outlet.

The stream of cold water surged over his hands and he splashed his face. It was time Paula Hobson found out what she was up against.

*

It was twenty-five past twelve and she was going to be late.

Paula jogged along the corridor. By the time she reached the changing room, she was out of breath. She was pulling on her scrubs when one of the staff nurses joined her. The nurse told Paula there had been a death that morning. There was something in the girl's voice that made Paula suspicious. She made her way into the unit and let Nancy give her the hand-over, before she dragged her deputy into the office.

'How come all the staff know?' she said, standing with her back to the radiator.

'Know what?' said Nancy, looking bemused.

'Know about what we've been talking about.'

'Less of the – we – please.'

'There has been another death, hasn't there?'

Nancy shrugged.

'It could be one of the sisters,' Paula muttered it to herself.

Nancy shook her head. 'Jeez, you're really starting to scare me,' she said. 'You're getting this way out of proportion.' Nancy stood next to the table and crossed her arms. 'Apart from the fact that the guy had just been admitted, he was in cardiogenic shock. It's amazing he got this far and anyway Karen was the only person on duty who'd been at that meeting. You're not suggesting it's her, are you?'

'No, of course not,' said Paula, 'but the more I think about-.'

'Maybe,' said Nancy. 'That's the problem. You're thinking too much.' And then, in an attempt to lighten the conversation, she added. 'I know we're bloody good, but miracles take a little longer, as they say.'

'This isn't funny.'

Nancy sighed and picked up a set of records from the table. 'I'm sorry, but I think it's a coincidence. However,' she said. 'Because I thought you might mention the incident, I've been through the guy's notes and I've spoken to Karen. There were never less than two people with him at all times. So unless you are saying there is some sort of conspiracy-.' She dropped the notes on the desk and leaned against the filing cabinet, fiddling nervously with the key. Paula didn't move.

'Look, Paula,' said Nancy. 'I've agreed to keep an eye on things, but I think you're being a little paranoid.' She waited for a response. Paula glared.

'Maybe you're over tired,' said Nancy. 'You're obviously worried about your mother. Then there's Duncan. Perhaps you should take a couple of days off.'

'Have you finished?' said Paula. She picked up the notes, flicked through them and then slammed them on the desk. 'How bloody dare you? Who the hell do you think you are telling me what to do?' Their voices were so loud they could be heard in the unit.

'I thought I was your friend,' Nancy said. 'But if you want my professional opinion, you shouldn't have had that meeting. The nurses are all over the place. It's not just Maureen who thinks they are being accused. They all feel under suspicion.' Nancy flicked at the key. 'And - if you are so sure about it - why don't you go to management or the police?'

'If you're not going to help,' said Paula. 'Then I don't need *your* opinion - and while I'm at it, who has been telling everyone? I made it perfectly clear at the meeting.'

'What the hell did you expect?' said Nancy. 'You can't drop a bombshell like that and then expect them to keep quiet. For God's sake, Paula, the whole bloody hospital probably knows by now.'

Paula struggled to keep her emotions under control. She'd had disagreements with Nancy before, but nothing like this. 'I made it perfectly clear at that meeting. What I said was confidential and if I find out who has – I –I,' she stuttered with temper. 'I'll discipline them.'

Nancy flushed. 'Oh, yeah, that would be just great,' she said. 'Let the whole bloody world in on your paranoia and what if – sister bloody smarty-pants - you're wrong, eh? For one minute, suppose this bizarre theory of yours, is wrong. What do you think is going to happen, eh? You'll have put everybody through all this hell for nothing.'

'I'm not wrong.'

'Okay,' said Nancy. 'Let's say you're right. Tell me, who would do such a thing? I'm bloody certain it's none of our staff. Even better tell me how - how the hell could anyone get away it?'

'I'm not wrong,' Paula repeated stubbornly. She lost

her temper and swept her arm across the desk, scattering the contents. They both stared at the mess.

Nancy spoke first. 'You know you can't go on like this, Paula' she said, picking up the papers.

Paula hesitated a moment, but then stormed out of the office, slamming the door behind her.

Chapter Seventeen

So much for getting off on time, thought Paula as she changed out of her scrubs into mufti. They'd had an admission an hour before the end of shift. Having nothing to rush home for, she'd stayed back to help clear up. The argument with Nancy had been playing on her mind all afternoon and she'd made her mind up to try and sort things out. Heaving the laden backpack over her shoulder, for a split second, it crossed her mind that Duncan would be worrying. Then she remembered. The backpack dug into her ribs. Paula knew if she was caught removing the files from the hospital, she would be in big trouble. She shrugged the bag higher onto her shoulders and left the changing room. It was well after ten-thirty pm when she made her way along the theatre corridor. Someone had turned off the main lights, casting ghostly shadows along the walls. Paula had done her fair share of nights and the half darkness didn't worry her.

She was approaching theatre's main, equipment storeroom when she thought she heard a noise. The room held the expensive anaesthetic machinery and so she decided to take a closer look. The door was slightly ajar. It was supposed to be locked. Paula couldn't see anything through the gap. She pushed it open with her foot. A shiver trickled down her spine. She told herself to get a grip and tried to find the light switch by running her hand up and down the inside wall. Unable to find the switch, she rummaged around in her bag until she found a pen-torch. Paula used her backpack to prop open the door and let in what little light there was. The storeroom was probably one of the largest in the hospital and the glow from her tiny torch proved to be totally ineffectual. She could just to say make out the outlines of the large wire-metal trolleys. Arranged in rows, they held a multitude of neatly stacked sterile instrument packs. Spotless anaesthetic machines lined the walls. She heard a loud clunk echo up from the far end of the room.

Paula called out. 'Hello, is anybody there?' She

hesitated, looked back towards the door. It would be more sensible to go and phone security, but then she'd have to make a report and everyone already thought she was paranoid. A bogus security report wouldn't help her cause. She slowly began to make her way along the middle aisle, edging deeper into the darkening space. The beam from her torch was less than useless and by the time she was three-quarters of the way into the room, Paula knew it had been a big mistake. All her instincts told her to run. She muttered to herself. 'Don't be silly - nothing's going to happen.' She shouted into the gloom. 'Hello – it's Sister Hobson – I know somebody's in here?' There was the distinct rustle of clothing. Whoever it was, they were hiding at the bottom of the aisle. She shook the torch in a desperate effort to get more light out of it.

'I know you're there,' Paula said, peering into the darkness. She inched her way forward. 'Come on out.' She tried to make her voice sound authoritative. Suddenly, there was a noise from behind. Before she could turn round, an arm swung around her throat and pulled her off her feet. Paula could feel herself falling, her arms flailed in the air as she tried to regain her balance. She struggled; she stamped; she kicked at her attacker's shins; she tried to grab his arm, but her fingers failed to gain a grip. The vice tightened around her neck until she could hardly breathe. Paula tried to scream, but the pressure on her windpipe allowed only an inaudible gurgle to escape her lips. She felt something soft clamp over her nose and recognised the distinct sickly smell of anaesthetic mixed with rubber. Her legs buckled and she fell into a nightmare.

Paula's only connection with reality was the cold concrete floor beneath her flaccid body. The world hissed in her ears and spun through her brain like a tornado. She tried to grab the mask, but her limbs failed her commands. A disjointed voice drifted through what little remained of her conscious thoughts.

'I know you can still hear me, Paula,' he said quietly. 'I want you to listen very carefully - I don't want to hurt you, but you've got to stop.' The icy whispers floated round her head. 'No one believes you.' She could feel something pressing against her throat 'You're making a fool of yourself.' Paula realised he was massaging the nerve in her neck, which would to slow her heart rate. In that part of her mind separate from the fear, she wondered if he was trying to kill her. At least, she now knew that she'd been right all along. For all the good it would do her. Her heart pounded against the membranes of her ears, like drum. His soft voice penetrated her thoughts.

'Paula,' he whispered. 'I do really like you, but you must consider the consequences of your actions. You must know that cannot get the better of me. There is no proof.' His words drifted back and forth. 'They think it's all in your imagination. Give it up, Paula.' She wanted to scream, but couldn't move.

'If you continue to interfere in things that don't concern you - it will be bad for your career and you never know - it could be very bad for your health.' His voice seemed familiar, but she couldn't place it.

'This is not a threat, Paula,' he continued. 'It's a promise - I know where I can find you and I can get to you any time I want.' He spoke so quietly that his last words were drowned out by the hiss of gas and the pounding of her heart.

Consciousness returned in spasms, along with an overwhelming feeling of pain and nausea. She was disorientated and grabbed the nearest trolley to help her up, but it rolled away and she fell back to the floor. She decided to remain on hands and knees until her head cleared. A searing pain shot through her left hand, making her groan. She stayed like that for several minutes, until she was able to pull herself up with the aid of the trolley. A rip-tide of nausea flowed over her as she staggered toward the light. In the corridor, she leant against the wall. Her vision was blurred, but she could still make out the crepe bandage covering her hand. Paula knew she ought to go and find help. The unit was nearest, but she couldn't bear to face Maureen. She needed time to think. She needed to go home.

The continuous bleep of the answer-phone made her get up from the sofa where she been since staggering into the house. She punched the play button. There was a message from Duncan. He repeatedly asked her to pick up the phone. The message ended abruptly after he shouted. 'All right, please yourself.' Paula considered ringing him, but decided against it. He was liable to do something silly. There was also a message from her father. She deleted them all and poured herself a drink of Duncan's brandy. Returning to the sofa where Barnum had claimed his usual corner, she unravelled the bandage. There was a large, blood-soaked dressing covering her palm. She stared at the wad of cotton, not daring to remove it. Blood began to trickle down her wrist.

Eventually, she plucked up the courage to peel off the dressing. There was a clean surgical incision that started between her thumb and index finger and then traversed diagonally across her palm, ending at her wrist. The edges had been neatly reunited with a series of steri-strips. The blood began to dribble down her arm and drip from her elbow. She raised her hand in the air and took a slug of the brandy. Paula knew she should go to A&E and have it stitched, but how could she explain what had happened? Who would believe her? Besides, she felt too sick to go anywhere. She couldn't even remember driving home.

Collecting the first aid kit from the kitchen, she rummaged around the old biscuit tin, which contained half a dozen Elastoplasts, an unopened bandage, a new rugby gum-shield and a squashed tube of Anthisan. The blood continued to dribble from her elbow as she scoured the house for something to replace the dressing. In the end she used one of Duncan's large cotton handkerchiefs that an elderly aunt had given him for Christmas. It was difficult bandaging with one hand, but in the end she managed a reasonable job. After she'd cleared away the mess, she found herself a couple of paracetamol, washed them down with the brandy and topped up the glass. Paula lay back against the cushions and stroked her cat. Thoughts swirled through the whirlpools of her mind. None of it made any sense. Why? Why would he do such a thing? Thoughts of Duncan, her mother, the attack, threats, and death, all spun on a merry-go-round of despair and pain.

Chapter Eighteen

James Bentley was about to enter the ICU when Paula barged through the double doors and nearly knocked him over.

'Morning, Paula,' said the fresh-faced consultant, cheerfully.

Paula stared through him. James waved his hand in front of her face and repeated the greeting, adding. 'Is anybody in there?'

'Sorry, yeah hi,' she said.

The consultant looked from her face down to her hand. 'Are you all right?' he said. 'What have you done to your -?'

'I'm fine thanks,' said Paula, cutting him off. She had only been on duty a couple of hours and was already sick of everyone asking about her hand. James blocked her way. She averted her eyes. 'Look, sorry James, but I'm in a hurry,' she said as she tried to push past him. James reached over and opened the door. He stared after her receding figure.

Despite daylight, the terror of the previous evening flooded back as she entered the corridor. She tried to take her mind off the rising panic by considered whether James could have been her attacker. He had been on call the previous evening, but then so had Ravi and they'd both known she was on shift. Paula couldn't believe either capable of such aggression. The same could be said for all the doctors she worked with. Brian Pollard was an elder statesman and a gentleman. Alan Charlton and Lennox Telleman were both first rate anaesthetists and then there was Philip. He lived on a different planet to everyone else. She knew they were all capable of spitting out their dummies if they didn't get their own way and she'd seen them at their worst, but she was sure none were capable of hurting her.

She had just started to think about the junior doctors, when she found herself outside the theatre store room. The doors were open and she could hear someone moving around inside. Her hand flew to her throat and she broke out in a cold sweat. She had to take several deep breaths, before she could force herself to go inside. She looked for the light switch and realised that if she had only gone a little further, it had been within reach. A noise made her jump. A young orderly was working at the end of the row of trolleys. A surgical mask dangled from his neck, blood-splatters covered his wellies. He whistled a nondescript tune as he loaded the sterile packs onto glass trolleys and stopped when he saw Paula approach.

'Bloody hell, Sister you made me jump,' he said.

'Sorry.'

She grabbed the nearest trolley with her good hand and hid the other one behind her back while she scanned the room. The orderly asked if she was looking for anything in particular.

'No,' she said, trying to smile. 'I - is everything okay?'

He frowned. 'Yes thank you,' he said. 'And you?'

She struggled to keep her composure. The orderly stared at her, waiting for her to say something else.

'Have you noticed anything odd?'

'Such as -'

'I don't know,' said Paula, 'something out of place - a mess maybe?'

'Nope,' he said, shrugging. 'Should there be?'

'No.'

The office of the theatre manager was like a goldfish bowl. When the Venetian blinds were open, it had a commanding view of the operating theatre suite. However, Charles Edmonds rarely opened the blinds, preferring to watch the comings and goings through the slats. If the ambitious manager was not at a meeting, his time was mainly taken up by placating irate surgeons.

Paula walked past the window, knocked on the door and entered without waiting for a response. The tweed jacket on the back of the door dislodged the flat cap that had been resting on top of it. Paula bent down, picked it up from the floor, slapped it on her thigh and returned it to the hook. She sat on the chair next to the manager's desk. Charles switched off his computer screen and swivelled his chair to face her.

'Did we have an appointment?' he said.

'I didn't think I needed one,' said Paula.

Charles pushed the keyboard to one side. 'So, what can I do for you, sister?' he said. His eyes took in her bandaged hand. Before Paula could say anything, he added. 'If you don't mind me saying, you don't look too good. What have you done to your-'

'I cut it on a broken bottle,' snapped Paula. She'd told the lie so many times; she was beginning to believe it herself. Lack of sleep made her feel nauseous and her hand throbbed. She handed him a copy of the audit and cradled her hand whilst he read it. Charles flicked through the pages then put it to one side.

'Thanks for that.'

'It's only a draft,' she said.

'Well come back when it's finished.' He tried to give it her back.

'I want you to read the summary,' she said.

'I'd rather wait until it's finished.'

'I think someone is practicing euthanasia in the ICU.'

The paper fluttered to the floor. 'What?' he exclaimed. He bent down to pick up the report. His flushed face blotched as his blood pressure rose. 'What?' he repeated.

'I said,' said Paula. 'Someone is practicing euthanasia in the ICU.'

It seemed to take Charles some time before he regained the power of speech. 'Wow,' he said. 'And who have you told about this?'

A shiver of dismay passed through Paula's body. 'You,' she said. 'You, - I'm telling you.'

'Yes, yes,' said Charles. 'What I mean is – who else – and why hasn't any of the consultants said something to me before now?' He removed his rimless glasses and nipped the bridge of his nose.

'I've been trying to catch Brian or Lennox,' she said. 'But they're both in theatre.'

Charles fiddled with his specs before putting them on. He flicked to the back of the report and began to read.

'Nancy knows,' said Paula. 'And I've mentioned it to the Sisters, but I've given them strict instructions not to tell anyone.' What she didn't say was that the gossip had already spread throughout the hospital like an infection.

'Wow,' said Charles again. 'This is mind-blowing.' He tapped the ends of his fingers together and examined the Senior Sister closely.

'Right,' he said to himself. 'The question is do I take this to the chief exec?' To Paula, he said. 'How sure are you and have you any idea who's doing it?'

'Yes, I'm sure,' she said, She bit her lip.

Charles thumbed through the pages of the report. 'Where are your graphs?' he said.

'I haven't put them in yet.'

'I can't take this to the CEO as it is.'

'You've got to be kidding.'

'These figures don't mean much on their own. You need to be able to show it graphically,' he said.

'Well, it's more of a trend,' said Paula 'and -.'

'Hang on a minute,' said Charles interrupting. 'You mean you haven't got any real evidence?'

'Charles, I'm not making this up,' she said. 'He is-'

'He, he, who?' said Charles.

Paula wanted to tell him about the attack, but she knew if she tried to explain, it would only make her look paranoid. She tried to convince him to take her seriously, but her head had started to throb in time with her hand and she lost her train of thought. In the end she lamely said. 'Put it down to instinct, Charles, but please - you have to believe me.'

'Right, okay,' said Charles. He peered at her over the top of his specs. 'Leave it with me. I'll sort something out and get back to you.'

'But-'

'Don't say anything to the consultants. I'll have a word with them myself.'

'Please, Charles you have to believe me.'

'Yes, yes of course I do,' he said. 'Look, Paula, I am sorry, but I'm already running late for a meeting. I will talk to the consultants, but you must understand we have to be very careful about this sort of thing.' He placed the report on top of a large pile in a wire tray and twisted his chair to face the desk.

Chapter Nineteen

The four consultants, annoyed at being dragged away from their lists, entered the office muttering. Charles swung his chair round to greet them. He was holding a clipboard that held Paula's report.

'Ah, come in, gentlemen,' said Charles. 'Thank you for coming at such short notice. Please take a seat.' He waved his arm across the office, which was a little short on chairs.

Alan was the only one to take up the offer. He chose a seat in the corner of the room, crossed his legs and immediately looked at ease. Lennox folded his thick, hairy arms and leant against a row of khaki-green filing cabinets. James and Philip flanked the door. The seat nearest the desk remained empty. Lennox spoke first.

'Dr Pollard sends his apologies, Charles,' he said. 'He can't find anyone to cover his list.' It was a lie. Brian's actually words were. 'Tell that trumped up little nonentity to piss off.'

'Ahem,' Charles cleared his throat. 'Sister Hobson came to see me this morning.'

'Oh, for God's sake get on with it, man,' said Lennox.

'Yes, yes sorry,' said Charles. 'But this is a rather sensitive issue.'

'Charles,' barked Lennox.

The presence of the senior doctors seemed to fluster the manager. Lennox's obvious bad temper didn't help. 'I'm afraid we have a rather serious problem, gentleman,' he said. Charles clung to the top of the clipboard and looked at each of the doctors in turn. Their faces remained impassive. He approached the subject tentatively 'Have any of you been made aware of any issues concerning the ICU?'

Philip removed his flimsy theatre cap from his thinning hair and scratched his scalp. 'Charles, some of us have patients waiting,' he said.

'Apparently, Paula suspects - someone is - oh dear – erm,' said Charles, struggling. The words eventually tumbled out in a rush. 'She thinks someone is practicing euthanasia.' The manager reached behind him, grabbed a pencil from the desk and began to fiddle with it. 'I know this all sounds rather fanciful, but she is insistent about it and I have to say -'

'Bollocks,' said James cutting in. He started to laugh. 'She's having you on.'

'Please Doctor,' said Charles. 'This is serious and as far as I am aware Paula is not prone to paranoia.'

'Is this what you've dragged me out of theatre for?' James said, shaking his head. 'Bloody hell I thought somebody had declared war.' He pushed himself off the wall and grabbed the door handle ready to leave. 'Tell her to take more water with her whiskey next time.'

'Please hear me out Doctor Bentley,' said Charles, more forcefully.

'Yes shut up, James,' said Alan, 'or we'll never get out of here.' James grunted and resumed his position by the door.

Before continuing, Charles nodded gratefully toward Alan. 'I agree with you, James,' he said. 'It does sound rather farfetched, but we do have to take something like this very seriously.' Charles twiddled the pencil between his fingers. 'I have looked at her figures and although there are one or two slight anomalies, I think they could probably be easily explained. However, even if this does turn out to be a flight of fancy, as I suspect it will, we are still left with the problem of,' he tapped the paper with the pencil to stress the point, 'what do we do about Sister Hobson?'

'Can I just say something here?' said Alan. 'In my opinion, Paula is a well balanced person and not someone prone to flights of fancy.' He flicked a piece of fluff from his trousers. 'Although I do find her claims a little hard to swallow. There are far too many people around the ICU for someone to get away with that sort of thing.'

'She is very set on this idea,' said Charles. 'It could be she is having some sort of breakdown so we need to think about what is best for the ICU.'

'That's your problem, mate,' said James.

'Maybe,' said Charles, 'but I'm sure I don't need to tell you all, it would not do your department's reputation much good, if she went to the press or police with this.' He began doodling thick concentric circles on to Paula's report.

'You'd better get it sorted then,' said Lennox.

'Yes well,' said Charles. 'I have spoken to Sister Coleman. Apparently, Paula has a few personal problems at the moment, which are putting her under some considerable stress.'

'What are these so called problems?' said Philip, speaking for the first time.

'To be perfectly honest,' said Charles. 'I don't really know. I did try to find out, but Sister Coleman wasn't keen to elucidate. I have to say though that when Paula came to see me this morning, she looked absolutely terrible. She looked as if she hadn't slept for weeks.'

'She's hurt her hand,' said James.

'Yes, I asked her about that,' said Charles. 'She said something about cutting it on a wine bottle.' The manager scratched his scalp with the blunt end of the pencil and then smoothed the tuft of hair back over his bald patch. 'You don't suppose she has a drink problem, do you?' he added.

James blew out his cheeks. 'She certainly looks rough at the moment,' he said, 'but I don't see Paula as an alky.'

'I would find it hard to believe,' agreed Alan. Lennox pulled a noncommittal face and Philip turned his attention to the ceiling.

'So, gentleman,' said Charles, 'any ideas?'

'Charles, as far as I can see this is a personnel matter,' said Lennox, sounding exasperated. 'You are the manager so I suggest you get on and manage it.'

'I thought I'd explained all that,' said Charles. 'If we dismiss her allegations without making, at least, some effort to investigate, we could find ourselves in deep water. I am, as you kindly pointed out, a manager and no expert in ICU matters. Gentlemen, my inclination would be to take this to the CEO. If it did turn out that there was substance to what she is saying, he'd be very upset if I hadn't informed him. However, if it is some aberration in Sister Hobson's mind we would all look rather silly.'

'No, Charles,' said Lennox. 'We wouldn't - you would.'

Philip suggested they get Paula over and have it out with her, but James pointed out that if she was in the middle of some sort of breakdown, being intimidated by them would put her under even more pressure. He suggested they make some preliminary investigations before making any snap decisions. At that moment, the door flew open and Mr Stone, the General Surgeon, stormed in demanding that his anaesthetist return to theatre immediately.

'Before you all go,' said Charles, as the doctors made for the door. 'Can I just confirm? We agree that at least for time being, I will defer contacting the CEO. In the meantime, one of you – you can decide who, between yourselves - will look into the allegations and in the meantime I'll contact Nancy to arrange for her to come in for a meeting.'

'I'm in the middle of some important research,' said Philip. 'I haven't time to deal with that sort of thing.' He began to relieve an itch in his groin. The others averted their gaze.

In the end, they agreed that the meeting with Nancy should be restricted to the manager and whichever consultants available at the time.

'In the meantime, gentlemen,' said Charles. 'I suggest we keep this between ourselves.'

The consultants were out of the door before he finished speaking.

Chapter Twenty

Paula hadn't cleaned for weeks. The living room was a mess. Reams of paper and computer printouts cluttered the coffee table and floor. Multi-coloured post-it notes protruded from patient records heaped in untidy piles. Charts and graphs had been fastened to the white walls with Blue-tack. Barnum sulked on the sofa because she'd scolded him for scattering the papers.

She had stopped answering the telephone or returning calls, even from her family. Paula felt guilty and kept promising herself she'd drive down to the bungalow to make up for it. But the truth was she just couldn't face either of them. Her mother's vacant eyes and lack of recognition and her father's condemnation of her neglect overwhelmed her with feelings of guilt, self reproach and anger.

The cut on her hand was a festering reminder of the attack. Reluctant to heal, it oozed continually. Paula kept it hidden under a bandage. She was grateful that her attacker hadn't found the notes in her backpack. Without questioning her motives, the anaesthetic secretary had been retrieving the notes for Paula. In every case, she had found the ICU charts to be missing. The loss of the charts was a major blow. She'd spent hours trawling through the data, but was no further forward. The trouble was she wasn't even sure what it was she was looking for. Paula had little appetite for food and so decided to go for a walk in an effort to clear her mind. She grabbed her Berghaus from under the stairs and found a pair of Duncan's woolly gloves to stretch over her bandaged hand. It was Saturday afternoon. Normally, she'd be standing on the sidelines watching Duncan play for his club.

She walked aimlessly for over an hour. The river Lye split the town into two distinct halves. The west hosted the golf course and more affluent properties. The east bank played host to run down council estates, ear-marked for regeneration, and several industrial estates. Head bowed against the chilly wind and oblivious to the icy-cold drizzle, Paula made her way along tree lined avenues. She reached the river and wandered along the grassy embankment, watching the wind chase the water. She looked up. The distant, snow-topped hills seemed to beckon.

She found herself in the Victorian park, adjoining the rugby club. In the summer, it would be crowded with noisy families, but for now it was deserted. She passed the dilapidated band stand and crossed to a large wire enclosure. A selection of birds shared their captivity with a collection of mop-eared rabbits. They continually hopped around the collection of rabbit food and bird shit. Doleful eyes followed Paula as she ran her hand along the wire. She realised that she showed all the classic signs of burn out, but knowing about it didn't change anything.

She made her way over to the empty children's playground, sat on one of the swings and pushed herself back and forth, letting her shoes slide over the hard muddy ground. The cold had penetrated the open-weave of her gloves, making her hand ache. Saying she'd cut it on a bottle had not been one of her better moves. The rumours were that she'd been drunk, but even if she'd told the truth, they wouldn't believe her. At the moment, no one was giving her the time of day. She felt like a pariah. Despite her protestations of support, even Nancy wasn't convinced by her arguments. Whoever this man was, he must be having a good laugh at her expense. She wanted to fight, but if she couldn't find the evidence what chance had she. Paula felt desperately alone. She needed her mother.

Lyedale Amateur Rugby Club was playing at home. Shouts drifted through the ether. Paula climbed the small hillock that separated the park from LARC's field. A lone sycamore offered shelter from the icy breeze. She let its branches envelope her, shifted some of the leaf-litter and eased herself down onto one of the roots. A carpet of snowdrops spread out in front of her. Their milky heads hung in sympathy with her mood. She was able to make out the home strip of blue and white beneath caked mud. A small crowd of supporters stood on the far side of the pitch. The teams were well into the game and had broken off for an injury. She could see Duncan jumping up and down to keep warm. Occasionally, the referee's voice was carried up to her on the wind.

'No hands - hands away – scrum – crouch and hold –engage.'
Deep grunts exploded from the pitch as burly men collided in
the scrum. Despite herself, Paula couldn't help but be sucked
into the excitement of the game. She watched as the away
team pushed the blue-and-whites toward the touchline. Deep
in the home quarter, the ball emerged from the scrum. Paula
found herself gritting her teeth, silently urging her side on.
Duncan intercepted a pass and sprinted down the wing. Three
burly defenders blocked his way. He glanced over his shoulder
looking for support. Paula stood up, straining to see as he side
stepped the first defender, held off the second with an
outstretched arm. He was just short of the try line when the
remaining fullback crunched into him. Paula winced.
Duncan's strength and adrenaline were enough to take him
over the line. She couldn't help herself and punched the air,
shouting his name, but her voice was carried away on the
breeze. The try was converted and the referee blew full-time.

Without thinking, Paula had started to make her way
down the hill, but then saw that Duncan had been surrounded
by his team-mates. She stopped and watched them hoist him
onto their shoulders in a triumphant melee, before taking him
into the clubhouse. It appeared that her ex was doing fine
without her.

Chapter Twenty-One

Charles was out of breath when he entered the newly decorated seminar room. The manager had arranged for the meeting to be held on the fifth floor, well away from the ICU. The floor space could be divided into two sections by a large concertina door. One half of the room was given over to an informal area with small round coffee tables surrounded by low-slung easy chairs. The other side was set up as a formal lecture theatre with state of the art presentational equipment. The doors had been left open and Charles tugged on the handles to try and close them. He only managed to drag the heavy structure a few inches before giving up.

Brian Pollard, had refused to be involved in what he saw as 'underhand action', but Charles had managed to persuade Lennox, Alan and James to attend the meeting. He'd asked them to arrive fifteen minutes prior to Nancy, to give them plenty of time to discuss the situation before she arrived. He'd also arranged for a large flask of coffee and a plate of assorted biscuits and was fussing around the refreshments as the doctors entered.

'Coffee,' he asked as they took their seats. Lennox declined. The others assented.

'No milk for me,' Alan said, arranging his chair so as to put space between himself and the manager.

'Thank you for coming,' said Charles 'I asked you here a little early, because I think we need to decide a strategy before Sister Coleman arrives.' He served the coffee. 'I'm sure you've all had time to realise the seriousness of these allegations and the impact they could have on the hospital and especially your department. I've had a quiet word with the CEO and he agrees with my assessment of the situation, which is that unless there is some proof to these claims, it would be better for all concerned if we nip this in the bud.' He raised his eyebrows, looking for agreement. The doctors nodded. 'Gentleman, I don't need to tell you,' he continued, 'what would happen if the media got hold of such spurious accusations.' He stood up and handed round the biscuits. 'And take my word for it, gentlemen, most of the flack would be aimed at you. So do I have your agreement that we deal with this in-house so to speak?'

Alan took a sip of the sharp caffeinated coffee. He pulled a face and returned the cup to its saucer. 'I have taken a look at the statistics,' he said, 'and although I don't want to be the one to discredit Paula, I am afraid I can't find any validity to her claims.' He put the cup and saucer on the table. 'There are a handful of deaths that have happened at a similar time of day, but in the main, they were patients that were expected to die. It's the sort of anomaly we'd expect to see now and again.' He rubbed his chin. 'I'm afraid I don't find any significance in her figures.' He then added. 'For Paula's sake, I am sorry.'

'Can I add something here,' said Lennox. A crumb of biscuit clung to the corner of his mouth. He said, to Alan, 'I am sorry that Paula's having problems, but I'm not sorry you haven't found anything.' He turned to the manager. 'And I also agree with you Charles. It is unthinkable that these fantasies are real.' He wiped away the crumb. 'Although I have to say – that even if someone has taken it upon themselves to help one or two patients on their way, I'm sure it was all done with the best of intentions.'

'Excuse me?' said Charles, looking horrified.

'Well, it's all right for you managers,' said Lennox. 'You sit in your little ivory towers and pass judgement on everyone else, but we live in the real world. Nowadays we can prolong life virtually indefinitely. Sadly it's not always to the benefit of the patient and it can leave us with some very difficult decisions.' He bent forward conspiratorially. 'If someone has - and of course I'm not saying they have – but for arguments sake let us say her claims were true. I'm sure whoever had been doing such a thing - would know by now that they've been rumbled and would have put a halt to whatever -'

'I don't think I like what I'm hearing, Doctor,' said Charles. 'Are you saying there is some truth in what she's saying?'

'No, no - not at all,' said Lennox.

They continued to discuss the matter until interrupted by a tap on the door. Believing she was late, Nancy had taken the stairs two at a time and was out of breath.

'Sorry I haven't changed,' she panted. 'We're busy and it was difficult to get away.' She noticed the half empty cups. 'Am I late?'

'Do you want one?' said Charles, picking up a clean cup.

'Please,' Nancy said. While the manager poured a coffee, she took the opportunity to pull up a chair. Nancy grabbed two Jammy Dodgers, smiled sheepishly and put them onto the side of her saucer. 'So what's this all about then?' she asked, picking up a packet of sugar. When she ripped the top, brown granules splattered over the table. 'And why all the secrecy?' she added dusting the sugar onto the floor.

Lennox lounged back in the chair, which was too small for his big frame. James and Alan avoided Nancy's gaze. She looked from one to another.

'Right then, Sister Coleman,' said Charles, addressing her formally. 'First of all, I would like to thank you for coming today. I know you are a very busy person.'

Nancy frowned.

'We are here,' continued Charles, 'to talk about the problem with Sister Hobson.'

'What problem with Sister Hobson?'

'We are aware that she is under a lot of pressure at the moment,' said the manager. 'You know this as well as anyone. But I believe I'm right in my understanding - and do correct me if I'm wrong - her mother has a terminal illness and Paula herself has some personal problems. Obviously this puts her under a lot of stress so it's hardly surprising it is beginning to affect her work.'

'Hang on a minute,' said Nancy. 'Don't you think you should be talking to Paula, not me?'

'We want to help,' said James.

'We have to find the best way of make things easier for her,' said Charles.

Nancy spilt some of her coffee onto the Jammy Dodgers. 'I'm sorry,' she said. 'But if you are going to discus my boss. - I really think she should be present.'

'Have you seen her lately?' said James. 'She looks bloody awful.'

'We're trying to find a way to take some of the pressure off,' added Alan.

Nancy sucked the air in through her teeth and slouched back on the chair.

Charles picked up from where he'd left off. 'So we're agreed,' he said. 'We need to find the best way to take the pressure off Paula.'

They looked at Nancy.

'I won't do anything behind her back.' she said, cautiously.

'Of course not,' Charles assured. 'So, without breaking any confidences, can you give us a breakdown of the main issues?'

Nancy picked up a soggy jammy dodger then thought the better of it and replaced it on the saucer. 'Well,' she said. 'For a start, someone needs to take her seriously about this audit. It hasn't helped that you lot are avoiding her.' She threw the doctors an accusing look.

'I'm afraid that's my fault,' said Alan. 'I'm sorry, but I wanted to look into things before anyone spoke to her and you know what it's like. Its takes time to gather this sort of information together,'

'I understand she hurt her hand?' said Lennox.

'Yeah,' said Nancy. 'I've seen it and it's pretty nasty. She should have had it stitched, but you know how bloody minded she can be. She's stuck it together with steri-strips.' She regretted the words as soon as she'd spoken them.

'Mm,' muttered Lennox.

'And her mother?' said Charles.

'Alzheimer's,' said Nancy. She felt decidedly uncomfortable, but didn't know how to get out of it. 'But the rumour about her boyfriend dumping her is way out.'

'Oh I thought that was true' Lennox said.

'They've split up, but it was Paula's decision,' she said. 'I want to stress that none of these things have affected her work.'

The door opened and a fresh faced junior doctor rushed in. He looked round. 'Oops sorry,' he said. 'I take it this isn't the resuscitation lecture?' He disappeared before anyone had a chance to reply. Charles got up and closed the door. Returning to his chair he looked sternly at Nancy.

'Do you think someone's harming the patients?'

'No, well I don't think so,' she said. 'But the timing thing is a bit odd.'

'But you do agree that it is worrying if she's injured herself,' Charles said. 'Do you think she might be drinking?'

No way,' she protested.

'She's showing all the signs of burnout,' said James, 'anxiety, insomnia, accidents even paranoia.'

Charles tapped the end of his pencil on the clip board where he'd been making notes. He looked up. 'I can have a quiet word with the occupational health doctor,' he said. 'We could try and get her to take some sick leave. Although I understand your staffing levels aren't very good at the moment.' Nobody spoke. 'Other options, gentleman – Nancy.'

'You can't make her take sick leave,' said Nancy. 'That's her decision, not yours.'

Charles banged the pencil on the paper, breaking the point. 'Sister Coleman, we're trying to do our best here and you are not helping,' he said, angrily.

'He's right Nancy.' said Lennox. 'We have to do something about her.'

'You must admit, morale isn't very good at the moment' added Alan.

Nancy chewed her fingernail.

'There is another option,' said Charles. 'In fact, I think it might be the best thing all round and she wouldn't need to take time off or lose face.' He took a sip of coffee and appeared to enjoy it. 'I'm sure I could find her a project to work on.'

The consultants nodded approvingly.

'What,' said Nancy? 'You mean you're going to take her out of ICU?'

'You have to admit,' said Lennox, 'these accusations are very disruptive. I agree with Alan. The patients have to be our priority.'

'You can't do that to her,' she said. 'You cannot take her out of the unit. Anyway, what if she's right?'

'Come on, that's not a reality, is it?' said James. He leant forward and added, sympathetically. 'I know you're not convinced.'

'Of course, you will get acting up pay for the duration,' said Charles.

Nancy ignored the offer of a bribe and pushed her chair back in disgust. 'This is a set-up,' she said. 'You'd made your minds up before I got here. I can't believe you'd such a thing.'

'You said it yourself,' said Lennox. 'She's unlikely to accept sick leave as an option.'

'I don't agree with any of this,' said Nancy. She stood.

'Sit down, Sister,' Charles ordered.

She flopped onto the seat and folded her arms. The manager removed a fountain pen from the inside pocket of his jacket. He unscrewed the top and wrote bullet points on his paper. 'I think that's the best solution,' he said. 'It won't be a permanent move. As soon as she's better, Paula can go back. In the meantime, Nancy I expect you to take charge in her absence.' He glared at her. Nancy matched his stare, but made no comment. The manager continued. 'You will say nothing of this meeting to anybody, especially Sister Hobson. If you do - you could find yourself on the wrong end of a disciplinary hearing. Do I make myself clear?'

'Perfectly-'

'Good,' said Charles. He smiled. 'I will be in touch with you over the next few days with the details.'

'Is that it then?' she said. 'Can I go?' Without waiting for a reply, she grabbed a handful of biscuits from the plate and stormed out.

Chapter Twenty-Two

Marty hadn't seen a client for over a week. HR's blood money had gone some way to make up for the trauma to her body. Even so, she knew one day he would go too far. It wasn't worth the risk and Marty seriously considered whether she'd service him again. The two young mothers had allowed the kids skip school. While Jude continued to work, Marty treated Robbie and Amber to a day out at Adventure World along with several sessions at the local baths, not to mention the time spent browsing the shops, although Robbie hadn't been so keen on that part of their adventure. She eventually felt guilty about keeping them off and sent them back to school.

The small heater had been on all day. The room felt unusually warm and cosy. For once, the television was silent. Amber and Robbie were laid on the floor with colouring books and crayons. A mouth-watering smell drifted out of the kitchen area. Not noted for her cookery skills, Marty had sought help from the gay couple in the flat above. Evan had let her borrow a couple of pans and given detailed instructions on how to roast a chicken. Vegetables were simmering on the back burner of the old cooker and a large tub of ice cream had been secreted in the freezer compartment of the fridge. It awaited the addition of Smarties and chocolate flakes. When Jude entered the flat, Marty was attempting to make the gravy.

'That smells good,' said Jude. She picked Robbie up and began to spin him round.

Amber jumped up. 'Me - me – me,' she screamed.

Robbie staggered and fell. Jude continued to give turns to each child until neither could stand. She left them in a heap and crossed over to where Marty was scooping lumps out of the gravy.

'This isn't as easy as it looks,' she said.

Jude stuck her finger into the brown liquid. 'Who's bothered about a couple of lumps?' she said. She licked her fingers and nodded approvingly.

Giggling with anticipation, Amber and Robbie knelt in

front of the rickety table. Marty made them sit cross-legged then made a great performance of delivering the meal.

'I called into Johnnies this morning,' she said. The shop owner was an occasional client of both girls. He'd given Marty a discount on some second hand furniture. 'I got us a dining table and chairs and he's going to bring them round tomorrow.' A piece of chicken had fallen from Robbie's plate onto the table. Marty picked it up and popped it into her mouth. 'So in future we'll be able to sit at a proper table and I'll have to teach you some manners,' she said, licking her fingers. Robbie and Amber scooped up spoonfuls of gravy-laden turnip and carrot mash.

'Oh,' said Jude. 'I've just remembered something.' She left her half-eaten meal and rushed out to reappear a few minutes later with a copy of the local newspaper. 'You said that you thought you saw your mum at the hospital.'

'Shh,' Marty hissed.

Jude forked a lump of potato into her mouth before saying. 'What's your brother's name?'

'Why?'

'Well, Inny isn't his real name, is it?' said Jude. She turned and spread out the broadsheet on the floor.

Marty wasn't keen to be reminded of her family. 'Vincent Steven,' she said quietly. 'Why?'

Jude struggled with the pages of the paper. 'One of my punters left this yesterday,' she said. 'I was looking through it earlier while I was waiting for my three o'clock.' She found what she was looking for, folded the paper in half and flattened it out. 'And I saw this.'

Marty leaned over her shoulder.

'Read that,' said Jude, pointing to an article.

Accident Victim Improving

A nineteen year old man, critically injured following a fatal accident, remains stable according to a hospital spokesperson. Vincent Stevens of, the Poplars, Lyedale;, remains on a life support machine in the Intensive Care Unit at Lyedale General Hospital. The accident claimed the life of a Mr Alf Jordon. Age 56, of Marley Rd, Ridgebank. The father of three died when his Fiat Uno was involved in a collision with a stolen BMW and a Ford Fiesta on the Lyedale ring road on Tuesday 20th Feb. His wife, who was also in the car, is making a good recovery in hospital. Jason Wood. Age 17, believed to be travelling in the stolen BMW, also died at the scene. The occupants of the Fiesta were unhurt. A police spokesman said they are still waiting to interview Mr Stevens about the accident. They are also keen to speak to a young man seen running from the scene. He is described as 5'8' medium build, wearing dark clothing and a baseball cap. Police are keen to speak to anyone travelling on the Lyedale ring-road between 9.30 and 10.30 am on the morning of Tuesday 20th Feb. Anyone with information can call the police on 01063399425.

'Oh, shit,' said Marty. She snatched the paper from the floor to get a better look and re-read the article several times, trying to glean as much information as she could from it. Jude left her and started to clear up after the meal.

Marty stared at the paper and remembered the day her half-brother was born. She was seven years old, in desperate need of love and she became besotted with the new baby, but hadn't been allowed to hold him. Undeterred, she would sneak into his room, drag a chair up to his cot and lift him out. Despite the age difference, they became close friends, but Marty hadn't seen him since the day she left home.

Chapter Twenty-Three

Paula had been running on auto-pilot for so long, she no longer knew what day it was. In the vain hope, it would put a stop to the eddy of thoughts swirling through her brain; she'd been spending as much time as she could with the patients. It also meant she could keep a close eye on them. By now, it seemed as if everyone was aware of her *'predicament'* and either looked at her accusingly, or even worse, with pity.

The Neurosurgeon, following a sustained barrage from Mr Stevens, had agreed to come and take a look at Vincent. It had taken a significant effort on Paula's part to gather the appropriate doctors for a full case conference. In the end, a veritable throng of medical personnel had descended on the ICU. For once, the solicitor appeared to be satisfied with their efforts.

No sooner had the masses departed than a call came through about an imminent admission. Shortly after that a gurney crashed through the battered ICU doors. The pint-sized junior anaesthetist clutched her stethoscope as she tried to catch up. Paula looked at the female patient who was conscious, but only just. The woman's dank hair clung to her plump steroidal face.

'Now then, you old bugger,' said Paula. 'You just can't stay away can you, Linda?' The forty-nine year old asthmatic was well known to the ICU team. This would be Linda Scott's fourth admission in the last six months. Linda came from a family of renowned hawkers and was a formidable woman who, despite their deleterious effects, refused to give up the fags and booze. Her colourful language and evil stares put the fear of God into some of the less robust doctors and nurses. Despite this, and the woman's total disregard for her own health, Paula had become very fond of Linda. She knew that for all Linda's bravado there was a frightened woman hiding underneath. A smile tugged at Linda's lips as Paula took hold of her hand. George gratefully accepted his boss's offer of help.

Ravi rushed into the unit. 'These blood gasses are very bad, Sister,' he said, holding out a sheet of paper to Paula. 'I think we need to ventilate the lady.'

George went into the store cupboard to fetch the intubation trolley. Paula bent over and spoke quietly to Linda.

'I don't know whether you heard that,' Paula said. 'Ravi's looked at your results. He thinks it would be better if we put you to sleep until we can stabilize your asthma. Is that okay?' Linda squeezed her hand. 'I know you've been through all this before, but I'm still going to tell you what we're doing.' Linda squeezed her hand again. 'You're going to have to give me my hand back for a while,' she said. 'I'm already down to one.'

*

The office was one of many that had been packed into the fourth floor. The small room contained a standard desk, complete with computer, chair and a single filing cabinet, which had been pushed up against the unadorned, pastel-green wall. The doctor only used his office as a refuge and repository for his drugs horde. He rested his feet on the open bottom draw of the filing cabinet while he peeled open a sandwich carton. Next to him on the table, a polystyrene cup of black coffee sat on top of a copy of the hospital phone book. He was about to take a bite out of the sandwich when his bleep alerted him to a call from Ravi, who told him about the admission. The doctor informed the registrar that he'd be along shortly, before replacing the receiver and picking up his sandwich. He knew Linda Scott and her drunken husband, very well and in his opinion, the woman was a waste of time, effort and resources.

He knew Paula was on duty. She had looked tired. He decided that this could be an opportunity to remind her who was in charge. The doctor finished his sandwich while he worked out a plan. He made a quick detour to the theatre department before heading for the ICU. The theatre nurses were busy setting up for their afternoon lists. They took little notice as he removed a box of Propanolol from the drug cupboard. He called into the surgeon's changing room to draw up the beta-blocker into a syringe. When he entered the ICU, the doctor walked casually over to the bed space and stood next to the intubation trolley where a neat line of primed syringes lay on a green sterile towel. Empty ampoules sat adjacent to each syringe, indicating their contents. The doctor checked no one was looking and swapped over the syringes. It was then Ravi noticed his presence. His heart skipped a beat. Paula looked up and smiled. She still looked drawn. The doctor sucked in his adrenalin and savoured every second.

'Thanks for coming,' said Ravi. 'She's in severe bronchospasm. I have started Aminophylline and Ventolin infusions, but her blood gasses have been getting progressively worse. I'm afraid we have no choice, but to ventilate.'

'It looks like you have everything under control,' said the doctor. He returned Paula's smile before adding. 'Don't let me hold you up. I'll call in later to see how she's doing.' He nodded and then left them to do his dirty work for him.

Paula picked up a syringe from the trolley and passed it to the registrar.

'Linda,' said Ravi. 'I'm just going to give you something to make you sleepy.' He injected half of the fluid into the drip, held the mask over Linda's face and waited for the sedation to take effect. A couple of the nurses wandered over to watch. After a few seconds, a strange high pitched screech could be heard coming from the mask. Ravi eased it away from Linda's face. The noise seemed to be coming from her. The anaesthetist looked horrified. He replaced the mask and glared at Paula, looking for help. She shrugged and shook her head. Ravi gave the rest of the sedation and tried to squeeze the oxygen into Linda's lungs, but her chest had become so tight her lungs refused to move. The black rubber bag expanded like an over inflated balloon. Ravi loosened the valve to allow the oxygen to escape.

'I can't get anything in to her,' he said, panic creeping into his voice. Linda's heart-rate slowed. The monitor's alarm sounded.

George pressed the silence button. 'She's going into a bradycardia,' he said.

'Atropine' said Paula 'and bring the arrest trolley.' She grabbed Ravi's stethoscope from around his neck, put the ends in his ears and held the resonator over Linda's barrelled chest. A frown creased his forehead as Ravi listened.

Whenever he nodded, Paula moved the disc to another part of Linda's chest. The registrar shook his head in disbelief.

'Nothing,' he said. 'Nothing is moving at all. I cannot get any oxygen in, Sister. Please, give her some muscle-relaxant.'

Paula grabbed a syringe of Pancuronium from the trolley. 'I don't think she's asleep yet, Ravi,' she said. Her hands are clenched - I can't paralyse her if she's still awake.' Linda's eyes were open, but unseeing. Her body seemed to be in total spasm. Cold clammy sweat, oozed from every pore.

'I've given her all the sedation,' said Ravi.

'I know, but look at her,' Paula said, taking hold of Linda's hand. She sounded calmer than she felt. 'It's all right, Linda, everything going to be okay.'

'I'm sorry, Sister,' said Ravi, 'but I must get this tube in. Please, give her the muscle relaxant.'

Paula hesitated. She thought that to be awake and paralysed must be terrifying.

'Please.' Ravi urged.

Paula injected the drug. 'I know you can hear me, Linda,' she said. A tear trickled down the asthmatic's temple. 'This must be really frightening for you, but we need to get this tube in. The injection I've given you will make your muscles relax. You won't be able to move.' Paula looked to Ravi, who was easing his hand under Linda's neck. 'I know you're scared, but it won't be for long,' she continued. 'George is getting you some more sedation and we'll put you to sleep as soon as we can.' A look of desperation passed between doctor and nurse. Paula shouted over her shoulder. 'Hurry up, George.' The male nurse hurried over and passed Paula the syringe. But it made no difference. Nothing they did made any difference.

Chapter Twenty-Four

Paula's stomach told her she'd missed lunch, again. On returning to her office, she found a hand delivered envelope on her desk. It had been placed squarely in the middle of her doodle pad and was addressed to *Senior Sister Paula Hobson, c/o Intensive Care*. She sliced open the brown envelope with her finger and removed the contents. It was a curt, official note from Charles Edmonds, requesting she attend a meeting the following week. It also advised that she may wish to be accompanied by a union representative. Paula frowned and slumped into her chair. Why would Charles send such a letter, unless it signified some sort of disciplinary action? But she hadn't done anything wrong. She re-read the letter and then stared at the notice board. Whatever this meeting was about, her enemy, for that is how she saw her attacker, must be behind it. It had turned into a war of attrition and Paula knew that, at least for the moment, she was on the losing side.

Clutching the missive in her fist, she stormed over to Charles's office, only to find it empty. Unable to find him anywhere, she sought out his secretary who told her that he was on leave and wouldn't be back until the day of the interview. The secretary claimed to have no knowledge of the appointment or its purpose. Paula was in no doubt that Charles had arranged it so she couldn't get to him before the meeting. Returning to her office, she slammed the door, scrunched up the letter and threw it at the waste bin, muttering 'bloody little coward.' A sharp knock on the door made her start. She retrieved the paper from where it had landed on the floor, smoothed it out on the desk and took a deep breath before shouting.

'Come in.'

'Paula there's a -.' George stopped in mid-sentence and stared at his manager. She looked pale and drawn. Her cheek bones were beginning to stand proud of her face. 'Are you okay?' he said.

'I'm fine,' said Paula, folding the letter and then

putting it in her bag. 'I was just trying to think if there was something we missed yesterday with Linda.'

The male nurse crossed his arms and leaned back against the door. 'It was bound to happen sooner or later. You can't say we didn't try,' he said. George chewed the inside of his cheek for a second before adding. 'Don't mind me saying this, boss, but you look like absolute crap?'

'Subtle as ever, George,' said Paula. 'Thanks for that.' She was fed up of people telling her how ill she looked. 'I'm fine.' He didn't look convinced. 'Did you want me for something?'

'Oh yes,' he said. 'I nearly forgot. There's a woman at the door. Says she's Vincent's sister? - I didn't think he had one.'

'He hasn't,' she said. 'His mother told me he was an only child. I presumed that's why they're so overprotective.' A headache threatened, but after a moment's reflection, she added. 'I suppose it can't harm to find out what she wants. Would you mind bringing her down for me, George please?'

He opened the door to leave and then turned. 'I don't wish to be rude about this girl,' he said, 'but she doesn't look like she belongs to the Stevens family, if you know what I mean. She asked if his parents were here.'

'Oh, well, let's see what she has to say for herself.'

After George had left, Paula crossed over to the mirror that hung on the back of the door. He was right, she looked awful. Dark, panda-rings encircled her red rimmed eyes. Her head had started to pound behind her, now virtually permanent, frown. She tried massaging her temples, but it didn't make any difference. She ran her fingers through hair.

Marty's hips swung provocatively as she sauntered along the corridor in a pair of torn jeans, t-shirt and old anorak. Her trainers left black marks on the freshly scrubbed floor. George showed the young woman into the office, raised his eyebrows and left.

Paula stood and held out her good hand. 'Hi, I'm Paula Hobson, the Senior Sister here,' she said. 'Please take a seat.' George was right. The girl didn't look as if she belonged to the Stevens' family, although there was something familiar in the tawny-brown eyes. She noticed the girl's thick makeup hid several fading bruises.

Marty remained standing, 'You have Vinnie Stevens?' she said.

'We have a young man called Vincent Stevens,' said Paula.

'He's my brother.'

'We've been led to believe that he doesn't have a sister.' Paula wasn't sure what to think. It was obvious the girl was a prostitute.

'Yeah, well they're lying,' said Marty. 'I am his half-sister.'

Paula rested her hands in her lap and waited with a patience she didn't feel.

Marty broke the silence first. 'I had to leave home because- well, just because,' said. 'I wanted to keep in touch with him, but you know how it is.'

Paula wasn't sure she did know how it was, but couldn't see any reason why the girl should lie. Thinking it would give her time to think things over, she offered her a drink. Marty seemed to be taken aback by the offer.

'Sugar please?' she shouted after Paula.

Paula took her time. By the time she'd finished, because it would only cause more trouble with the parents, she'd made her mind up not to allow the prostitute to see Vincent. 'I'm afraid I can't-' she began.

'Vinnie'll vouch for me,' said Marty, butting in. 'You ask him. He'll want to see me,'

'I'm sorry.'

The prostitute looked crestfallen.

'I'm not proud of what I did,' she said. 'I got into drugs and all that stuff.' She sniffed and rubbed her nose on the back of her hand. 'Joan calls herself a mother, but-'

'You have to understand,' said Paula. 'We can't get involved in family disputes.' She took a sip of her tea and peered over the rim of her mug. 'Vincent can't tell us what he wants because he's under sedation. I'm afraid you're going to have to wait until he comes round.'

'He'll be alright, won't he?'

'He still has a long way to go, but -' Paula smiled, reassuringly. 'He's doing fine,' she said. She instinctively warmed towards the young woman and could understand why someone would want to run away from Russell Stevens. 'Honestly, he's doing fine.'

'So what's wrong with him then?' said Marty. 'When's he going to wake up?'

Paula had already told the young woman more than she intended. She pushed the blunt end of a pen into her temple in an attempt to relieve the persistent nag. In the end she gave in and told the girl what she wanted to know.

'Can I go in then?' said Marty when Paula had finished.

Paula hesitated. 'I shouldn't really.'

'Go on nurse, please, he's my brother.' pleaded Marty.

'Normally, I'd go by what his parents wanted,' said Paula. 'What if they come in while you're here?'

'I'll keep out of the way,' said Marty. 'I don't want anything to do with them.'

'I suppose in the circumstances,' Paula sighed. Did she really need the trouble?

'Please.'

Paula decided to take the risk. 'Oh, go on then,' she said. 'You're going to have to be careful, though.'

'You can ring me when they've gone and I'll come in then.'

'You don't ask much, do you?' said Paula. 'Look, I'll tell you what I will do. Your parents don't visit that often. If you ring up and ask for me, I'll try and give you some sort of idea of what's happening and the best time to come.'

'Thanks,' said Marty.

'Your mother and step-father would be very angry if they found out,' said Paula. 'So it won't happen when I'm not on duty. Do you understand? It wouldn't be fair of me to ask the staff to do it.'

'Yeah, okay,' Marty sparked. 'I can show him a picture of his niece He doesn't even know he's got one let alone seen her.' She began to scramble around in her bum-bag. 'He can tell us what he wants when he comes round,' said Paula. 'Until then, you'll have to be careful. I'll take you in and you can leave the photo with the nurses. They'll keep it in his locker for him. In the meantime, I'm sure he'd love to hear all about his niece.'

Marty grabbed Paula's good hand and pumped it up and down.

'Don't be put off if he doesn't respond to you.' said Paula, pleased to have made someone happy for a change. 'That doesn't mean to say he can't hear you. '

She escorted Marty into the unit. George raised his eyebrows at Paula. She shrugged and pulled up a chair. Marty talked to her brother, nonstop, for an hour. The tube in his mouth had been replaced with a tracheostomy. The facial swelling had reduced sufficiently to make Vincent, at least, look more like his old self. Paula explained her decision to the nurses, but told them not to say anything to the parents about Marty.

Chapter Twenty-Five

Paula, arms wrapped around her knees, sat on the rug in front of the fire. She'd pushed the coffee table out of the way and rested her back against the sofa. A CD sang quietly to itself in the background. She stared into the flames lapping at the chimney breast. After a while she noticed a small brown-edged mark on the rug. She rubbed her fingers against the roughened edges and recalled the night they'd baked chestnuts on the open grate. One had burst, showering Duncan with red-hot shards.

The cat had curled up under her legs. It was as if he felt her misery and kept close for comfort. A log collapsed and spat loudly. Paula leant forward, added another log from the stack at the side of the hearth and kicked open the damper. Her investigation had come to a complete standstill. Piles of notes lay undisturbed on the dining table. The walls of her living room remained covered with sheets of paper. Neat tables showed personnel, cross referenced to patients. She pressed the heels of her palms into her red-rimmed eyes in an attempt to stop the flow of tears.

Jennifer had phoned earlier to sarcastically thank her for her help and to tell her that their mother was going to be admitted to a Psycho-geriatric ward. Paula felt as though she had let everybody down. Simon and Garfunkel sang Bridge over Troubled Waters. 'When you're weary, - feeling small - when tears are in your eyes, I will comfort you.' Her troubled waters felt like a tsunami.

The doorbell made Paula jump. She pulled herself up on the arm of the sofa then hesitated. What if it was Duncan? What if it was her attacker? Did he know where she lived or was she just being paranoid? The doorbell persisted. Still she hesitated. There was sharp tap on the window. She turned off the stereo, crossed to the bay and tentatively pulled back the curtain. Nancy was jumping up and down outside, arms pumping at her body. A deluge of fine snow swirled around her head. Paula nodded and made her way to the front door.

Nancy made a perfunctory scrape of her feet on the doormat, before pushing passed her friend into the sitting room.

'Bloody hell,' she said, heading for the fire. 'You took your time. I could've become a snowman out there.' She dumped a carrier bag, unceremoniously onto the coffee table and rubbed her hands before stretching them in front of the flames. 'Have you eaten yet?'

Paula was surprised to see someone who had spent the last few days assiduously avoiding her. She hovered by the door. 'No, not yet,' she said.

'Good,' said Nancy. 'I've brought fish and chips.' She lifted her duffle coat and pushed her bottom toward the fire. 'Okay - I've done my bit. You go and get the plates and a corkscrew.' She wiggled her bottom and moaned with relief. 'There's a bottle of red to be going on with. I'll just stand here for a bit and thaw out.'

Paula dutifully went into the kitchen while Barnum greeted an old friend and wrapped himself round her legs. As Nancy bent down to pick him up, she noticed the unusual wallpaper.

'So what's your mum been up to then?' she said, removing her coat. She slung it over the back of the chair as she walked over to the charts. Paula came back from the kitchen carrying a tray and set it down on the chair whilst she pulled the table in front of the sofa. Nancy grunted as she scrutinised Paula's handiwork then pointed to one of the charts.

'Hang on a minute, you've got my name on here,' she said. 'You've got my name on your bloody list of suspects.' She turned to confront Paula. 'What the hell have you put my name up there for?'

Paula was sorting out the plates. 'I had to include everybody,' she said.

'Yeah, but you don't really think I've got anything to do with it.'

A row was the last thing Paula needed. She threw the fork she'd just picked up, back onto the tray, stood straight and crossed her arms.

'Do with what?' she said. 'You don't think there's anything going on so why should *you* be worried, because I've put your sodd'n name on a bit of paper.' Her face flushed with simmering temper. 'If you've come here for another argument, Nancy, I'd rather you left – now.'

Nancy put up her hands to fend off the barrage.

'Hey Kemosabe,' she said. 'I come in peace.' She smiled at her own joke. 'I was going to bring a peace-pipe, but as neither of us smoke.'

Paula sighed. 'I'm sorry,' she said, manoeuvring the sofa to make more room. 'Maybe, I'm a little sensitive at the moment.'

'I know.' Nancy weaved her way around the furniture to give her friend a hug. 'You look bloody awful,' she said.

'Thanks.'

'I'm so hungry so can we eat first and talk later.'

Paula was too tired to do anything but comply. Even though she'd brought plates, they ate their fish and chips from the paper. Barnum's whiskers twitched at the vinegar- laden smell. After a couple of mouthfuls, Nancy wiped her hands on a piece of kitchen roll.

'Chuck the wine over and I'll open it,' she said, discarding the chair for the floor.

Paula licked her fingers, reached over the back of the sofa and grabbed the bottle of Shiraz; she'd left on the sideboard. She handed it over. Nancy opened the bottle with the corkscrew and poured the wine into a couple of glasses. The pair ate in companionable silence. Nancy had made significant inroads into the meal and was chewing a mouthful of scraps when she said. 'When did you last have a decent meal?'

Paula took a gulp of the wine and wiped her mouth with the back of her hand before answering.

'Erm, the last time I had fish and chips,' she said, 'was probably - last year in Whitby. Duncan got his shoes wet.' She smiled. 'He sat with his feet against the blower all the way home.'

'Very nice story,' said Nancy, 'but that's not what I meant and you know it. If you get any thinner, the cleaners will start using you as a floor brush,'

'Don't exaggerate,' said Paula. Having eating as much as she could manage, she fed the cat a piece of fish and took her things into the kitchen. Nancy shouted after her.

'I'm not exaggerating'

*

The doctor had been hammering on the door of the flat for ten minutes, without reply. As he turned to go, he saw a young woman, carrying a plastic bag, coming up the stairwell. He leaned over the rail and pointed towards Marty's flat.

'Where is she?' he shouted.

'What do you want?' snapped Jude.

'What do think you stupid cow?' He jabbed his finger towards the flat door. 'I rang earlier. Where is she?'

'She's out,' Jude flashed her crooked teeth at him in a sarcastic grin.

'I pay good money.'

Jude edged her way up the steps. 'Trust me Hot Rod,' she said. 'She's had enough of your *good money*. If you touch her again, she's going to the cops.'

The doctor was unnerved by mention of the police. He hated women like Jude. At least Marty had more polish than most of the slogs around Lyedale. This one was definitely a slapper.

Jude flattened herself against the rails as he passed her on the stairs.

'Don't look to me, mate,' she said. 'Lay a finger on me an' I'll screw your balls into mincemeat.'

'You tell her I want to see her,' he said 'and next time I come, I expect her to be here.' As he headed down the stairs, Jude shouted after him.

'Go find some other mug to fuck.' Warming to her task, she leaned over the banister. 'Go screw yourself. You're sick you are. You should be put down.'

The doctor returned to his car. He still needed to find some release for his frustration, but quickly dismissed the idea of finding another hooker. Instead, he decided to go for a drive and joined the motorway, heading south. The traffic was light, giving him a chance to think and his thoughts naturally returned to his nemesis. For some time, he'd known that Paula had been removing patient's notes from the records department. Her efforts were doomed to fail, but she was becoming an irritation.

Chapter Twenty-Six

A lump of wood collapsed sending a flurry of sparks up the chimney. Before chucking a couple more logs onto the fire, Paula refilled Nancy's glass from the second bottle.

'How are you going to get home?' she said.

'I'm off tomorrow,' said Nancy, pulling herself up onto the chair. 'I'll take a taxi tonight and pick the car up in the morning.' She tested the new wine. 'Not bad,' she added.

'You wouldn't know the difference if it was vinegar,' Paula scoffed. She crossed over to the window and tugged back the curtain. 'It looks really icy out there.'

Nancy put her glass on the table. So,' she said.

'So,' echoed Paula.

A tension of expectation hung in the air between them.

Nancy began with a less contentious subject. 'How's your mother?' she said.

'Not good,' said Paula. She dropped the curtain and returned to the sofa. 'She's being admitted to St Mathews tomorrow.' She sat with her head in her hands.

'It must be hard for you,' said Nancy. 'I don't know how I'd feel if it was my mother.'

'You wouldn't stick your head in the sand,' said Paula, massaging her temples. 'Jennifer's furious with me. She thinks because I'm a nurse I should know what to do.'

'It's different when it's your own,' said Nancy. 'You can't possibly be objective.'

'Objective,' said Paula. 'I can't deal with it at all.'

'I don't understand why you won't talk to me.'

Paula thought for a moment before answering. 'I suppose it's because I'm frightened,' she said. 'If I let someone in, they might see me for what I really am.'

'Which is?'

'I don't know,' said Paula, 'a frightened kid – a coward – I can't bear to see my mum like that. It's as if her personality is being stripped away layer by layer. It's like she's naked - without identity. I can't go to see her in a hospital. Those places are like prisons. Christ, they don't even get their own clothes to wear. No personality, no dignity, no life. How can I watch mother go through that? And what sort of daughter am I if I don't?'

'You can't help how you feel,' said Nancy. 'I'm sure she'd understand.'

'Maybe,' said Paula. 'But Dad's not fit enough to look after her - Jennifer's got a family of her own to look after. I should be supporting them, not hiding in my own misery.' She took a deep breath and rubbed her face with the heels of her hands. 'You'll probably think I'm awful,' she said. 'I know she would hate to be like that. – I, I wish I could put her out of her misery.'

'I'm sure a lot of people in your position feel like that.'

'Yeah,' said Paula. 'But don't you see the irony? It's the same excuse he's using. Who am I to judge? - maybe he's right.'

Nancy pushed the coffee table out of the way and knelt in front of her friend, resting her hands on Paula's knees.

'It'll be all right,' she said.

'Do you know what I feel like?' said Paula.

'What?'

'Like a rabbit in the birdcage of life.'

'Uh?' said Nancy bemused.

'There's an aviary in the park,' said Paula. 'I was there the other day. There are these miserable looking rabbits in there. They spend all their time dodging bird crap.' She ran her fingers through her hair. 'That's how I feel – like a rabbit trapped in the bird-cage of life.'

'That's pathetic,' said Nancy, laughing.

Paula pouted. 'I know,' she said. She gulped down a mouthful of wine and wiped her mouth with the back of her hand. The tang of vinegar still clung to her fingers.

Nancy leant her back against the sofa. 'The difference between you and him is - you care' she said. 'Whoever this bastard is, I'm sure he's not doing it out of any sense of compassion for the patients.' She stretched over to remove the poker from the companion set and began to stab at the burning embers. 'I'm sorry,' she said. 'I know I've been avoiding you recently. Things have been a bit awkward and I didn't know what to do so I thought it easier if I kept my distance.'

'At least you seem to have come round to my way of thinking.'

'Oh no I- I don't mean that,' said Nancy.

'What? You still don't believe me.'

'No – no - well – yes,' said Nancy. 'Yes, I do believe you. It's partly that -'

'You're not making a lot of sense,' said Paula. 'I thought that was my prerogative at the moment.'

'They're trying to get rid of you,' Nancy blurted.

Paula was past anger. She didn't say anything, but got up to get her bag and retrieved the letter from Charles. She dropped it into Nancy's lap, saying. 'I think I've had a hint.'

As she read the letter, Nancy chewed her fingernails. When she'd finished, she told Paula about the meeting with the consultants and manager. Handing the letter back, she added. 'Apparently they're either going to make you go off sick, move you or take you out of the unit to do some sort of project work.'

Paula was shocked by the revelation. 'Phew,' she said. ''Thanks for telling me. At least I know what to expect now.' She threw the letter onto the table.

'Don't thank me,' Nancy said as she examined her chewed finger ends. 'I feel bad enough already. I did try to stick up for you – actually, that's not true. I was so gob-smacked I didn't get the chance. I'm really sorry boss.'

Paula shook her head in disbelief. 'It must have been tough,' she said 'especially with that group of egos.' She stared into the fire. 'I can't believe they'd do that to me. I thought they were my friends. I've done nothing wrong, Nancy.' Tears filled her eyes. 'He must have got to them somehow.'

'Who?'

'Oh, we're not going to start all that again are we?'

'No, not at all' said Nancy, 'but how do you know it's a man?'

'Trust me,' said Paula, 'it's definitely a man.'

'I get the feeling there's something you're not telling me,' said Nancy. Paula didn't reply. It was the deputies turn to sigh. 'At least tell me how far you've got with the investigation?' she said, indicating the chaos of paper.

'Nowhere,' said Paula. 'Whoever it is, he's covering his tracks well.' She cradled her wine on her tummy and tried to make the glass sing by gently stroking the rim. 'It has to be one of the doctors.'

'Why?'

'Because no matter how much I want it to be a stranger – it can't,' said Paula. 'Or somebody would have noticed. Whoever it is I can't find any evidence.' She told Nancy about the vanishing ICU charts. 'I reckon, only someone with authority could do that.' She gave up trying to get a sound out of the glass. 'There is one thing I'm certain about,' she said.

'What?'

'He's killed at least ten,' said Paula.

'Oh, my God,' said Nancy. She grabbed the bottle of wine and emptied the dregs into her glass.

'There's no telling how long it's been going on,' said Paula 'I've only gone back six months so it could be more. I think the only reason we hadn't noticed sooner is because he was careful not to affect the mortality figures.'

. 'Look,' said Nancy. 'Don't take this the wrong way, but are you sure about this? I can't believe any of our docs would do something like that.'

'I'm positive.'

'This is Lyedale, not Los Angeles,' said Nancy. 'That sort of thing just doesn't happen here.'

'Trust me, it is happening.' Paula held up her hand. 'Did you believe I did this to myself?' she said. 'Did you think I slashed my hand to get attention or was I so off my head with drink and depression that I didn't know what I was doing? Because that's what he wants you to think.' She ripped the plaster from her hand and winced at the horrendous scar. Paula pushed her palm towards her friend's face. 'He did this to me Nancy - he put me to sleep - he sliced my hand and then neatly fastened it back together with steri-strips.'

Nancy looked horrified. Her eyes swivelled between Paula's hand and her face. She listened, in stunned silence, as Paula described the attack. 'Why the hell didn't you tell me this before?' she said.

'Because I knew you wouldn't believe me,' said Paula. 'Because nobody believed me – because - because he did it to frighten me. To play mind games - and because it worked,' she said, crossly. She was as much annoyed at herself as she was the attacker for letting him get to her.

'Oh, Paula, I'm so sorry,' said Nancy. She joined her on the sofa. 'So what are we going to do?' she said putting an arm round Paula's shoulder.

'For a start,' said Paula, her sense of humour returning. 'You can stop chewing your nails. It's getting on my nerves.'

Nancy sat on her hands. The phone rang. Paula glanced at her watch and frowned. It was just after eleven. She got up and made her way over to the sideboard. 'I hope it's not Jennifer,' she said.

'Hello.' Her legs buckled at the sound of the voice. 'Who is this?' she demanded.

Nancy put her glass on the table. 'Who is it?' she mouthed, silently.

Paula put her finger to her lips and returned to the sofa. She sat next to Nancy and urged her to keep quiet. Both girls listened intently to the disjointed robotic voice that crackled out of the receiver.

'Wasn't my warning enough for you?' it said. 'How is your hand Paula?'

She took strength from Nancy's company. 'I'm fine and I will not be intimidated by someone like you - whoever you are,' she replied forcefully. There was a prolonged silence; Nancy pulled the cordless phone closer to her ear.

'You should be, Sister' said the fragmented voice. 'I know what you've been up to. You can search as much as you like. As far as everybody is concerned those patients died a natural death.' he continued. 'Your career in intensive care has come to an end, sister. Maybe a position in a psycho-geriatric unit would be more suitable.' There was a snort of derisive laughter.

Paula snapped. Her voice shook with emotion. 'I won't let you do this,' she shouted. 'Leave the patients alone.' The phone crackled with laughter. Nancy tried to snatch it

127

from her. Paula shook her head.

'You're a very silly woman, Sister Hobson,' said the fragmented voice. 'You should have realised by now, you are no match for me. I can do as I like.' There was a pause. Paula could feel his smirk. 'What do you think happened with Linda Scott?' he said.

'What do you mean?'

'People like that don't deserve to live,' he said.

'What are you talking about?'

'All that money wasted on them,' he said. 'Someone has to put a stop to it.'

Both girls looked horrified. 'You didn't,' said Paula, panicking. 'You couldn't have. I was there.'

'Oh, Paula,' he said. 'Don't upset yourself. Not even you can stop me. You can search through those notes as much as you want, you won't find anything. It's all in your mind. Remember, I'm in the very fabric of the building and I am watching you.'

Nancy tried to snatch the phone. Paula pulled it away. She covered the receiver with her hand.

'Shh,' she whispered. 'Stop it. It's better if he thinks it is just me.' Paula removed her hand from the receiver and asked the caller what he wanted.

'What do you think?' The voice croaked. 'If I were you I'd take the chance to get out of ICU. These places can end up being bad for your health.'

'If I do, will you stop the killing and leave me alone?'

The phone went dead.

'Now do you believe me?' said Paula shaking. She turned off the phone and returned it to the stand.

'You have to go to the police,' said Nancy.

'With what?' she said. Paula shook her head. 'He is right I have no evidence.' She ran her fingers through her hair. 'I don't believe it's him. He can't have killed Linda.'

'You know who it is,' said Nancy.

'No, I don't.'

'You do,' said Nancy. 'Why won't you tell me?'

'It's just something George said,' said Paula. 'He told me about an early morning visitor.'

'Who?'

'No-one,' she said. 'Forget it - it couldn't possibly be him.'

Nancy suddenly bounced on the cushion and sent the cat flying. 'I know what it is - was.'

'What?'

'That sound,' said Nancy. 'I've heard it before. In fact I've messed about with one.' She smacked the air with her fist and shouted. 'Yes.' Nancy swallowed a large gulp of wine before elucidating. 'It's one of those mechanical voice-box thingies. They use them for patients who've had a laryngectomy. They sound like one of those robots on the Smash potato adverts. He can't get one over on me.' she said, smiling smugly. 'Where did you say the wine cellar was?'

'Under the stairs,' said Paula. She couldn't help but smile. 'Don't you think it's a little late to open another bottle?'

'You must be joking,' said Nancy. 'You don't think I'm leaving you on your own with that maniac around.' She looked a little unsteady as she stood.

Paula shouted at the disappearing figure. 'You'll have to fight your way through the scuba gear.'

Nancy returned within a few seconds. She was carrying two bottles. 'Anyway, we've got to decide what our next move's going to be,' she said as Paula handed her the corkscrew.

'Great that's all I need, Cagney and bloody Lacey on the case,' said Paula.

'Which one are you going to be?'

'Cagney,'

'Oh, no, that's not fair,' protested Nancy. 'I want to be Cagney. She gets all the good looking guys.'

'Exactly,' said Paula, holding out her glass.

Chapter Twenty-Seven

Marty liked the Sister. Unlike most people she'd met in authority, Paula hadn't tried to judge or patronise her and she'd kept her promise. When Marty had first seen her brother in the ICU, she had been more shocked than she let on. It wasn't just because he looked so poorly. The boy in the bed was no longer the brother of her youth. It had upset her to think that she hadn't been there for him as he grew up.

With Paula's help, she was able see Vinnie most days. Even the mean spirited Mrs Stott had been sympathetic and looked after Amber. Marty had told her daughter that she had an uncle and promised to take her to see him as soon as it was allowed. She did not mention Joan or Russell Stevens (she no longer considered the woman to be her mother). After conquering her fear of the machinery, Marty began to help with her brother's care. She teased him as she shaved the stubbly, bum-fluff from his cheeks and spent hours talking to him about his niece. Caring for Vincent made her feel useful. Once, when she'd been giving him a wash, she was sure he'd squeezed her hand. The nurse had said it was probably a reflex, but Marty knew different.

When Paula had told her that she was going off duty for a couple of days, Marty had intended to stick to her end of the bargain and not visit until she returned. But then Marty began to worry. What if Vinnie woke and she wasn't there? He might think she'd abandoned him again. His parents seemed to stick to the same visiting times and were always away by quarter to six. Marty made up her mind to take the risk and go without Paula's agreement.

Not owning a car, it took Marty three quarters of an hour to get to the hospital. After catching a bus into the town, she took a short cut through the back streets that brought her out at the rear of the Hospital. The lighter evenings had begun to untie their winter's bonds. It would be time to turn the clocks forward soon. Marty hated the dark and looked forward to the lighter nights. She approached the large wrought-iron gates. A thick chain and padlock secured them against a vehicle, but there was a gap, made by kids, in-between the post and galvanized metal fence. Marty had no problem squeezing her slender frame through the gap. The only downside of using this way into the hospital was that to get to the main entrance you had to pass the mortuary. A continuous hum from the laundry disturbed the quiet night air. It might have been her imagination, but the dark, poorly lit area, felt cold and spooky. A shiver ran down her spine. It wasn't difficult to resist the temptation to peer through the scratched frosted windows of the morgue. Marty quickened her pace and skirted round the side of the building. She started to climb the steep, overgrown slope leading to the car park. The flimsy tread of her worn trainers combined with mud and rotting leaves made it difficult to keep her balance. She slipped and had to stop herself from falling by putting out her hand. It became caked in mud. She was wiping it on her jeans as she rounded the corner of the building.

A series of massive arc-lights flooded the car park. As Marty looked up, she could see Russell and Joan Stevens. They were stood outside the main entrance. Marty retreated behind the wall. After a few minutes, she sneaked another look and saw that they were talking to a man. He had his back to her and was wearing a white coat. Presuming he was a doctor, she felt sorry for him. She couldn't hear what they were saying, but by the body language it was plain they were having an argument. Her step-father's temperament obviously hadn't improved. She hunched shoulders and thrust her hands deep into her pockets and crept nearer. The trio were so caught up in the argument they took little notice of anyone else. Marty strained to hear the conversation. As she watched the frame of the man in the white coat began to take on a familiar shape.

The fact that HR was a doctor came as no surprise to Marty. Most of her clients were so-called professionals. They were all like her stepfather, scrape the polished surface and you find a bastard underneath. Whoever HR was, she didn't want him anywhere near her brother. Still unable to hear what they were saying, she took a gamble and walked over to join a group who were milling around the concourse. Keeping her back to her parents, Marty sidled as close as she dare. Snatches of conversation drifted across the icy air.

'I am sick of different doctors every day,' said Russell Stevens. 'Being told something different every time – such a crass manner -'

Marty chanced a glance at her mother. Age had not been kind to Joan Stevens. Heavy streaks of grey coursed through the dark hair. Deep crevices had ground their way into the skin around her eyes and mouth. Joan clung onto her husband's arm. The hairs on Marty's neck stood to attention.

'I am sick of repeating myself -' said HR.

Marty made her mind up to find out who the man in the white coat was. She thought that with a bit of luck she might even be able to exact a little revenge for the beatings. The police might not be bothered about justice for a prostitute, but the local press would be interested in the sordid life of a hospital doctor.

In due course the altercation came to an end. Russell and Joan headed off to their car. White coat entered the hospital. Marty followed at a distance. Thankful that he chose the stairs rather than the lift, she turned the corner just in time to see him exit onto the third floor landing. He disappeared along a short passageway behind the lifts. A sign on the wall read 'Anaesthetic Department'. Marty watched HR enter a room halfway along the corridor. She looked round. The place seemed deserted and decided to take the risk. She wandered along the corridor as if she had every right to be there. She stopped outside the room, examined the nameplate, did an about turn and retraced her steps.

Chapter Twenty-Eight

When first built the Victorians would have been impressed by the grand imposing asylum. Over the years the building had sprouted several tentacular add-ons and morphed into the ragged structure, which was St Mathews Psychiatric Hospital. Paula passed through a thick set of oak doors into a marbled hall and her footfalls resounded across the high acoustic ceiling. Poor signage meant that it took her an age to find the reception. A harassed clerk searched through the computer records for evidence of her mother's admission. Paula was eventually directed to one of three annexes that were in the grounds.

Retracing her steps across the driveway, she thought the gardens appeared in better condition than the dilapidated buildings. A squirrel gambolled round the trunk of one of the two great oaks, which stood in the middle of a circular lawn. She crunched across the gravel path until she came across Beech House. It was surrounded by shrubbery trees, and flower beds. Paula wondered why the unit had been named after a tree not found in the grounds.

A pair of transom windows flanked the door. One held a sheet of paper stuck on the inside. The notice, written in thick black marker pen, advised the visitor to 'Press Bell and Wait'. Paula, fighting the urge to run, stood for several minutes before obeying the command. Her summons was eventually answered by a short, rotund girl who was dressed in a uniform that had seen better days. She removed a bunch of keys from her pocket to unlock the deadbolt. The door-handles were situated at the top and middle of the frame. She had to stretch her arms to reach them and open the door. Paula flinched at the smell of stale urine mixed with hospital cooking. She introduced herself and the nurse mumbled for her to follow. The nurse indicated to a door at the far end of the corridor.

'She's in the dayroom,' she said. She turned and left Paula to find her own way.

The nearer she got to the room the stronger the stench of urine and cabbage. Paula unconsciously gritted her teeth as she opened the door. Three large picture windows gave the room a light, airy feel. They commanded a clear view of the gardens. A sideboard played host to a ghetto-blaster, which was playing a compilation of wartime melodies. Winged, high-backed chairs with Melamine topped trays slotted into the armrests, secured the occupants into their individual mini gaol. Paula's attention was drawn to an old man who sat slightly apart from the others. He sagged into the chair, legs splayed, penis exposed. The old man wrestled the tray that imprisoned him. A frail old woman wearing a pair of pink fluffy mules shuffled up to him and started to dust his chair with a handful of paper tissue. The old man screamed obscenities at her. Paula did an abrupt about turn and exited the room.

Paula tapped gently on the door marked kitchen. Someone shouted 'come in'. There was a clatter of crockery as she opened the door.

'There's a gentleman in the day room needing attention,' she said.

A young girl, leaning on the sink replied. 'We'll be there in a minute,' she said.

'Actually,' said Paula, more forcefully. 'He's got his willy out and it's upsetting some of the visitors.'

An older woman stepped forward. 'That'll be Bert,' she said in a soft Scottish brogue. 'I'll come and sort him out.'

The woman reminded Paula of ma' Larkin. She recognised the uniform to be that of a staff-nurse.

'You must be Grace's daughter?' the staff-nurse said, smiling. 'It's Paula, isn't it? We hear you're a big cheese at the LGH,'

'I am not,' said Paula. She wondered what her father had been saying about her.

'Intensive Care,' said the nurse. 'Cutting edge of medicine, they say.'

'I doubt it,' said Paula. They reached the doorway of the dayroom. She gestured toward the patients. 'I don't know how you can do this.'

'Oh, it's not that bad,' said the nurse. 'Bert can be a

bit naughty sometimes, but he can't help it. He used to be an accountant.' She let Paula go on ahead. 'I'm sorry the place is in such a mess,' she said. 'We're a wee bit over crowded at the moment. We've had to double up with Ash House whilst they're being refurbished. Then it's our turn.' She led Paula to a pale skeletal woman in the middle of the group.

'They've been promising this upgrade for the last five years.' said the nurse. She bent over and spoke gently to the old woman. 'Your daughter's come to see you, Grace.'

Paula recoiled. How could she not recognise her own mother? She kissed Grace on the cheek and took hold of the stick-like fingers. 'Hi, Mum,' she said. 'I'm sorry I haven't been sooner.' Grace squeezed her hand.

'Please,' she said. Her mother banged Paula's hand on the tray. 'Pease - please,' she kept repeating the word.

Paula shouted over to the staff-nurse who was wrestling Bert back into his pyjama bottoms.

'I'm sorry,' she said. 'I know you're busy, but do you know what mother wants?'

'As soon as I've got this young man sorted out,' said the staff-nurse. 'I'll come and have a word with you.'

Paula extricated her hand from her mother's grip. 'I love you,' she sobbed. Grace nipped her arm. 'I need you, Mum - I need you now more than ever.'

'Please,' Grace said.

Paula couldn't help but think about her mother's request and her failed effort at carrying it out. 'I couldn't do it,' she said. Tears coursed down her cheeks. 'I tried, but I – I couldn't do it - I love you. – you know I'd do anything for you - but I can't do what you want,' she whispered. A hand on Paula's shoulder made her jump.

'Come with me,' said the nurse 'and we can have a wee chat?'

Paula wiped her eyes, kissed her mother on the forehead before following the staff-nurse into the Sister's Office. A young doctor joined them shortly after. It was the first time she'd been on the receiving end and Paula felt an overwhelming need to tell these people about her mother. She wanted to tell them about the funny, gifted, erudite, beautiful person her mother had been. Instead, she sat quietly, listening to the words of comfort she'd often spoke to others.

Chapter Twenty-Nine

The grey clouds darkened as night began its inevitable ingress into day. Yet another long lonely night in a cold empty house loomed before Paula. The visit to her mother had taken a lot out of her and she shivered as she climbed out of the car. Opening the front door, the house felt warm. Paula checked her watch; the heating wasn't due on for another half hour. A stream of light trickled under the sitting room door. Another shiver ran down her spine, but this one wasn't due to the cold. Paula had ignored his threats believing them to be scare tactics. She now wondered if she made the biggest mistake of her life. Panic gripped at her stomach and she looked around for a weapon. Her dive knife was upstairs, the air tanks and other heavy gear, in the garage. The only thing within easy reach was Duncan's umbrella. It wasn't much, but better than nothing. Clutching the umbrella in her good hand, she gingerly opened the door. The crackle of flames in the fire caught her attention. Surely her attacker wouldn't light a fire. She stepped into the room just as Duncan emerged from the kitchen, wine bottle in one hand, two glasses in the other. Her arm flopped to her side.

'Is it raining?' said Duncan, as if he'd never been away.

Paula tossed the umbrella onto the chair.

'Nope,' she said, smiling to herself for being so silly.

'I thought it was time the mountain came to Mohamed,' said Duncan. Paula's lip trembled. He put the wine on the table and jumped over the sofa. Taking her in his arms, he wiped a salty tear from her cheek with his thumb. 'Hey, I didn't think seeing me, would be that bad.' he said.

'I'm sorry,' she sniffed.

'I've missed you.' He kissed the tip of her cold nose then rubbed it with his finger. 'Nancy rang me,' he said. 'I know what's happened.'

Paula unravelled herself from his arms and removed her jacket, which then followed the umbrella onto the chair.

They sat beside each other on the sofa.

'You have to promise me,' said Paula. 'You won't get on your high horse about all this.'

He leant over, kissed the nape of her neck. 'As if I would.' he said.

Paula gave him a stubborn look and pushed him away. Duncan held up his hands in surrender.

'I swear on the plonk.' He picked up the bottle. 'By the way, my wine cellar seems to have been rather depleted.' The cork slid out with a satisfying pop. He handed her a glass.

'Blame Nancy, not me,' she said.

'No, I've learnt my lesson,' said Duncan 'and I'm really sorry about your mother.' The wine glistened in the firelight as he placed his glass on the coffee table. He stood with his back to the fire. 'I love your mother,' he said 'and I love you. I never want to lose you and I will do anything - I mean anything - to have you back in my life.' The light from the flames cast his athletic figure in silhouette and Paula thought he'd never looked so sexy.

'I've missed you too,' she said, sounding more composed than she felt. 'But - if I thought you were only coming back because I'm in a mess - because you think I need a hero to rescue me then-'

Duncan knelt before Paula and took her injured hand into his. 'I never wanted to go in the first place, remember.' He kissed the ugly, pink-edged scar. 'I want to come back because I love you, but I won't lie to you - if I ever get hold of the bastard that did this - I will kill him.' he said, running his lips over her hand.

Paula extricated herself and rested her hand on his chest. 'My hero,' she said, kissing him on the nose. They snuggled together and watched the flames lick at the chimney breast.

'You should have heard Nancy,' he said, breaking the spell. 'She gave me a right rollicking. - I know now that I added to the pressure.' He sniffed and wiped his eye on the sleeve of his rugby shirt.

Paula took his hand in hers. 'Maybe it's time we made up properly.' she said, pulling him onto the floor.

*

The doctor couldn't remember a time when he had not been in command, a master of his own destiny. But lately, things seemed to have slipped from his grasp. He needed to regain control and it was time to consider his options.

The solicitor was playing a game of one-upmanship with the life of his son. If he allowed the transfer to go ahead, at least he would be rid of the obnoxious, irritating little man, but it would also mean that Stevens had won. He could not allow that to happen.

After what happened the other evening, it seemed the prostitute wanted to defy him. She wasn't a threat, unless she went to the police, but even if she reported him, she didn't know who he was. It wasn't as if whores were in short supply, he could easily find another, but it would be inconvenient. One day he would do something about her, but it would have to wait.

Then there was Paula Hobson. The doctor found it hard to believe that someone with such an inferior intellect to himself could become such a nuisance. Arrangements to have her removed from ICU were progressing, but more slowly than he would have liked. He decided to leave matters as they were for the time being, but if the manager didn't get his act together; he would be forced to act.

*

The couple giggled like a pair of naughty school children that had been caught playing hooky. The cat jumped onto the bed, only to receive a short, sharp shock from Duncan's foot. Paula relaxed for the first time in ages. She pulled the sheet over her naked body and prodded Duncan's hairy stomach.

'You're getting a beer belly.'

Duncan pouted. 'You leave my tummy alone,' he said, stroking his midriff. 'It's taken me years to perfect this.'

Paula plucked one of his hairs making him wince. 'I was on the hill on Saturday,' she said. 'I saw you score the try.'

'Did you?' he said, feigning a touchdown over her shoulder. 'Wasn't I good?'

'Modesty becomes you,' she laughed and then became serious again, adding. 'Promise you won't leave me again?'

'I promise,' said Duncan.

'Even if I kick you out?'

'I promise.' He kissed the end of his finger and planted it on her lips. 'So, who do you think it is?'

Paula didn't need to ask what he was talking about. 'I don't know,' she said. 'I wish I did.'

'You must have some suspicions.'

'I'm pretty sure it isn't any of the nurses,' said Paula. 'It has to be someone in authority. Otherwise I wouldn't have been called in to see Charles.'

'Then it has to be one of the doctors.'

'I think it has to be.' Paula rolled over and rested on her elbow. She looked into Duncan's hazel eyes. 'I can't see any of the juniors having the confidence, never mind influence, to do it. So that leaves the five consultants, two senior registrars not to mention all the registrars. That's ten anaesthetists in all. Then there are the surgeons, physicians, orthopods - they all have equal access.' She felt the knot in her stomach return. 'Any of the doctors could get in and do it.'

'It's unlikely to be someone from wards, though?'

'Yeah,' said Paula. She rolled onto her back and covered her eyes with her arm, and added, 'which brings us back to the anaesthetists.'

'Sorry,' said Duncan. He reached over and grabbed the bottle of wine from the bedside table. 'Would you rather not talk about it?'

'No, no it's all right,' she said as he filled her glass.

'So who -'

'At the top of the list,' she said. 'Would have to be Ravi, Mark, James, Alan, Philip, Lennox and Brian, I suppose. But Duncan, I've known these guys for years -on my life - it can't be any of them.'

'Lennox has to be odds on favourite.'

'Maybe,' said Paula. She sat up against the pillows and took a mouthful of wine. 'Oh, I don't know. Just because he's bad tempered and I know he's a dreadful communicator, but it doesn't mean to say Lennox is a killer.'

'From what I've seen,' said Duncan. 'He's also a racist, a sexist and a bigot.'

'He can be a prat sometime,' she said. 'And he doesn't work well with anyone who hasn't fully mastered the English language, but that still doesn't make him a killer.'

'Okay, Alan then?'

She laughed. 'Alan's a gentleman as is Brian. They care about what happens to the patients and their families. Brian has a temper, but you can say that about ninety per cent of the consultants. They're all under a lot of pressure.'

'Okay,' said Duncan, plumping up his pillows before propping himself against them. 'What about the others?'

'James,' said Paula. 'He was around when I was attacked - oh God what am I saying - he wouldn't do anything like that - neither would Philip.'

'Now there's a nutter if ever I saw one.'

'Why? Just because he picks his nose and scratches his goolies,' said Paula, laughing. She shook her head. 'Mark - Ravi I've been through them all,' she said. 'Most of them are happily married with families and none of them would attack me - It has to be an outsider.' She tugged at her hair in frustration. 'This is driving me insane. The guy said he killed Linda - I've been through that morning, time and time again, but -'

'Oh, yeah, Nance mentioned something about that.'

Paula looked at him. 'How long have you been talking to my friend behind my back,' she said, pouting.

He kissed her on the nose.

'What about post mortems?' he said.

'There haven't been any,' she said. 'I went through the death certificate book. None of them were referred to the coroner. Anyway, he wouldn't use anything that would show up on autopsy.' She pulled up her knees and hugged them protectively. 'I need to catch him at it.'

'Go to the police?'

'There's no point. I haven't' got a scrap of evidence,' she said. 'Management obviously don't believe me, and I am up for a disciplinary – so I can't see how I could ever convince the cops. No, it's me against him.'

Duncan rested his hand on her knee. 'I know you don't want me to interfere,' He turned her face towards his. 'But he's already hurt you. I can't help but worry. Please don't take him on - I can't bear to lose you.'

Paula stroked the stubble on his chin. 'He might be a bully, darling, and he has some warped sense of compassion, but I'm certain he isn't a cold blooded killer.' she said, with more confidence than she felt. 'I need to catch him with the drugs in his hand.'

'How can you say he's not a killer?'

'I said he's not a cold blooded killer,' she said. 'He's doing it out of some misguided sense of humanitarianism.' She ran her fingers through her hair. 'There is something you could do for me?'

'Sure.'

'You have an analytical brain,' said Paula. 'Can you go over the figures for me? See if I've missed anything.'

'Okay, what am I looking for?'

'Anything out of the ordinary,' she said, 'patterns - any correlation between deaths and specific personnel. There might be something I've missed.'

'What are you going to do?'

'Get the nurses on side,' said Paula.

Chapter Thirty

Unusually for Paula, she had made a special effort with her appearance. She stood in front of the mirror and examined the results. The panda-rings around her eyes had virtually disappeared overnight. A light dusting of make-up had further reduced the dark circles. She'd flicked a little mascara onto her thick curling eyelashes, highlighting the depth of colour in her eyes. Satisfied, Paula pulled a comb through her unruly hair and smoothed the skirt of her freshly laundered uniform. There was little she could do about the weight loss except use a safety pin to shorten her petersham belt. She gave her silver buckle, a present on qualification from her parents, a quick polish with the heel of her hand. The appointment was for ten. It was a little after a quarter to and she was decidedly nervous. The harsh buzz of the office phone made her jump. The calmness of Paula's voice belied the increase in her heart-rate.

'Good morning,' she said. 'ICU, Sister Hobson speaking.'

'It's me.'

Paula let out a long breath. 'Is this important, Nancy?' she said. 'I'm just about to go over to theatre to see Charles?'

'I know,' said Nancy. 'But didn't the letter say you could take someone with you. I wondered if you wanted a bit of moral support. '

'No, I'm fine,' said Paula. 'Anyway, I don't want him to know you're on my side.'

'Who, Charles?' said Nancy.

'No, you idiot, the killer,' said Paula. 'If he thinks we're on to him, he'll go to ground.' She tugged at the hem of her skirt. 'And besides, if you come, Charles will know you've told me about the meeting. It's bad enough with one of us in the dog house.'

'Yeah but –'

'Trust me,' said Paula. 'I can handle Charles. But our friend is obviously pulling his strings - the last thing I want is him getting wind of what we're doing.'

'Okay, but be careful.'

'Thanks, I will,' she said. 'Will you keep working on the staff for me?'

'Sure.'

Paula glanced up to the clock. If she didn't hurry she was going to be late. 'Don't forget to tell them - if anyone - and I mean anyone - comes into the unit when they're not supposed to be there - they must page me. I don't care what time it is. I can be there in five minutes - they mustn't leave anybody alone with the patients. Make it really clear to them.'

'Maybe we should take turns to be on call.'

'No, it'll only complicate matters,' said Paula. 'Anyway, it takes you too long to get in. - I have to go now. I'll talk to you later.'

'Good luck.'

'And Nancy-'

'Yeah -'

'Thanks for talking to Duncan,' said Paula, tellingly.

'Ooh - '

She could hear the excitement in her friend's voice as she disconnected the call.

Paula noticed the blinds were closed as she past the office window and knocked on the door. Obeying the muffled command to enter, she stepped into the room with, if not total confidence, at least with resolve. Charles was sitting at his desk talking on the phone. Flush-faced, he was obviously in the middle of a heated discussion. He gestured for Paula to take a seat. She smiled inwardly at his discomfort.

'Yes, sir' said Charles. 'Yes, yes, I'll definitely have it on your desk by the end of the week. Yes, thank you – goodbye.' The manager shuffled uneasily in his seat. He took his time replacing the receiver then played around with some papers as though he was giving himself time to compose a speech. Eventually, he swivelled round to face Paula.

'Right,' he said, forcing a smile.

'Not finished your audit yet, Charles?' tutted Paula.

He ignored the question and positioned himself in the counselling mode, leaning forward with hands on knees. False sincerity seemed to ooze from every pore.

'So how are you today?' he said.

'Fine, thank you,' Paula was determined to make things as difficult as she could for him. She echoed his posture. 'And you?' she said.

'Yes, good,' he replied.

Paula had never seen her manager look so uncomfortable. She almost felt sorry for him, until he said. 'I was sorry to hear about your mother's – erm – illness.'

She cut in sharply with. 'Thank you.'

'How is she?'

'She has Alzheimer's, Charles,' she said, her voice full of sarcasm. 'She tends to be rather confused.'

'I am sorry to hear that.' Charles crossed his legs and clasped his hands round his knees. 'I imagine it must be very hard now especially as you are on your own.'

The comment was obviously in reference to her break up with Duncan. Paula sat in stony silence as Charles continued.

'You've been under an awful lot of pressure, Paula and people are very concerned for your welfare.'

'Really'

'Of course,' he said.

'I'm fine.'

'It's obvious you have lost a lot of weight,' he said. Charles looked her up and down then added, more thoughtfully. 'Although I must say it does suit you.'

'I am fine,' she repeated. 'However, as you already know I do have concerns over-'

'The audit,' he interpolated. 'My point exactly, on top of everything else you had the audit. I am well aware of what sort of pressure that can put one under. It would be difficult for anyone, never mind a -' he stuttered to a halt.

'A what?' she said.

'Nothing,' said Charles. 'I just meant difficult for anybody. We all feel pressure at times, even me. It's very easy to get things out of perspective.'

Paula thought to herself. 'You are a supercilious arse, Charles.' But what she actually said was. 'So this meeting is about my audit findings?'

'No, not really,' he said. Charles continued to say how worried everybody was about her health and how it might be having an effect on her judgement.

'As far as my judgement is concerned,' said Paula, struggling to keep her temper under control. 'I don't know how those statistics could be interpreted any differently.' Charles straightened his back, picked up a pencil and started to doodle.

'I didn't actually want to get into all this audit business,' he said. Neat concentric circles began to cover the page. 'However, as you have brought the subject up, I have to tell you that there has been a full investigation and your findings were not supported.'

Paula wondered how anyone could have performed a full investigation when the patient's records were still, unofficially, at her house. She frowned. 'So, who did this investigation and why wasn't I told about it?'

Charles banged the end of the pencil on his desk. 'That is no concern of yours, Sister,' he said. Taking the sharpness out of his voice, he added. 'I wanted to put your mind at rest about it, that's all.'

Paula stood. 'Okay then,' she said.

'I haven't finished yet,' said Charles. 'Sit down.'

Paula complied with his request, but took up a defensive position by crossing her legs and folded her arms.

'You cannot go around throwing silly accusations at people,' said the manager.

'I'm not throwing anything at anybody,' said Paula. 'And the last thing my allegations are is silly.'

'It's bad for morale-' Charles scraped the pencil along the paper. The lead broke. He threw the pencil onto the desk. 'Not to mention, sister, downright foolhardy - for goodness sake - what if the Press got hold of it?'

'So, maybe we should go the police before the press get hold of it,' said Paula.

'Don't you dare,' said Charles, threateningly. All pretence at civility disappeared. 'If you go to the police you can say goodbye to your career, young lady.'

Paula matched his stare without blinking. Charles picked out another pencil from a holder, scribbled something on a note pad and forcefully underlined it.

'We –you have two choices.' he said, glancing in her

direction, before averting his eyes. 'I'm sure your GP would view the situation favourably. You can take some sick leave.' Paula remained silent. Charles continued. 'Or, if you prefer, you can have a six month secondment to the personnel department. You could benefit from some project management.' He looked at her stony-faced. 'Not only would it be good for your career, it's about time Sister Coleman got some management experience.' The pencil flipped through the air.

Paula pretended to give his proposals due consideration before replying. 'No thanks,' she said, smiling politely.

It wasn't what Charles expected.

Sorry,' he said.

She inhaled deeply. 'Look, Charles,' she said. 'I'm not the first person to work when their mother is sick - I am not ill - and I'm sorry to disappoint you, - but I don't have any burning career ambitions in management - I do not want a secondment.' She uncrossed legs and sat back against the chair. 'Thank you, but I'm perfectly happy where I am.'

'What about Sister Coleman?' he snapped. 'She'd definitely benefit from the experience.'

'If Sister Coleman is that desperate for a senior post,' she said. 'She can look in the Nursing Press.' Paula knew she had him on the run. She put her hands onto her knees, ready to stand. 'Can I go now?'

'I want you to think seriously about what I have said.'

'Is that a threat, Charles?'

'No,' he countered 'I'm just saying. If certain people think your behaviour is disruptive - you might not get a second chance.'

Their eyes locked. 'Just try it, Charles,' she said. 'I can see the headlines - nurse sacked for raising concerns over suspicious deaths.'

The manager was first to break eye contact.

'Are we finished?' said Paula.

'Yes,' he hissed. 'But I am warning you, Sister- if you continue with these silly claims. I will take disciplinary action.'

With the threat ringing in her ears, her return to the

unit wasn't exactly triumphant. Save for several post-it notes stuck onto the doodle-pad, the office was as she left it. Most of the notes were reminders to return calls. Two were from Vincent's sister. Apparently, Marty wanted to talk to her urgently. Paula stuck the notes together and put them in her pocket.

*

The doctor watched Paula leave the manager's office and thought she didn't look very upset considering what was supposed to have happened. In fact, she looked quite smug. Presuming Charles had failed in his task, he snatched the mask from his face before making his way into the office. Charles Edmonds swivelled his chair to face the new visitor.

'Hi there,' said Charles.

'How did it go with Paula?'

'It appears she is a lot better.' said the manger.

'Are you telling me, you think that woman is in her right mind?'

'I can't make her go off sick,' said Charles.

'We had an agreement.'

'I know we did doctor, but I have to follow hospital policy,' said Charles. 'I can't make a precedent by excluding someone just because there's serious illness in the family. If I did that I'd have no staff left.' Charles picked up his notes and began to tidy them up.

'You, you agreed to sort her out,' the doctor said, through gritted teeth. 'I told you - she is having a disruptive influence in the unit – she's a danger to the patients,' he thundered. 'How bad do things have to get before you manager's take action?'

Charles looked surprised. 'Don't you think that's a little strong?' he said.

'The woman's unstable, man. It wouldn't surprise me if *she* was killing the patients,' said the doctor. 'I take it; you have given her an official warning and started disciplinary proceedings against her.'

'I'm afraid we have no grounds for taking disciplinary

action.'

'Then suspend her.'

'I'm sorry,' said Charles, 'but I don't have any grounds for that either. If I tried, the unions would wipe the floor with me. I promise I will get her out of there as soon as I can, but it might take a while.'

The doctor stormed out of the office.

Chapter Thirty-One

The young accident victim's return to consciousness had turned into a struggle of confusion and demons. Overall however, Vincent was making good progress and was managing to breathe on his own for increasing periods of time. A tracheostomy had replaced the tube in his mouth, but because it bypassed his vocal chords at times communication was difficult and frustrating. The nurses had moved him into the side-ward to give him some privacy. Despite his son's obvious improvement, Russell Stevens insisted the transfer to a private facility go ahead. Paula was having difficulty organising the move, not least because the hospital did not have a bed available. She'd spent most of the day on the phone. In the end, she managed to secure a provisional arrangement for the following week. By the end of shift, Paula had had her fill of admin work and was keen to get home to Duncan who'd reserved a table at their favourite restaurant to celebrate their reunion. Paula was making her way out of the building as Marty tottered round the corner on a pair of rather muddy high heels.

'Oh boy, am I glad to see you,' said Marty, breathlessly. She had snagged her stockings on the wire fence then fought her way up the grassy slope.

'Hi, Marty,' said Paula. 'Your brother's had a really good day today. He'll be pleased to see you.' The sister remembered the post-it notes in her uniform pocket. 'I'm sorry I didn't manage to get back to you.' Paula tried to side step the prostitute. 'I'll catch up with you tomorrow.'

Marty blocked her way. 'Have – to - talk,' she gasped. She bent over, rested her hands on her knees and gulped down a lungful of air. 'I've been trying to get hold of you for days.'

'Yes, sorry,' said Paula, 'but I'm off duty now and I am in a hurry.'

'No, no,' said Marty. She clutched at the pain in her side.

'Are you all right?' said Paula.

'Stitch,' Marty said, in way of explanation. She grabbed hold of the sister. 'You don't understand - I have to tell you something.'

Determined not to be delayed, Paula eased Marty's fingers from her arm. 'I have an appointment, Marty.' she said, firmly.

'No, really you don't understand. One of your doctors is a punter.'

'Uh,' said Paula, thinking she'd misheard.

Marty took a deep breath and repeated the statement.

Paula's eyebrows flipped.

'Oh,' she said. 'I'm not sure you should be telling me this.'

Marty insisted Paula listen. The sister was astonished by the revelations. At the same time alarm bells began to ring as she made connections.

'You might have been mistaken.' she said. 'It could have been another doctor.'

Marty pointed to the Accident & Emergency. 'Last time he smacked me about I ended up in here.'

Paula recalled the fading bruises.

'I saw Hot Rod talking to Vinnie's parents,' said Marty. 'I'd know him a mile away.'

Paula bit her lip to stop a snigger escaping. 'Hot Rod?' she echoed

'You laugh if you want,' said Marty, 'but this guy is a piece of work.'

*

The doctor had been looking out of his window at the heavy clouds. Watching them as they slowly crept over the terrace houses, stretching out before him. He was about to return to his desk when a familiar figure in the car park, caught his eye.

'What the f-?' he said. Leaning closer to get a better look, the doctor's warm breath misted the window pane. He began to rub at the condensation with the heel of his hand. Just at that moment, Paula glanced up. The doctor leapt back as if electrocuted. He could not understand how the two women could have met. Returning to his chair, he sat down heavily and tried to make sense of the new development.

He had to presume the prostitute would tell Paula about his indiscretions. The question was could Paula make any mileage out of the information? The sister had already proved to be more resilient than expected. Despite the ineptitude of Charles Edmonds, he was still confident that in the end his plan to have her removed would succeed. According to Maureen Dent, the nurses were becoming increasingly disgruntled with their boss. He'd encouraged the night sister to take every opportunity to cause trouble. After some consideration, he decided that the meeting could actually work to his advantage. He went back to the window and watched them talking. At one point Paula actually laughed. He touched the glass with his fingertips and smiled.

'Two birds - one stone.' he said.

*

Paula pulled Marty to one side.

'It can't be him, he's got a couple of kids.' she said. 'Are you certain?'

Marty, shrugged. 'They're all happily married with kids,' she said

'Sorry, I didn't mean to be condescending,' said Paula. 'Thanks for letting me know.'

'What're you going to do about it?'

Paula blew out her cheeks. 'Phew.' She needed time to think. 'To be honest, Marty I don't know. I'm not sure that I can do anything. ' she said, truthfully. 'You should go to the police.' She suggested they get out of the cold. The two girls went into the main foyer where the short skirted, mud-strewn prostitute received several raised eyebrows from passing workers who had finished for the day and were on their way home. Paula returned their looks with a glare.

'I won't go to the cops,' said Marty, 'but if I have to, I will tell Russell Stevens. He'll do something about the slime-ball. I don't want HR anywhere near my brother.' Marty bristled with indignation and pulled herself up to her full five-foot one and half, but she still only reached as far as Paula's shoulders.

'Look,' said Paula. 'I know what I'm about to say isn't what you want to hear, but if Vinnie goes to the private hospital then Hot Rod can't look after him.'

Marty looked even more aggrieved.

'If you don't want to go to the police,' said Paula, trying a different track. 'What about writing to our chief executive? At least I can help you with that.'

Marty shrugged.

Paula was running out of options. She pushed her hands into the pockets of her jeans. 'Look, I'll do what I can,' she said, 'but unless you make an official complaint, I don't think they'll do anything.'

'Then maybe our lad will be better off someplace else,' said Marty, angrily. She turned to leave. Paula called her back. She felt she owed the girl at least some sort of effort.

'Give me time to think about it,' she said. 'Come in tomorrow afternoon - I promise by then I'll have worked something out.'

As they talked, questions had been flitting through Paula's mind. If HR was the killer, how could she continue to believe his motives were out of compassion? Why hadn't she followed up on the conversation with George? The answer came easily. Because she could not believe that someone she thought of as a friend could be capable of killing.

Chapter Thirty-Two

Paula could hear a man coughing.

'Is that you, Nance?'

'Who else would answer my phone?' said Nancy. The comment was quickly followed by a snort, a giggle and a whispered, 'get off.'

'You're obviously busy,' Paula said, to a background of stifled giggles. She raised her voice slightly and spoke slowly in hope of gaining her deputy's attention. 'But I thought you might want to hear this.' She paused. By the sound of the continuing giggles, it hadn't worked. She tried again. 'I know who is doing it.'

There was a mutter, followed by a scuffle, a bang and then silence. A moment later, Nancy returned to the phone.

'Did you just say what I think you said?' she said.

'Yes.'

'Wow' said Nancy. 'All right, you've got my total, undivided attention. Come on then don't leave me in suspense.'

Paula told her about the conversation with Marty.'

'Oh, my god,' said Nancy. 'Do you trust her?'

'I don't have reason not to.' Barnum was getting under Paula's feet. She nudged him out of the way.

'She might be out to make trouble.'

'I hope we're not getting into all that again.' said Paula.

'What?'

'Not believing me.'

'Hey, this isn't the same,' said Nancy. 'She's a prostitute.'

'Prostitute or not, she has no reason to lie to me.'

'Maybe it's a ruse to stop Vinnie being transferred.'

'Just the opposite,' said Paula. 'She'd rather have him transferred than looked after by one of her punters. I saw the bruises, Nancy and it fits.' said Paula. She had taken time out from getting ready for her date to speak to her deputy. 'You'll never believe what he calls himself.' She told Nancy about the pseudonym.

'You're joking.'

'I am not,' said Paula. 'Can you imagine doing the ward round - *could you get me the x-rays, Sister – of course, Hot Rod - anything you say, HR.*' There followed a few moments of light hearted banter. Eventually, Paula became serious again. 'I need you to do me a favour,' she said.

'Go on.'

'Duncan and I are going out for a meal,' said Paula. 'And I'm already late; otherwise I'd do it myself.'

'Don't let it be said that Nancy Coleman got in the way of true love.'

'Yeah, right, said Paula. 'Thanks.' She turned down the damper. 'I've checked the rotas. HR isn't on call and we don't have any patients that fit his criteria,' she said, putting the guard over the fire. 'I'm pretty sure he won't do anything. George is on tonight. Would you mind giving him a ring and asking him to keep his eyes peeled? Don't go into the details. I'll sort all that out tomorrow.' She sat on the sofa next to the cat. 'Tell him to page me if he's worried about anything.'

'No problem,' said Nancy.

'Tell George it doesn't matter what time it is. I'll come in.'

'Yup – got that.' said Nancy. 'What are you going to do tomorrow?'

'I don't know,' said Paula, stroking Barnum's ears. 'To be honest, I'm way out of my depth. I've asked Marty to come in after lunch. If it's all right with you we'll spend the morning putting something together and then take her to see the chief exec.' Paula heard a sharp intake of breath on the other end of the phone. 'I'll pound on his bloody door until he lets us in.' she said.

'Heavy stuff,' Nancy said. She sounded worried. 'What about Charles? If we leave him out of the loop we'll be burning all our bridges.'

'I've been there, done that remember,' said Paula 'It's either that or we have to catch HR in the act.' She ran her hand through her freshly washed hair. It crackled with static. 'I think our only hope is to persuade the CEO to take us seriously. Unless you have any bright ideas?' she added.

'Not really.'

'I have to go now,' said Paula. 'We'll talk it over properly in the morning.'

'Sure,' said Nancy. 'And Paula –'

'Yeah-'

'Have a good time with Dunc the Hunk.'

*

They occupied a table in a secluded corner of the restaurant. Duncan had ordered an extremely large T-bone steak and was devouring it with great relish. Paula had never been able to compete with his sizeable appetite and was struggling with Peking duck. She set her elbows on the table and rested her chin on the back of her hands.

'I'm still worried about you,' said Duncan, chewing on a piece of gristle.

'I'm good,' she said, watching him eat. At that moment she thought her boyfriend was the sexiest man in the world. 'He wants to destroy my career, not me.'

Duncan gave up the battle with the gristle. He took it out of his mouth and put it on the side of his plate. 'You say that, but he's already the belted hell out of the prostitute,' he said 'and attacked you. So don't tell me he's not violent.' They spoke in hushed voices so as not to be overheard.

'That was to scare me,' she said 'and don't get me wrong -it worked, but if he'd really wanted to hurt me he wouldn't have put me to sleep.'

He grunted.

'Duncan, don't forget I've known this man for years,' she said. 'Whatever his motives are, I know he cares about people. I might be naïve, but I can't believe he's a cold blooded murderer.'

Duncan took a wooden toothpick from the container and started to chew on it. 'What do you call it then?'

'Mercy killing,' she said. 'Modern medicine can be really cruel. A few years ago most of our patients wouldn't have reached hospital never mind ICU. We put people through all sorts of hell and then they still die. It can be heartbreaking to watch.'

'It is still murder, Paula,' Duncan said, quietly. He leant over to refill her glass.

She covered it with her hand. 'I'm driving, remember,' she said.

'I think you're underestimating him,' said Duncan. 'Bugger your CEO -you should go straight to the police.'

Paula pushed her plate away and rested back in the chair. 'They'd probably say I was certifiable,' she said, wiping her mouth with the napkin. 'Let's see what tomorrow brings. If I don't get anywhere then I promise I'll contact the police.'

Duncan didn't look convinced by her reassurance. He placed his knife and fork neatly on the plate. Apart from the bone and one piece of gristle it had been wiped clean.

'Thank goodness we don't have a dog,' said Paula. 'The poor bugger would starve.'

The waiter seemed to appear from nowhere and began to clear their plates. Paula had hardly touched hers and had to assure him there had been nothing wrong with the meal. Duncan ordered a desert. She asked for a cappuccino.

She was about to take her first sip of the coffee, when a piercing command interrupted them. Duncan's spoon hovered halfway to his mouth. People turned to see where the noise was coming from. The couple stared at each other in shock. Paula was stung into action and grabbed her bag. Her hands shook as she removed the bleep. She studied the message as it stuttered across the small grey screen.

'Oh, shit,' she said. 'It's from George.' Her chair scrapped the floor as she pushed it back. 'I have to go.'

Duncan dropped his spoon. 'I'm coming with you' he said, wiping his mouth.

Paula scooped up her belongings. 'No don't,' she said. 'Darling, there isn't anything you can do. You'll only be in the way - please – I promise, nothing's going to happen to me - the night staff are there and I'll ring you as soon as I can.' She stroked his cheek and gave him a lingering kiss. 'Do you mind taking a taxi home,' she said.

'Go,' he said. 'Go, before I change my mind.' He grabbed Paula's hand as she turned to leave and pulled her back. 'Please, darling, be careful.'

'Stop being so melodramatic,' she said, kissing him again.

Duncan stared after Paula as she rushed from the restaurant.

Chapter Thirty-Three

Having celebrated his twenty-fifth birthday the previous evening, George was feeling decidedly fragile. Maureen had allocated Vincent into his care for the night and the male nurse was looking forward to a quiet shift. Having set up the television in the side-ward, his intentions were to settle down with his patient to watch snooker; but George's intestines were making him suffer and he was forced to make several excursions to the changing room. He was on the way back from the latest of these when he noticed the door to the sideward had been closed. Certain he had left it open and seeing all the other nurses busy in the main ward, George quickened his pace. The door opened before he reached it.

'Hello, George.'

The male nurse froze in his tracks. 'I didn't think you were on call tonight,' said George.

'Just passing through on my way home,' said the doctor. He patted the pockets of his white coat and added. 'I thought I would pop in to make sure all's well.' He frowned. 'Are you all right, George? You look as though you've seen a ghost.'

The male nurse opened his mouth to say something then changed his mind. He turned and shouted to the Night Sister. 'Sorry, Maureen I need to go again,' before rushing out of the unit. Instead of heading towards the changing rooms, George sneaked into the Sisters office and closed the door. He crossed to the desk, picked up the phone, dialled zero and asked the switchboard to page Paula.

Maureen joined the doctor and fell in beside him as he made his way out of the unit.

'I hope I don't have that effect on all your staff,' he said.

'Gippy-tummy,' said Maureen, in way of explanation. 'You're in very late tonight?'

'Had a couple of post ops to see on the ward,' he said. 'I'm going to pop up to my office and then I'm off home.' The doctor seemed to be in a really good mood and patted Maureen's hand in an avuncular manner. 'I hope you have a quiet shift. Goodnight, everybody.' he said waving to the nurses.

*

The town centre was relatively quiet considering it was a Friday night. The drive from restaurant to hospital took Paula less than ten minutes. She gripped the steering wheel so tightly her knuckles hurt. She passed the Friday night revellers staggering from pub to pub, looking for a final drink before chucking out time. Paula had never been particularly religious, but she muttered a prayer under her breath.

'Please God, don't let him hurt anyone - please let me be wrong – please - please let me get there in time.' The VW skidded on ice as she turned into the eerily deserted car park. The high security lights cast a pale yellow glow over the empty expanse. The night workers' vehicles huddled together close to the hospital entrance. Paula pulled up in front of A&E, slammed the car door and ran past an abandoned ambulance. She took a short cut through the A & E department and hardly noticed the numerous bloodied casualties who were awaiting their turn. Lisa Gower came out of the changing rooms. They nearly collided.

'Whoa,' gasped Lisa. She had to hold on to Paula to steady herself. 'What's the rush?' she said.

Paula spun her colleague round. 'Sorry, Lisa can't stop. I'll tell you later,' she said, running off.

By the time she reached the first floor landing, Paula was out of breath and had to slow to a fast walk. She sensed something was wrong as soon she opened the outer doors and broke into a run again. She crashed through the airlock.

'Where is everybody?' Paula demanded of the nurse standing by the desk.

'They're in the side-ward,' she said. 'Vincent's arrested.'

Paula felt sick. She struggled out of her neat tailored jacket and threw it, along with her handbag, onto the nearest chair. On opening the sideward door, she was horrified by the scene being played out. George was knelt on the bed, performing heart massage. Maureen stood at the head, squeezing oxygen into the tracheostomy tube. A third nurse was busy opening emergency packs and Ravi held the defibrillator paddles in the air as if he'd just given a shock. The gleaming steel hovered, menacingly, over Vincent's chest. They looked up. There was only George who was not surprised to see their boss.

'When did it happen?' said Paula.

'A few minutes after he left,' said George, his arms pumping the young boy's heart. 'He went into ventricular fibrillation.'

Ravi re-positioned the two gel-pads to protect the patient's chest from burns. He flicked the charge switch on the defibrillator, saying.

'Charging two-hundred and fifty joules-'

George climbed off from the bed. Paula looked to the monitor. Where Vincent's heart trace should have been, a squiggle white line traversed the screen. Ravi positioned the paddles.

'STAND CLEAR,' he shouted. After checking that no one was touching anything, he pressed down firmly onto gel-pads.

'ALL CLEAR'

Wham.

A bolt of electricity thumped into Vincent's body. His torso jerked. His arms flailed. Nobody moved. All eyes remained fixed on the monitor. The screen went blank. A second felt like minutes. Everyone held their breath. And then, looking as if it had been drawn by a child, an uneven, jagged white line sluggishly made its way across the screen. Vincent's heart had not restarted.

'Shit,' said George. He climbed back onto the bed and continued the chest compressions 'One - two- three – four -.' He looked to Paula 'I'm sorry boss, he was in before I could do anything,' he said.

'Keep going,' said Paula. She grabbed a syringe and ripped off the sterile wrap.

'Ravi, you're going to have to trust me,' she said as she took twenty millilitres of blood from the arterial line.

'Keep on with the CPR,' said Ravi. 'I'm going to give another shot of adrenaline.' Out of the corner of his eye he could see Paula fill two identical specimen tubes with blood. 'What are you doing?' he asked.

'I haven't time to explain,' said Paula. She left the bottles on the trolley and made her way round to the other side of the bed. 'I'll take over, George.' Swapping positions with the male nurse, Paula looked conspicuous in her white blouse and black trousers. 'Can you get me a dextrose and insulin infusion, please?' she said.

'Fifty mils?' queried George.

'Please.'

Maureen leant over the bed. 'What the hell do you think you're doing?' she said. 'You can't come here and take over my shift.'

Paula ignored her and continued with the straight-armed compressions. She looked at the anaesthetist. 'Ravi, he's been given a deliberate overdose.' she said.

Ravi stared in horror. 'Charging three-hundred joules-' he said 'an overdose of what?'

'Of potassium-'

'STAND CLEAR.'

Paula jumped off the bed. 'You have to give him some dextrose and insulin to counter it,' she said, urgently.

The young man's erect brown nipples stood out against his ashen skin. Despite gel-pads, large circular wheals were beginning to appear where the electricity had entered his body. Ravi adjusted the pads again and placed the paddles on top of them.

'ALL CLEAR'

Wham. No change except that Vincent's heart was beginning to show signs of weakening. George rushed in with a large, fluid filled syringe.

'Please, Ravi' Paula urged. 'You have to trust me.'

'Take no notice of her, Ravi,' said Maureen. 'She's out of her mind.'

George held out the syringe. The registrar looked from one nurse to another.

'But-'

'We don't have time for buts, Ravi,' she said. 'Trust

me - give him the reversal.' Sweat was dribbling down her back with the exertion and the cotton blouse stuck to her skin. George pushed the syringe closer to the registrar. Still, Ravi hesitated.

'How much has he been given?' he said.

'I don't know,' said Paula. 'I've taken blood so we can sort the levels out later,' she stopped the massage for a moment. 'Give it,' she said, forcefully.

Ravi took hold of the syringe. 'I - it might kill him,' he stuttered.

'He's dead if you don't.'

Maureen reached over and grabbed his hand as he connected the syringe. Don't,' she said. 'Don't listen to her.'

Paula slapped the Night Sister's hand out of the way. 'For God's sake, Rav,' she said. 'Give the fucking injection.'

'If it helps, I believe her.' said George.

The anaesthetist squeezed the plunger. They watched the fluid trickle into Vincent's circulation. Paula continued to pump his heart. Damp hair clung to her scalp and a drop of sweat dribbled from her temple. George noticed Paula's fatigue and offered to take over again.

'No, I'm all right,' she said. 'I will not let this happen - come on, Vinnie, fight.' The room seemed to shrink until there was only her and the boy. 'Come on, damn you – he can't do this to you - don't let the bastard win.'

They all stared at Paula and then followed her eyes as she looked at monitor. Whenever she squeezed Vincent's heart, the trace shot up the screen only to return to the uneven squiggle when she released the pressure. Ravi turned to charge the defibrillator.

'Charging three-hundred-'

'STAND CLEAR.'

Paula slid off the bed

'ALL CLEAR'

Wham.

The screen went blank.

'Shit,' said Paula. She climbed onto the bed and began to position her hands one on top of the other. She was about to restart the massage when Ravi put his hand over hers.

'Hang on a minute,' he said.

163

A wide irregular complex flashed across the monitor. The group waited, eyes transfixed to the screen. Another complex appeared and then another and another. They all held their breath as they watched the young man's heart struggle back to life. Eventually Ravi was able to feel a strong pulse on Vincent's neck and his smile broke the tension. Paula slid off the bed.

'What has just happened here, Sister?' said Ravi.

A loud sucking whoosh announced Vincent's first long, deep breath taken via the oxygen bag.

'Wow, that's just how I feel,' said Paula, squeezing his hand. As the boy's strength recovered, Paula felt hers diminish. She picked up the specimen tubes from the trolley and clutched them to her heart, muttering to herself. *'Gotcha - you bastard'* to the others, she said. 'I'll explain everything later.'

Paula guided George out of the side-ward and gave him a hug. 'Thanks,' she said.

'Any time, boss,' said George, 'especially if I get a cuddle.'

'You put your neck on the line for me.'

'Just as well really, wasn't it? Otherwise we'd have lost him' said George. He shook his head in disbelief. 'I can't believe he'd do such a thing.'

'I was sure he wouldn't,' said Paula. She wiped a hand across her damp forehead. 'I know he wanted me out of here, but I never thought.' She couldn't finish.

'If I hadn't gone to the loo,' said George.

'Don't worry; it's not your fault. I should have done something,' she said. 'I should have made people listen.' She put the bottles of serum on the desk, rolled up her sleeves and walked over to the sink. Paula turned on the mixer-tap with her elbows and allowed the fast flowing water to glide over her fingers. The male nurse stood next to her and followed suit.

'Will you do me a favour?' said Paula, squirting hand cleanser from the dispenser.

'Sure.'

'Can you bag everything up,' she said. 'Sharps boxes - rubbish bags that sort of thing.'

'Why?' George adjusted the taps to lessen the flow.

Paula checked to see where the night sister was before replying. 'He must have prepared the potassium somewhere else and brought it in with him,' she said, thinking out loud. 'But he has to dispose of the syringe somewhere.' She shook the loose water from her fingers and grabbed a couple of paper towels. 'It would make sense to chuck it into the sharps box.' Paula wiped her face and neck with the damp towel before depositing it in the bin.

'Are you going the cops now?' said George.

'I think I'll wait until we get the results back first,' said Paula. 'Sorting Vinnie out has to be our priority. If you give Ravi a hand, I'll take the blood to the lab.'

'Why did you take two lots?'

'Just in case one gets lost,' she said. 'I'll put the other somewhere safe.'

George re-tied the cotton belt of his scrubs before heading back to the side-ward. He passed Maureen as she came out.

The night sister said to Paula. 'I want a word with you.' Her voice was filled with hate.

'It'll have to wait,' said Paula, pushing past. 'I've things to do.' She took two clear, zip-topped bags from a drawer in the desk, wrote Vincent's details on each of the specimen bottles and then she deposited them into the bags and closed the seals.

'How dare you?' hissed Maureen. 'I'm in charge on nights and don't you fucking forget it.'

Determined not to be forced into an argument, Paula didn't reply, but glared at the Bat before carrying on with what she was doing. Maureen walked round the desk and jabbed a finger into Paula's shoulder.

'Don't you ever - ever do that to me again,' she said.

Paula deposited one of the specimens into her handbag then turned to the night sister.

'If I ever hear you swear again, Maureen, at me or anyone else' she said. 'I'll have you out of here as quick as you can say old Bat.' She paused for effect. 'Do you understand me? And if you have a problem with that - I suggest you find yourself another job.'

Maureen's lips trembled, her face and neck glowed beetroot red. Paula thought that if it could have been physically possible, there'd be steam coming out of her ears.

'Sadly, I doubt if anyone else would put up with you,' said Paula. A stifled snort came from behind the bed screen. 'So, if you don't mind, Sister,' she said. 'I want to get this specimen to the lab as soon as possible - then I'm going to phone the police - then I'm going to phone the CEO.' She lowered her voice so that only Maureen could hear, '- but not necessarily in that order -' she said.

Maureen looked as if she was about to reply, but before she could, Paula waved the plastic bag in front of her face. 'I'd be grateful,' she said, 'if you'd call the biochemist. Tell him it's urgent and I'll be waiting outside the lab - I take it you can manage that.' She added sarcastically.

The night sister glowered.

'I'll only say please once,' said Paula. 'There's been enough shouting for one night and I don't think you'll want to explain your actions – or more accurately - non actions - to the Chief Executive, do you?'

'I'll do it in the office,' said Maureen. She stormed off.

'I think that went well,' said Paula, to no one in particular. She walked over to the side-ward where George was carefully packing things into plastic bags. He wrote *Evidence - Do Not Remove* on them and left them outside the room.

'How's he doing?' Paula said, to Ravi who was stood by the breathing machine.

'He's stable, but to be on the safe side I think I'll put him back on the ventilator overnight.' said Ravi. Paula leant against the door frame. The registrar crossed over to join her

'I thought I should ring the consultant on call to let him know what has happened,' he said. The doctor looked as though he was still in shock. 'Did someone really give him the potassium on purpose?'

'Believe it,' said Paula.

Chapter Thirty-Four

The doctor sat two floors above the ICU. The stakes had gone up and so had his adrenalin. He had never felt so alive. He tried to play solitaire on the computer, but couldn't concentrate. He tried to visualise the ICU. The panic as they tried, in vain, to save the wretched boy. It had been the right call, deciding to terminate the hooligan. There'd be one less thug on the streets and the father had been taught a lesson in humility. The doctor considered returning to watch the disaster unfold, but it might look suspicious and so he returned his attention to the card game.

*

Maureen muttered to herself as she sat at Paula's desk. She lifted the telephone out of a mess of papers and set it down in front of her with a clatter. Her temper reached boiling point and the night sister chuntered to herself. *'How dare she order me around - I'll teach the bitch to humiliate me in front of everybody.'* She picked up the receiver, dialled zero and waited for the operator to respond. Later on, Maureen would say that she had intended to ask for the biochemist. What she did was request to be put through to the doctor.

*

The incessant bleep interrupted his thoughts. He closed the card game, before answering the call and grunted as he picked up the phone.

'I have a call for you,' said the operator.

'Hello.' There was no reply. He shouted impatiently. 'Hello, who is that?'

'It's, it's Maureen.' the Bat kept her voice to a whisper.

'What,' he said. 'Speak up woman, I can't hear you.'

'It's Maureen - Maureen Dent.'

'I'm not on duty, Sister,' he said. 'You'll have to get the consultant on call.'

Maureen raised her voice to a loud hiss. 'I know you're not, doctor' she said, 'but I thought you would want to be told what's happened.'

He thought she was going to tell him that the kid had died. Curiosity got the better of him. 'Told what?' he said.

'Vincent arrested and-'

He cut in before she could go into detail. 'That's terrible, Maureen' he said. He removed a grainy photograph from the pocket in his white coat. It was of a young woman and little girl. 'I'm very sorry he's died, but I've just got home so you'll have to get somebody else to sort out the paper work.' He'd taken the picture from the drawer in Vincent's room. The woman looked familiar.

'But-'

The doctor turned the photo over to see if there was anything written on the back. 'Goodnight Maureen,' he said. The receiver was no more than a few centimetres from his ear, when he caught the words.

'He's not dead.'

'What did you say?'

'I never said he was dead,' said Maureen. 'I said he'd arrested.'

He returned the picture to his pocket. He'd think about that later. I'm sorry, Maureen' he said. 'I obviously misheard you. What happened?' The night sister gave him a long rambling account of the cardiac arrest.

'And then Paula stormed in -'

'What.'

'Thankfully, Vincent's all right,' said Maureen 'but that's no thanks to her.'

'What are you talking about, woman?'

'Paula came in sprouting some sort of nonsense,' said Maureen. 'I can't believe what Ravi did.'

'What did Ravi do?'

'Hid did exactly what she asked,' she said, 'and now they all think she was right all along.'

The doctor banged his fist on the table.

'What was that?' said Maureen.

'Nothing, I dropped something, that's all,' he said. 'What's she doing now?'

'Apparently, once she gets the results, she's going to call the police.'

'What results?' His mind was in overdrive.

'Paula took a blood sample before they gave the dextrose and insulin,' said Maureen. 'It was just a coincidence - wasn't it?'

'I'm sure it was,' he said. The doctor remained calm. It was as if his brain was split in two. One side was able to deal with irritating woman on the phone, whilst the other considered his options. If Paula had taken blood before they gave the antidote. It would show the abnormal levels of potassium that could have only got there by an injection. He had to get hold of the sample before it reached the laboratory.

'Has it gone off to the lab yet?'

'Paula's gone there to wait for the biochemist,' said Maureen. 'She sent me to call him. You should have heard the way she spoke to me. It was so unprofessional. It would serve her right if I didn't bother – she can stand in that poky basement until the cows come home, for all I care.'

'I'm sure there's no rush,' he said and then after a moment's pause, he added. 'Listen, Maureen, why don't you let her stew. I need to talk to the biochemist about another patient so I'll ring him for you and you can go get yourself a cup of tea.'

She hesitated.

'I'm sorry if I was short with you earlier, Maureen,' he said. 'I'd just got home and you know what it's like - you want a drink - the bleep goes.' He turned off the computer. 'My wife's brought me a drink so I've plenty of time to make the call.' He smiled to himself. 'And, Maureen - you did the right thing. This hospital needs more sisters like you – goodnight.' He cut the connection before she could reply.

The doctor stared at the phone as if it had stung him. How could that interfering bitch have known? He took a moment to compose himself and then retrieved his briefcase from the floor. Flicking the catches with his thumbs, he opened the case and removed a pair of surgeon's gloves. The doctor opened the packet as if he was about to perform a sterile procedure and slid the latex over his fingers. The gloves fitted like a second skin. He unlocked the desk drawer, took out a blue-handled scalpel and pressed the flat blade against his lips. Returning his attention to the drawer, he removed a syringe from the back panel where it had been secured with surgical tape then closed the case and slipped the items into the pocket of his white coat.

Chapter Thirty-Five

Whoever thought of putting the pathology laboratory in the basement had obviously never worked a night shift, thought Paula. She took the lift. It shuddered to a halt. The doors opened onto a dimly lit network of corridors that dog-legged their way beneath the hospital. The dank air was filled by the drone of the heating system. The walls of the passage that led to the laboratory had been plastered and painted a grubby apple-white. The concrete floor covered with durable linoleum. Halfway along the passage all semblance of domesticity stopped, revealing the assortment of pipes, some bare, some lagged. These were the veins and arteries of the hospital. Parallel gutters flowed along the edges of the concrete path. A constant dribble of grungy fluid trickled alongside Paula as she headed toward the laboratory. At its furthest point, the corridor culminated at the mortuary. The underground access allowed for the movement of bodies away from the public eye.

Paula reached the set-back alcove and pressed the intercom bell, in the hope the technician had already arrived, but there was no answer. Because of the heating pipes the corridor was overly warm. Despite this, Paula shivered. She looked around the alcove. A dilapidated cork notice board filled one wall. Opposite, a row of three plastic-backed chairs offered rest for the visitor. Paula jammed her hands into her pockets and began to walk round in a circle, kicking her heels.

A door banged from somewhere above. Pretending she wasn't spooked by the noise, Paula hummed to herself. She soon became bored and looked at her watch. It was half-past eleven. She'd already been waiting fifteen minutes. By now, Duncan would be worrying because he hadn't heard from her. She made a mental note to ask the technician if she could use his phone. Paula poked her head out of the recess and looked up and down the empty corridor. She glanced at her watch again.

There was no warning. Paula didn't hear anything.

One minute, she was kicking her heels, the next he was stood in front of her, a creased white coat covering his Moss Bros suit. Several inches taller, he glared down at Paula. She took a step back and tumbled into the chairs. She tried to regain her balance, but he edged closer.

'Alan,' she said, shakily. The front of the chair dug into the back of her legs.

Alan Charlton didn't move.

'Paula.'

She tried to push the chairs away, but he put his foot out and blocked them. Paula tried to act as if everything was normal. 'I thought you'd gone home?' she said.

'You'd have liked that Sister,' he said, snatching the specimen bag. He put it into the pocket of his white coat. 'You couldn't leave things alone could you, Paula?'

She had stretched out her injured hand to stop her from falling. The doctor put his hand on top of hers and squashed it against the wall.

'I'm waiting for the biochemist,' she said, more assuredly than she felt.

'Do you think he's going to turn up?'

'Yes, Maureen rang him for me,' said Paula. He grinned sardonically and increased the pressure on her hand. 'Alan, please you're hurting me.'

'Not the first time,' he said.

A tsunami of fear flooded into Paula's veins. 'There's no need for this,' she said. 'We can sort it out,'

He pulled her hand away from the wall and turned it palm up. With his free hand, he took the scalpel from his pocket and removed the cover with his teeth. His eyes were icy cold as he stroked the blade over the scar. Paula shuddered.

'Let's go back to the unit and talk,' she said, trying to sound calm.

The consultant smiled. He raised the knife to her face and began to caress her cheek. 'It's too late for that, Paula,' he said.

'Please, Alan you're scaring me.' She couldn't believe what was happening and tried to back off, but the chair was cutting into her legs.

'Am I, Paula?' he said. 'Am I really scaring you?' He

tilted his head to one side and peered into her eyes. 'Has anybody ever mentioned your pretty eyes?' The blade slid under her chin. 'Your boyfriend, he must have said it -what was his name?'

Paula bit down on her lip.

'I asked you,' he said, quietly. 'What is his name?'

'Duncan.'

'Yes, Duncan, how could have I forgotten.' The blade glided over her silky skin. 'How does it feel now he's left you?' he said.

Paula's knees gave way and she landed heavily on the nearest chair. The high pitched scrape of metal on floor, echoed along the corridor. Alan let go of her and looked out of the recess.

'I do believe you're right, Sister,' said Alan, when he returned. He grabbed Paula by the arm and pulled her off the chair. 'We need to go somewhere more private.' He gestured with the knife for her to pass.

This man had been her friend. He was so cold and controlled. Paula could smell the hate on his breath. She headed towards the stairs. Alan dragged her back.

'Wrong way,' he said, pushing her in the direction of the mortuary. 'We wouldn't want to be disturbed while we have our little chat, would we?'

Paula turned to face him. 'Please don't do this Alan.'

He prodded the knife into her arm and a trickle of crimson blossomed onto the white of her blouse.

Chapter Thirty-Six

After paying the taxi driver, Duncan let himself into the house. He unwound the charcoal-grey cashmere scarf that had been a Christmas present from Paula, along with the black leather bomber jacket he was wearing and threw them over the back of the chair. He sat heavily on the sofa, kicked off his shoes and put his feet on the table. At the restaurant, he'd been about to suggest he sell the flat and move in with Paula on a permanent basis. Only the bleep had rudely interrupted. Duncan rubbed at stubble on his chin for several minutes.

The fire had gone out. He got up and tried to re-light it, but failed dismally. Paula always managed to get it going first time by using old newspapers and a coal scuttle to draw the embers. Whenever Duncan tried the same technique, despite having spent the greater part of his youth in the Scout movement, the paper inevitably caught fire and disappeared up the chimney. He persevered and eventually managed to force a few pieces of charcoal into a thin drizzle of smoke. After making a coffee, he switched on the television to catch the end of the news, but couldn't settle. In the end, he turned off the television and threw the controller onto the chair in frustration. Piles of paper and notes littered the table. The fact that they had not been able to find anything in the records, only added to Duncan's conviction that the killings were carefully planned. Despite Paula's reassurances, he was becoming increasingly worried. He kept telling himself, she would be furious if he tried to interfere, but in the end he couldn't help himself. He got up from the sofa, added a small log to the pitiful flames and jammed the fireguard against the chimney breast. Duncan gathered up his scarf and jacket. Not wanting to risk driving, he scoured the under-stairs cupboard for a pair of gloves before setting off on the short walk to the hospital.

He followed the same shortcut as the prostitute and had a hard time squeezing his burly frame through the small gap in the fence. As he passed the mortuary, Duncan thought he heard a noise. It unnerved him and he quickened his pace.

When he reached the outer doors of the ICU, Duncan ignored the *'Please Ring and Wait'* sign and passed through to the airlock. He peered through the small porthole window of the inner door. At first glance the place looked dark and empty. He opened the door gingerly and poked his head into the ward.

'Hello,' he said, in a voice slightly above a whisper. By now his eyes had adjusted to the dim lighting and he could make out the angle poise lamps above each bed space. The room took on the appearance of a deserted sci-fi film set. The distinctive hiss, squeak and buzz of machinery only added to the eerie atmosphere. Duncan noticed a light streaming out from an open doorway.

'Hello,' he said, more loudly. His body followed his head into the ward. 'Is there anybody here?' Several nurses seemed to appear from nowhere. A tall, immaculately turned out nurse strode towards him.

'How did you get in? ' said Maureen. She shooed him off like an errant child.

'I'm looking for Paula,' said Duncan.

His words were like a red rag to a bull.

'I don't care if you're looking for the Pope,' said Maureen. 'You're not allowed in here -get out.'

'You must be the Bat.'

Maureen blushed. She bore down on him like a charging rhino. 'How dare you talk to me like that?' she said. 'Get out of my unit.'

Despite his bravado, Duncan found himself backed up against the door. Maureen repeated the order and tried to physically push him out. The door opened behind Duncan and a female voice shouted over his shoulder.

'He's with us, Maureen.'

Duncan turned. 'Ah, the cavalry,' he said, breaking into a smile. 'Have you seen Paula?'

Nancy was accompanied by a man who matched the ruby player in height and build. Nancy stood on tiptoe and gave Duncan a peck on the cheek. 'Isn't she here?' she said.

'No,' said Duncan.

Nancy made her way over to the nurses' station. The two men followed. Maureen slammed the doors and stormed off in the opposite direction.

'Dunc, this is Jeff,' said Nancy. 'Best police sergeant Lyedale Constabulary can offer.' She stressed the word constabulary for Maureen's benefit. 'This,' she indicated to Duncan, 'is the 'great one's' boyfriend.' Duncan peeled off his gloves and shook hands.

'What are you doing here?' Duncan said to Nancy.

'George rang me,' said Nancy. 'He said Paula was going to call the police and as Jeff happened to be with me at the time, I thought he was as good a plod as any, especially as he already knows Vincent.' She turned to the night sister. 'So, Maureen, what have you done with her?'

George emerged from the side-ward and joined them. Nancy turned her back on Maureen and addressed the male nurse.

'How's Vinnie?' she said.

'Thanks to Paula, he's fine,' said George. Indicating with his thumb and index finger, he added. 'We were this close to losing him. I've never been so -'

'I'm sorry to interrupt your analysis,' said Duncan, 'but where is she?'

'She's fine,' said George. 'She's gone to the path lab with a blood sample and she's going to wait for the results.'

Jeff asked George if Vincent was up to answering questions, but the male nurse told him that it would be some time before he'd be up to it.

'I'd like to speak to him as soon as,' said Jeff. 'In the meantime, you can tell him from me that we've managed to catch up with his mate. Not only has the little sod confessed to driving the car – he also told us that Vincent didn't even know the car was nicked.'

George stretched his back. 'I've rang his parents about him going into cardiac arrest,' he said. 'I told them the docs would have a chat with them, but I don't think they're coming-'

The phone rang. The night sister beat Nancy and snatched the receiver. A brief, troubled conversation followed. The Bat's hand shook as replaced the hand-set and she flopped onto the nearest chair.

'What's up with you?' said Nancy.

Maureen didn't reply.

'Was that, Paula?' said Duncan.

The night sister glared straight ahead. 'No,' she said, her face ashen. 'It was the biochemist. He wants to know where the blood specimen is.'

They stared at her.

'What do you mean?' said Nancy.

'I thought you said she'd gone to meet him,' said Duncan.

'He-he said that she wasn't there,' stuttered Maureen. 'He hasn't seen her.' She covered her face with her hands and her body began to shake. 'What have I done?'

'What do you mean?' Duncan snapped. He stood over her with fisted hands. Jeff pulled him back.

'What have you done?' said Nancy.

'I wouldn't have said anything,' Maureen said, through her fingers. 'He told me he was at home.'

'Who-' Nancy said. She tugged at Maureen's little finger in an attempt to get her to take her hands away from her face. 'Who was at home? You don't mean Alan, do you?'

'You're hurting me.'

'What have you done?' said Nancy.

'I'll do more that hurt you if you don't tell us what's happened.' said Duncan.

'Threatening her,' said Jeff 'isn't going to get us anywhere, Duncan. Back off.' He gestured for Nancy to move then crouched in front of Maureen. 'Tell me what happened,' he asked, gently.

'Honestly, I was going to ring the biochemist,' said Maureen. 'I was sure she was wrong. It was just a coincidence.' She looked at the police officer for support. 'I thought Alan should know what she'd been saying, especially as it concerned him.' Her sob came out as a hiccough. 'I'm sure he hasn't – he - he wouldn't do anything to her – he can't he's at home.'

'Where is she?' bellowed Duncan.

'Shut up and let her get on with it,' said Jeff. He leant closer. 'Take a deep breath and tell us exactly what happened?'

'I went in the office to ring the biochemist.'

Maureen's hands fell from her face into her lap. 'Alan came in earlier. We were busy. George was useless; he kept disappearing to the loo. Alan did a quick ward round. He often does pop in to check on the patients. He prefers to do it on his own. I was busy.' Strands of hair had escaped her bun and the night sister tried to tuck them in. 'He was the last one in the sideward before – before Vincent arrested - I thought it only fair he should know.' The hair broke away again. Maureen gave up with it. She looked totally despondent. 'He told me he was at home,' she said, defensively.

'When you rang him,' said Jeff. 'Did you tell him where Paula was?'

'He asked me.'

'Did you tell him?'

'Yes,' said Maureen. 'I told him she'd gone to path lab and he said he'd ring the biochemist for me. Alan said he needed to talk to him.' She looked to Duncan. 'I'm sorry,' she said. 'But I did - I did ring him.'

'Ring who?' Jeff said.

'The biochemist,' said Maureen. 'Even though Alan said he would – just in case he forgot, I rang the biochemist when I got back from the canteen.'

'You went to the canteen,' said Nancy.

'It's not your fault, Maureen,' said Jeff. '

'Not much, it isn't,' growled Duncan, through gritted teeth. 'If she's hurt I'll -'

Jeff stood up and pulled Duncan to one side. 'You are not helping here, mate. I know what I'm doing. The less you say the quicker we'll find out what's happening, okay.' Duncan reluctantly nodded and crossed his arms. Jeff returned to the night sister. 'Okay, Maureen. Thank you for being so honest with me,' he said. 'Now, do you know where they are?'

'How should I know?' said Maureen. Some of her bravado had returned. She looked at the disbelieving faces. 'Alan told me he was at home. I don't know where he is. Paula should be at the lab.' She reached for a box of tissues from the desk and tugged out several. 'I – I suppose he could have been in the hospital when he rang -I don't know.'

Jeff stood and faced the others. 'He might have tried to intercept her,' he said.

'Okay,' said Duncan. 'Let's go.' He turned to Nancy. 'How do we get to this lab?'

'I'll show you,' she said. Nancy glared at the Bat who looked as if she was feeling very sorry for herself.

'Oh no,' said Jeff. 'You're not coming with us. You can tell us how to get there.'

'No way,' said Nancy. 'I'm coming with you and you can't stop me. She's my friend and I know my way around.'

Jeff tried to argue, but Nancy didn't budge. George shouted after the trio as they headed for the door.

'Do you want me to come with you?'

'No,' said Jeff 'but you can ring the station for me. Tell them what's happened and ask them to send back up.' The policeman crossed to where George was stood by the nurses' station. He lowered his voice so no one else could hear. 'Tell them, I said that this guy is dangerous.'

'Come on,' shouted Duncan. 'You're wasting time.'

Nancy led the way as they raced down the stairs, but Duncan followed the signage for the pathology laboratory and arrived at the alcove ahead of the others. The door was locked and there was no sign of life. He left his finger pressed against the intercom button. A white-coated biochemist eventually answered the incessant summons. A bright florescent light flooded the recess when he opened the door. Jeff flipped open his ID card.

'Hi there,' he said. He read the technicians name badge. 'Dave, I'm sergeant, Jeff Palmer. I need to know if you have you seen either Sister Hobson or Dr Charlton?'

The biochemist seemed taken aback by their presence. 'I've just got here,' he said. 'What's going on?'

'We need to know if you have seen either of them,' said Nancy.

'No, I told you I haven't been here long. I haven't seen anybody.' he said. 'Mind you, I'm pretty sure someone has been here.'

'What makes you say that,' said Jeff.

Because when I got here,' said Dave. 'The chairs were all over the place.' He indicated the broken seat propped up in the corner. 'The leg on that one's been bent. It wasn't like that when I left.'

Jeff picked up and examined the chair.

'I thought it might have been kids,' said Dave.

'Could it have been caused by some sort of struggle or something?' asked Jeff.

'I don't know,' said Dave. 'We sometimes get kids in the basement, looking to make trouble and the occasional down-and-out looking for somewhere warm to kip.' Dave looked to the sister. 'What's going on, Nancy?'

She didn't answer. Nancy had seen something on the floor and crouched down to examine it. She ran her fingers over the floor's greasy surface and rubbed them together. Looking up to the others, she took a sharp intake of breath.

'It's blood.' she said, showing them the dirty red smudge on her finger.

Jeff turned back to the biochemist.

'Could that have come from your lab?' he said.

'I doubt it,' said Dave. 'I haven't had anything in or out tonight.' He nodded to Nancy's finger. 'And that's fresh.'

'I'll kill him,' said Duncan.

'We don't know its Paula's.' said Jeff, trying to sound positive. 'It's only a drop it could be from anything.' He stuck his head out of the recess then turned back to the technician. 'Dave, where does this corridor lead?'

The biochemist stepped out and pointed. 'That way goes to the changing rooms and back out the way you came,' he said. 'And that way leads to the mortuary.'

There was an icy silence as they stared along the dark passageway.

Nancy broke the spell. 'You don't think he'd take her down there, do you?' she said.

'Is it open?'

'It shouldn't be,' replied the technician, shaking his head. 'Not unless the porters have taken a body down there and forgotten to lock up.' He shrugged. 'I wouldn't really know. It's nothing to do with me.'

'Do you have a key?'

'There is one in the lab,' said Dave. 'But I can't let you have it. It's against hospital policy and anyway you still haven't told me what this is about.'

Duncan nudged Nancy out of the way and grabbed his

collar. 'We haven't time for this crap,' he said. 'If anything happens to her because you're being a prize idiot -' He wasn't allowed to finish. Jeff pushed in-between them.

'Look, mate,' said Jeff. 'Duncan's right we don't have time to go into it right now, but we do have to find Sister Hobson - and quickly.' He took out his warrant card. 'I've shown you my badge - you know Sister Coleman.'

The scientist hesitated. 'I thought you were looking for Dr Charlton as well. - I don't understand.'

'Dave, please,' said Nancy. She smiled at him. 'You know me I wouldn't ask if it wasn't important.'

They watched him disappear into the maze of rooms. Dave returned a few minutes later with a bunch of keys and a couple of heavyweight torches.

'You might need these,' he said.

Jeff and Duncan took one each.

Chapter Thirty-Seven

The building throbbed overhead. Whenever Paula's pace slowed or she tried to talk, he dug the scalpel into her skin. Despite the heat of the basement, the constant trickle of blood down her back made her shiver. The droplets spotted the begrimed floor. When they reached the mortuary lift, Paula stopped. Alan pushed her forcefully toward the stairwell. She turned and tried to reason with him.

'I don't know what,' she said. He lashed out at her arm. She backed off, saying. 'You don't want to do this, Alan - please.'

'Get up there.'

Paula raised her hands in submission and climbed the narrow staircase. At the top, Alan produced a key and inserted it into the grey metal door. She could smell his acidic breath and turned her head away from his face. His latex gloves stuck to the Yale and he struggled to open the lock. Alan swore. The door finally opened and rebounded off the wall. He pushed her into the darkness.

'Where did you get the key?' she said.

Paula didn't see his icy smile, but could feel the strength of his contempt. 'It's a master key. The head porter obligingly leant me his when I locked myself out of the office.' He spoke as if she were a stranger. 'You never know when these things might come in useful so I made a copy.' He found the light switches.

Paula had to blink before she was able to look round the large rectangular lobby, which was empty, save for three battered, cadaver-trolleys lined up against the wall. In a poor attempt at disguise, they had been covered with washed-out counterpanes. The near-side wall was taken up with the large refrigerated cabinet. It housed up to eighteen cadavers at any one time. A combination of her own fear and the stench of dead bodies, post-mortems and disinfectant made Paula feel sick. She could see an emergency exit at the far end corridor that led off from the lobby. Alan stepped in to block her escape.

'I don't think we'll be disturbed in here,' he said. Opening the nearest door, he ushered her into the autopsy room with a wave of the knife. There was a row of switches along the inside wall. Alan turned them all on. The lights flickered a moment before flooding the room and glinted off the multiple stainless-steel surfaces. The air conditioning unit began to hum. A lone dissecting table occupied the centre space.

'Please, Alan, think about what you are doing,' said Paula.

'Please, Alan,' he mimicked. 'You appear to have forgotten who you are speaking to.'

Even though the room was cold in comparison to the basement, Paula had now begun to sweat.

'I'm the consultant,' Alan said, quietly. He began to pace a circle with Paula as the centre point. 'And I'm in charge here.'

'You're the one with the knife.'

'You're supposed to respect your consultant, Sister' he sneered. 'Something you seem to have forgotten lately.'

Paula followed him with her eyes. Her sweat was mixing with the dried blood on her back.

'Maybe you need a lesson in respect,' said Alan. He weaved the scalpel in the air, as if conducting an unseen orchestra.

'Alan, you're frightening me.'

'Those were my patients,' he said, ignoring her pleas. 'I decide their fate.' He jabbed the knife at her. 'You dear Paula - you interfered in something that had nothing to do with you.'

'You can't go around killing patients because you -'

He didn't let her finish. 'No - no, you see that's where you're wrong. I can and I do what I have to. I help these poor unfortunates to a natural end.'

'There's nothing natural about what you are doing?' said Paula. She was praying that by now someone had realised she was missing and knew her only chance was to keep him talking.

'I do what others dream of, but don't have the balls to

go through with.'

Paula tried to back further into the room, but came up against the dissecting table. She clung onto the cold steel to give her strength.

'Some would call it murder.' she said, thinking of Duncan. For once, she hoped he hadn't listened to her.

'I put them out of their misery, like you would a dog,' said Alan. 'I save the relatives' days of weeping and wailing. - I save thousands of pounds in wasted treatments - I save you lot.' He pointed the knife at her heart. 'Time and effort -I make space for viable patients who deserve the beds. – You - should be grateful.'

'Linda didn't deserve to die,' said Paula.

'-I should be honoured for what I do.-'

'What about Vincent?'

'-I should be recognised for my services to this God-forsaken country.-'

'He's just a boy,' she said. 'And he was getting better.'

Alan stopped and leaned towards her. Forgetting that Vinnie had survived the attack, he said.

'If you hadn't interfered, Madam, I might have allowed him to live.' He straightened. 'They were all worthless pieces of shit. The world is a better place without them.'

'I don't believe you,' said Paula. 'I couldn't believe anybody could do it. When I found out it was you - at least I thought you'd done it because you cared.' Tears welled in her eyes. 'But you don't – do you? You don't care about anyone but yourself – why, Alan -why?'

'I don't have to explain myself to the likes of you.'

If she'd seen it coming, Paula might have had time to avoid the blow. His arm whipped round. The back of his hand slammed into her face. She staggered and grabbed the table to stop herself from falling. Her teeth had sunk into her bottom lip. The metallic tang of blood flooded her mouth. Paula knew she had to do something soon; otherwise he was going to really hurt her. She'd noticed a large stainless-steel bowl at the far end of the autopsy table and began to edge toward it. Alan pulled at the cuff of his latex glove and let it thwack back onto his wrist. He looked at Paula and lifted the knife to her face.

'Say you're sorry.'

She couldn't believe this was the same man she had known, liked and worked with for many years. A man she thought of as a friend. He flicked the knife at her skin wanting a response.

'I don't know what I've done wrong, but I'm sorry,' she said, inching along the table.

'That's better,' whispered Alan. He lowered his hand. 'Respect, Sister, that's what it's about.' All of a sudden, he leant over Paula until his face was inches away from hers. He dug the point of the blade under her chin. 'You see, Paula, the only trouble is,' he said. 'It's all a bit late, isn't it?' He twisted the knife into the soft tissue of her chin. The pain seared through Paula's head. She grabbed his hand and tried to pull it away, but the more she pulled the more he twisted.

'Please, Alan, you're hurting me.'

'It would be good to see the mortuary technician's face tomorrow morning,' he said. 'When he comes in and finds an extra body on his slab - I could even save them the bother of a post-mortem.' He laughed. 'How's that for dedication?'

Alan's face was so close to hers, she could see the individual beads of sweat on his brow. Paula knew he was trying to break her will. She struggled to fight the terror that was threatening to overcome her. He reached into the pocket of his white coat and pulled out the blood sample he'd taken from her. Alan's eyes drilled into hers as he dropped the bottle and crushed it with his shoe. He stood straight and produced the primed syringe form his other pocket.

'What's that?' said Paula.

'Pancuronium.'

The colour drained from Paula's face. The words came out in a croak. 'You wouldn't do that to me.' Panic gripped her throat. 'Please, Alan, think about what you are doing.'

'Please, Alan,' he said, mimicking her plea. 'Isn't this where we came in?' Alan brushed his hand lightly over her breasts. 'Look at you, you're such a mess.' He undid the top button of her shirt. 'It's such pity you won't be able to tell me what it's like to be paralysed and awake.' The sound from his throat was almost a purr. 'Do you think you'll suffocate or die of blood loss?' He mocked and then grabbed her breast, painfully. 'However, before we get into all that, you're going to take the place of that whore. It's your fault, I'm afraid. You shouldn't have told her about me.'

'I didn't,' said Paula. 'It was the other way round.' She was getting desperate and prayed to any God who might be listening. 'They'll be searching for me,' she said, in hope more than certainty. Alan wiped the blooded scalpel on her blouse.

'Duncan expected me home by now,' she said. 'I told him to ring the police if I didn't get in touch.'

'Your boyfriend dumped you.'

'We made up,' she said. Paula could tell he was undecided. She pressed on. 'In fact we were at the restaurant together when they bleeped me.'

'Who bleeped you?' He jabbed the knife into her chin again.

Paula winced, 'George,' she said. Pointing to the mess on the floor, she added. 'And that's not the only specimen. I took two.'

, 'You're lying.'

'I'm not.' She stood on her tiptoes in an effort to reduce the pressure from the blade. 'Nancy was with me the night you rang.'

'I don't believe you.'

Paula felt the knife hit bone. She let out an involuntary cry.

'Nancy came to tell me about the meeting you had with Charles and the others.'

Alan didn't say anything, but the pressure on her chin eased. She tried to take advantage of his indecision. 'Your call confirmed what Nancy already suspected. Because of her I was ready for Charles. I knew what he was going to say,' she said.

The consultant had taken a step back.

'You're lying.' He flicked the knife into her flesh. She sobbed with the pain. Blood dribbled down her neck and drenched her blouse. Paula pressed the back of her hand under her chin in an attempt to stop the flow.

'I'm not.'

'You think you're clever.'

'You think you're invincible.'

'I know I am.'

Paula noticed the splattered blood on his coat and realised it was hers. The panic began to cloud her brain. 'You won't get away with it,' she said.

'Ah, but I will,' said Alan. 'You see, Maureen thinks I'm at home with my loving wife and my loving wife will confirm it.' He smiled. 'Your death will be put down to some deranged, psychopathic maniac. He attacked you in the basement and dragged you here for his pleasure before disposing of the evidence.' He flicked the knife at her blouse. 'Take your shirt off.'

'What?'

'You heard me,' said Alan. He spoke slowly, enunciating the vowels. 'Take off your shirt.'

'No.'

'I won't ask again.'

This time Paula saw the punch coming, but still didn't manage to move in time and the blow struck her on the temple. Consciousness waned. Paula thought she was going to fall. She saw his hand rise again and lifted her arm to protect herself. Alan grabbed her blouse. The strong fabric resisted his efforts to rip it. His hand slipped and he staggered backwards. Paula took her chance and slid along the edge of the table. She grabbed the metal bowl and swung it at his head. It shimmered in the light as it flew through the air. It connected to his skull, like a hammer against a gong. Alan stumbled. He lashed out with the scalpel. It caught Paula on the arm, before slipping from his fingers and skidding under the table.

Paula miss-aimed a kick to his groin and threw the bowl at his head before running for the door. She managed to reach the corridor before he tackled her. They both fell to the floor. Paula landed painfully on her elbow. She twisted her body and kicked out at him. Alan scrambled over to where the syringe had fallen. Paula used the time to struggle to her feet. Both shoes had come off in the mêlée and she careered along the slippery corridor as she made a bee-line for the exit. Paula lunged for the quick release handle, but Alan caught up with her before she could open the door. She screamed, thrashed, kicked and scratched with all her strength. He held up his arms in defence giving her time to dive for the door, but he caught up to her and kicked her legs from under her. Paula fell heavily and banged her head. He straddled her body and pinned her arms to the floor with his knees.

She could hear someone screaming. The sound seemed to be coming from above her head. Only it stopped when he sat on her chest and she found it difficult to breathe. Paula could see the syringe in his hand and twisted her body in an effort to get away, but he increased the pressure on her shoulders.

Paralysed with fear, Paula watched Alan as he took hold of the needle cover with his teeth, pulled it off, spat it out and darted the needle into her vein. He stared into her eyes as he injected the lethal substance.

Chapter Thirty-Eight

Joan Johnson had enjoyed a privileged upbringing, but then fell in love, and pregnant, to a man without money or ambition. Following her first husband's death, from cancer, the single mother struggled to cope until she met Russell Stevens. When they married, Joan had vowed never to say or do anything to jeopardise her new life. At the age of thirty-four, she became pregnant with Vincent and doted on her young son.

On the day of the accident, Vincent had been on leave from Sheffield University. Boredom had driven him into town to meet with friends. The next time his mother had seen him was when he was attached to all the paraphernalia of resuscitation. Over the interminable weeks at her son's bedside, she'd kept to her vow of silence whilst her husband ranted and railed. But Joan had been brooding for several days over the impending transfer.

She was getting ready for bed when she heard Russell answer the phone. A short while later he came up to the bedroom. He told her that the call had been from the hospital to say that there had been an incident.

'What sort of an incident?'

'The lad's had some sort of a turn.' said Russell. He removed his tie and began to undo the buttons of his shirt.

'What do mean?'

'The male nurse said something about his heart stopped briefly,' he said. Apparently he's all right.'

'It must have been serious or they wouldn't have rung.'

'It just goes to prove,' said Russell. 'The sooner we get him out of there the better.'

'Did you tell them we were on our way?' said Joan, reaching for her clothes.

'No,' he said. 'I told them we would see them in the morning.' He tugged his shirt from his trousers. 'I have an important client tomorrow and what I need right now is some sleep.'

Joan made her way downstairs and rang the hospital. George seemed reluctant to say too much over the phone, but told her that the doctors would be happy to explain things if they went in. For once, Joan Stevens was determined to have her way. The phone call might have been the catalyst for her revolt, but once the flood gates had opened there was no stopping and nineteen years of repression poured out of her. In the end, Russell agreed to drive her to the hospital. It was a quarter to midnight when they got into their car.

*

Duncan rushed ahead as they ran along the corridor. The drone of machinery reverberated along the tunnel and drowned out any noise from above. He followed the shimmering drops of blood his flashlight picked out from the dirt. Jeff and Nancy caught up to him at the stairwell and all three took the steps two at a time. Nancy stumbled halfway and had to be helped. Unsurprisingly, Duncan was the first to make it to the top. He crashed through the unlocked door into anteroom and the others tumbled in after him. The place seemed eerily quiet. At first, although the lights were on, they couldn't see anything. Nancy pushed forward, following the trail of red spots until she came to the open door of autopsy room which was covered in smeared blood. She dropped to her knees. Jeff pulled her up.

'Go get help,' he said pushing her toward the lift.

A sound made them turn, their eyes following the skid marks along the corridor. Alan Charlton was kneeling over something by the emergency exit. He saw them and stood. The bundle on the floor moved. Paula braced herself against the wall and tried to stand, but her legs were no longer capable of holding her weight. She looked at her friends as her hands began to slide down the wall. Duncan, Jeff and Nancy were frozen to the spot. Paula finally slid to the floor. Duncan moved first.

'You're too late,' shouted Alan. He reached out behind him, pushed down on the steel bar with his gloved hands and disappeared into the black of the night.

*

The drive to the hospital took forty minutes. That night there
had been a sharp frost and the roads were covered in black ice.
Russell Stevens was unusually quiet as he squeezed the
accelerator of his Mercedes. Having found her voice, Joan
seemed empowered and was pressing home her advantage.
They were approaching the hospital gates when she fired her
final salvo.

'I want a divorce;' she said 'and I'm going to take you
for every precious penny of that bank balance.'

Stevens overran the gated entrance and the Mercedes
took the corner too fast. Time slowed into frame by frame
seconds. The car skidded and then glided across the
shimmering metallic surface in a leisurely waltz. Neither of
the car's occupant's saw the man running until Joan shouted
the warning. A discordant sound of screeching brakes filled
the air. There was a loud bang, quickly followed by a bone
crunching smack. A man's eyes glared like a startled animal
until a web of cracks zigzagged across the windscreen. The
wipers started up automatically and smeared blood across the
cracked glass.

Chapter Thirty-Nine

Paula could feel the drug block the nerve endings and began to lose command of her limbs as her body sank into paralysis. She slid slowly down the wall. As she lost the power in her muscles, Paula's other senses heightened and she could hear panic in Duncan's voice as he shouted her name. She felt the floor vibrate as feet pounded along the corridor. Duncan skidded on his knees and lifted her gently into his arms. She tried to speak.

'Pa - vu – l –on,' croaked Paula. It was the only word she could manage before the paralysis affected her vocal chords. Jeff and Nancy joined them. An icy draught blew through the open doorway. Nancy shivered. Jeff took hold of her shoulders and eased her out of the way. He leapt over Paula's prostrate body and followed the consultant into the night. Nancy closed the door and knelt beside Duncan.

'What's he done to you?' said Duncan. Paula's shirt was drenched in blood. 'I'll kill the bastard.' He cradled his girlfriend in his arms and rocked backward and forward. Looking at Nancy, he said. 'She's not breathing. What do I do?''

Nancy appeared to be unable to answer. Duncan shouted at her. The pain in his voice jolted the deputy into action. She picked up the empty syringe and looked at Paula.

'Put her down.' she said.

'She tried to say something,' said Duncan. 'When we got here, she said –something to me.'

Nancy grabbed him by the shoulders. 'Quick,' she said. 'Put her down.'

He released his grip and Paula's body slipped to the floor. Her unmoving eyes stared ahead. Nancy felt for her carotid artery. Paula's pulse pounded beneath clammy skin.

'What did she say?' said Nancy. 'Duncan this is important - what did she say? '

. 'I don't know,' he said. Tears welled in his eyes 'Erm – it - it sounded like Avalon.'

Nancy stared at the flaccid body of her friend, willing it to tell her what she needed to know. Clots of blood clung to the cotton of Paula's blouse. The gash in her arm trickled a rivulet of red. A lone tear oozed from the corner of her eye and dribbled down her temple, ending in a tiny puddle in her ear. Nancy stretched over and positioned herself in front of Paula's unmoving eyes. She almost shouted the words

'Did he give you Pavulon?' she said. Nancy nearly missed the imperceptible flicker of Paula's eyelids. She pulled her body away from the wall and made Duncan swap places. Placing one hand under her friend's neck, she eased Paula's head as far back as it would go; pinched her nostrils; pulled down her chin; inhaled deeply and then sealed their lips together. Nancy exhaled slowly into Paula's mouth and watched her chest rise. She took another deep breath and repeated the process. After several respirations, she wiped her mouth.

'What can I do?' said Duncan. He had sat back on his heels. 'Don't let her die?'

'Shut up you idiot, she can hear you,' hissed Nancy. She checked Paula's pulse again and then raised her voice so her friend could hear. 'She's going to be fine - aren't you buddy?' She tried to make a joke. 'Mind you look like you've done ten rounds with Lennox Lewis.' Nancy's hands were sticky with blood. She wiped them on her jeans before continuing with the mouth to mouth. In-between breaths, she said to Duncan. 'Find a phone - dial treble three and tell switchboard there's a respiratory arrest in the mortuary - tell them to come through the underpass and bring portable oxygen and a re-breath circuit.' She gave another breath. 'When you've done that, try and find some dressings or something - we've got to stop this bleeding.'

Paula was in a waking nightmare of fear and pain. She listened to the conversation between Nancy and Duncan with a disconnected interest. It was as if they were in another room. The world floated around her peripheral vision. She could feel the adrenaline pumping through her arteries. Her heart pounded in her ears. It seemed that the faster her heart beat the slower time passed. Nancy had pulled her head so far back; her eyes were fixed on a scuff mark on the wall. The dirty smudge looked like it had been made by a shoe. She wondered how it could have got so high up. Her friend's face dipped in and out of her field of vision. Paula could feel Nancy's warm breath course through her trachea into her lungs. She knew this was all that was keeping her alive and wondered if it might be easier if she gave in to death.

'Come on, kid.' Nancy's words floated in the air above her head. 'Hang in there boss – come on, Paula, you've got to do your bit -I won't let you go -'

The pain in her chest was becoming unbearable; each breath seemed to stretch her lungs like an over-inflated balloon. Oxygen depleted thoughts began to swirl through her brain. A smudgy-grey spinning-top jumped out from the mark on the wall. It headed toward her head and then swerved upwards and split into giant spiders. They preceded a warm blanket of darkness. It smothered the spiders and offered her safety.

Nancy could feel Paula's pulse begin to slow. 'Don't do this to me,' she said, increasing the rate of breaths. 'I can't lose my best buddy – you can't have a Lacey without a Cagney.' She was beginning to tire. Duncan hurried back with his arms laden.

'This is all I could find,' he said, dropping the packets and a couple of clean pillowcases onto the floor.

'Did you get switchboard?'

'They're on the way,' said Duncan. He knelt next to Nancy who wiped her forehead with the back of her hand.

'I'm knackered,' she said, to Duncan. 'You can take over from me.' To Paula, she said. 'I don't want any rumours about you and me boss so I'm going to let the hunk have a go.' She leaned forward so Paula could see and smiled. 'At least you should be used to his big gob.' Nancy and Duncan swapped positions. She gave him instruction, adding. 'Don't forget you're bigger than she is - so don't overdo it.'

Duncan had just given his first breath when there was a loud bang on the door. They exchanged looks, before Nancy got up to open it. She could hear a muffled shout from outside and pushed the bar down to release the bolt. The police sergeant burst through the door. He bent over with his hands on knees and took in great gulps of air.

Jeff looked from Paula to Duncan and then to Nancy. 'I'm sorry I lost him,' he said. Straightening up, he added. 'How's she doing?'

Nancy had bent over to sort out a dressing from the pile. She gave him such a look of despair that the policeman nodded in acknowledgement.

'I'll give the station a ring,' he said. 'Nancy, I know you have to do, what you have to do – but you will try and remember this is a crime scene and don't touch anything unless you have to.'

Not taking his eyes away from Paula, Duncan said. 'Third door along on the left - there's a phone.'

'Cheers.' said Jeff, before he made a hasty departure.

Duncan tenderly kissed Paula lips as he eased his breath into her mouth. He glanced over to Nancy who was trying to stem the flow of blood from Paula's arm with a wad of dressings. 'Shouldn't they be here by now,' he said, anxiously, 'where are they – why are they taking so long?'

No sooner had the words left his mouth, than the lift doors clattered open. The emergency team bore down on them, like a herd of rhinos. They were loaded with bags of equipment. A nurse from coronary care and two medics accompanied George and Ravi. A porter brought up the rear. He trundled a large oxygen cylinder in front of him.

Paula could hear snippets of the conversation as she drifted in and out of consciousness. The voices familiar, the words floated above her head. She wondered who they were talking about. Maybe she should be doing something. She knew that she should be a part of the exchange. The sounds, smells and commands were all normal and yet she was in a dream. Pain like nothing she had ever experienced before. Burning embers had replaced her muscles. The spiders had gone from her vision and yet her eyes remained fixed on the same dirty mark on the wall. The smell of rubber was overwhelming. She wanted to push the mask away, but her hands wouldn't obey her commands. A familiar Indian accent drifted into her brain.

'I am sorry,' said Ravi. 'I don't have any neostigmine to counteract the Pavulon –I'm going to have put in an endo-tracheal tube.' The voice was disjointed and seemed to make little sense to her, '- be as careful as I can -.' Faces came and went. Voices drifted in and out of her hearing. Sometimes the noise became unbearable. Paula wanted it to go away. She wanted to scream at them to leave her alone, to let her die. Just leave her in peace.

She felt her head being pulled so far back she thought her neck was going to snap and then the cold blade of the laryngoscope slipped into her mouth. Paula felt a gag reflex, but nothing moved. She wanted to be sick, but nothing happened. The thick tube slid down her throat, allowing the cold gas to flow into her lungs and oxygenate the blood. The oxygen rich blood was then pumped through her arteries to the vital organs. It cleared her brain and tamed the turmoil.

Chapter Forty

Her head was gently lowered onto a pillow and she felt warmth of blankets cover her body. The roar in her ears drowned out any other noise, but she could still make out the sound of her own breaths. It was like breathing through a snorkel, but Paula knew she wasn't underwater. Patches of light and dark flashed overhead. Her body bounced on the trolley as it hit the uneven surface of the basement corridor. A hand found hers just before she lost consciousness.

Jeff stayed on in the mortuary, to take charge of the investigation. Duncan and Nancy trailed behind the trolley. They eventually reached the ICU, but no sooner had the team passed through the airlock, when a cacophony of bleeps erupted.

'RTA -- Road Traffic Accident - Accident and Emergency – please respond.'

Once everybody had got over the shock, of a second emergency the team split into two. Maureen was keen to keep out of the way and so volunteered to accompany the medics heading for A&E. George, aided by Ravi, wheeled Paula into the empty side-ward. Duncan wanted to stay with his girlfriend, as did Nancy, but George reassured them he could manage without them for a while. Nancy dragged Duncan off to the staffroom where the pair sat in shocked silence.

The male nurse had already contacted the police along with Lennox Telleman and senior management. Doctor Telleman was stood next to the nurses' station along with the CEO as they wheeled Paula into the unit. Lennox peeled himself away to join his registrar. Once they had seen the extent of her wounds, the doctors agreed to ventilate Paula while they treated them. Only the short acting drug was beginning to show signs of wearing off and Paula had already regained the ability to blink. George told her what they intended to do, but Paula had other ideas and managed to convey her dissent.

In the end she accepted a compromise and agreed to

have a shot of sedative while they treated her wounds.

The analgesic worked quickly as did the plastic-surgeon who had come in especially. He examined the numerous cuts to her back. There was a six inch laceration to her upper arm and a cut to the inside of her swollen lip. The surgeon painstakingly treated each of her wounds with immaculate suturing. The gash under her chin proved especially difficult and was going to need a skin graft. It was an hour and a half before he finally finished off with steri-strips to the cut on her forehead. As soon as the surgeon had finished, Ravi kept to his promise and gave an injection of reversal to neutralise any remaining muscle relaxant. It was three am before Paula was fully awake and able to move. Blood continued to ooze through the dressings. She refused a hospital gown and insisted on a clean set of scrubs to replace her blooded clothes. By the time Duncan entered the room, she was sitting on the edge of the bed, swinging her legs and holding her throat.

'Hi,' she croaked.

'You look bloody awful,' said Duncan, rubbing his eyes.

'I love you, too.'

He sat next to her on the bed and mirrored her footwork.

'Lennox and Ravi say you have to stay until morning.'

'No thanks,' she croaked. 'I've had enough of this place.' Her body felt as though it had been through a mangle.

'What if that drug's still in your blood stream?'

'You can give me mouth-to-mouth again.' She coughed and had to hold onto her ribs. 'I feel like the All Blacks have just done the Hakka on my head,' she said.

Nancy came in followed by Jeff who'd just got back from the mortuary. Paula looked at them and realised something was wrong.

'What's the matter?' she croaked.

'Nothing,' said Nancy.

'Where's Alan?'

No one said anything.

'If you're worried about the blood sample being broken?' said Paula. She wobbled on the edge of the bed. 'I took two; the other is in my bag, wherever that is.'

'Yeah,' said Jeff. 'We've got it.'

'So what's the matter?' she asked again. The pain killer was beginning to wear off. She dabbed the back of her hand against her chin. 'Did he get away?'

'Not exactly.' said Jeff.

Nancy pulled a chair up and sat. She rested a hand on her friend's knee. 'Alan's been in an accident, Paula,' she said. 'He ran out in front of a car.'

'Is he dead?'

'No,' said Nancy, 'but it looks bad - he sustained a massive head injury.' There was an awkward silence. She continued. 'The ironic thing is – it was Russell Stevens. They were on their way in.'

For some reason, Paula wanted to cry. She eased herself off the bed.

'I think I'll go home now,' is all she said.

Paula walked unsteadily out of the room and was surprised to see the ICU full of people. There were doctors, senior management and some people, she presumed were the police. She looked round the familiar and unfamiliar faces and noticed one missing. It looked like no one had bothered to call Charles. She saw the body of Alan Charlton lying on a bed at the far end of the room. The group surrounding him parted as she approached, barefoot. Paula stared at the man who'd caused her so much pain and felt robbed. She wanted Alan Charlton to be accountable for what he'd done. She stood there for several minutes before turning and walking away.

Chapter Forty-One

The news about his daughter had left Jack Hobson distressed. Paula thought her father had enough to worry about and had wanted to protect him from the publicity, but a local hack had got to him before she'd had a chance to phone. To allay his fears she'd let Duncan drive her down to see him. Despite her best efforts, there wasn't much she could do to disguise her swollen and bruised face. Even a polo-necked jumper couldn't cover the cut on her chin. They had given her a sling to rest her arm, but it stayed in her bag. In the end, she decided the best way to reassure her father was to go back to work as soon as possible. She'd returned to duty within a few days of the attack, but not wanting to frighten any relatives, Paula had pretty much stuck to the office, trying to catch up on paper work. The office is where Nancy found her. The deputy laid her hand lightly on Paula's shoulder.

'You didn't have to come back quite so soon, you know,' she said. 'We could have struggled on without you.'
The student entered carrying a tray holding two mugs of tea.

'Thanks Celia,' said Paula.

'I see you've got the sympathy vote.' Nancy teased. The student left. Paula swivelled her chair round to face Nancy and smiled crookedly.

'I've had to work hard for it,' she said.

'Today's the day then,' Nancy said, more seriously. 'His family have arrived.' She picked up one of the mugs and took a gulp. 'Do you want me to sort it out?'

'I'm not sure,' said Paula. 'Part of me wants to have nothing to do with him anymore. But it's not Sylvia's or the kids fault.' She cradled the mug in her hands and took comfort from the warmth. 'As the Senior Nurse I should deal with them.' She sighed. 'There again, if I go in looking like this,' she said, running her hand over her discoloured neck.

'Oh, I don't know,' said Nancy. 'I think it would do Sylvia good to see what he did to you.' She took another drink. 'She's still in denial - swears her husband wouldn't hurt a fly.'

'You can't blame her,' said Paula. 'It must be unbearable to find out you've been living with a psychopath.' Paula coughed.' Look how long-' She coughed again.

'Are you sure you're all right?'

'Yeah, I'm fine,' said Paula. She straightened her sagging shoulders. 'I have to do this,' she said, grabbing a handful of tissues from the box on her desk. 'How about we do it together, then if I screw up you can take over?' Paula said, and then drained her mug.

'Fair enough,' said Nancy. 'Lennox is waiting for us in the unit.'

The spring sunshine glinted and birds could be heard welcoming in the new season, through the grime-encrusted windows of the visitors' room. A police woman stood in the far corner, trying to look invisible. Sylvia Charlton, her son Benjamin and daughter Fiona were crammed onto the two-seated sofa. Benjamin tapped a cigarette on the edge of a full ashtray. Lennox and Paula took the two easy chairs. Nancy, sat protectively on the arm of Paula's chair. The policewoman shuffled her feet, anxiously.

'Terrible business, Sylvia,' said Lennox. He cleared his throat. 'You must be finding all this very difficult.'

Sylvia Charlton glared accusingly at Paula. Benjamin stared at the ashtray. His sister sobbed quietly.

'As you know,' continued Lennox 'We've done the brain stem tests again and I'm afraid it confirms Alan is brain dead.' Instead of letting the news register with the family, the consultant continued in his usual blustering manner. 'Normally, we would ask you about donating his organs – but because of the legal stuff and all that.' He floundered. 'So there's no use in carrying on - we might as well get it over with and discontinue his ventilation.'

'I'm so sorry,' said Paula.

'I don't want you in here,' said Sylvia Charlton.

Nancy was about to say something, but Paula grabbed her arm. 'It's okay, I understand.' She stood up to go.

'Actually, Sylvia,' said Lennox. 'I think Paula should stay. None of this is her fault.'

'No honestly, Lennox, it's all right,' said Paula. 'I'll

be in the office if you want me.' Paula found Jeff Palmer hiding in the restroom and took him into her office. 'What's going to happen now?' she asked him.

'The investigation will go ahead,' said Jeff. 'But it could take months, years even.' He found one of the mugs still had some tea in it and finished it off. 'We might never know for certain how many he killed,' he said.

Lennox and Nancy joined them. Lennox closed the door behind him.

Nancy blew the air out of her cheeks. 'They don't want to see him again,' said Nancy. 'Apparently they said their goodbyes last night.'

The consultant, two sisters and policeman entered the unit together and crossed over to the side-ward where Alan Charlton lay on the same bed in which Frank Hoyle met his death. The group stood in an uncomfortable silence and stared at the unconscious doctor. The only movement was the rhythmic rise and fall of the patient's chest in time to the ventilator.

Jeff took a step back. Paula made her way over to the ventilator and held on to it for support. Nancy stood beside her. Lennox faced them from across the bed. No one wanted to make the first move.

'Are you sure he's brain dead?' said Jeff.

Nancy glared at him. Lennox sighed.

'You were there sergeant when we did the tests,' he said. You've seen the paperwork. I can assure you, he is definitely brain dead.'

'Sorry,' said Jeff, taking another step back. 'I suppose it's a fitting end.'

'We can't put it off any longer,' Lennox said to Paula.

Nancy cancelled the monitor alarms. Paula reached down to the controls of the ventilator. She looked at Lennox. He nodded and she turned the switch off. The pulsating beat of the ventilator stopped. The room settled into a deathly silence. Lennox reached over the bed and disconnected the tube from the machine. There was no movement from the man in the bed; no sudden intake of breath; no flicker of an eyelid. The four watched the monitor as the heart-trace slowed, until only a straight white line traversed the blank screen.

Epilogue

Column from the inside pages of the local newspaper, six months later.

Death Accident, driver convicted.
Earlier this year, eighteen year-old Jason Reilly lost control and crashed his BMW into a Vauxhall car, killing two and leaving one young man with serious head injuries. In court Reilly, admitted to aggravated vehicle taking, dangerous driving, driving with excess alcohol and failing to report an accident. Judge Robert Jackman banned Reilly from driving for five years and sent him to a young offender's institution for three years. He told Reilly '...your crass stupidity has robbed two people of their lives. The consequences of your actions will have a long lasting effect on the families of these victims, who will never see their loved ones again. I hope you spend your time in custody reflecting upon this.'

Russell Stevens never recovered from the post-traumatic stress syndrome he suffered after driving into Alan Charlton. Although the solicitor continued to work, he lost the ability to strive for anything other than inner peace. Joan Stevens flourished in her new role as head of the house. Her only regret was the loss of her son. Although Vincent was now making good progress, he planned to live with Marty following his discharge from hospital. After spending time helping to care for her brother, Marty had decided she wanted to be a nurse and already signed on for night classes to gain the qualifications she needed.

*

Jack Hobson clung onto his wife's skeletal hand. Jennifer had wrapped a protective arm around her father's shoulder. Paula and Duncan sat opposite. Malcolm had driven up from the capital and was stood at the bottom of the bed. They all watched the fitful rise and fall of Grace's chest.

Paula's scars were healing, but she often woke in the night with giant spiders haunting her dreams. Management had offered counselling, but she'd refused. All the support she needed was sat next to her. They had been sat there for several hours after the nursing staff had rang to say Grace was close to death. Paula thought her father looked tired and persuaded him to go for a break. She told Jack that Duncan would get him if there was any change. Jennifer and Malcolm went with him. Paula swapped sides and kissed her mother on the forehead.

'Do you think it's serious between Jeff and Nance?' said Duncan.

'It's already lasted longer than most of her relationships,' said Paula. She stroked Grace's arm. 'You never know with Nancy, but yeah, I reckon it's serious enough.'

Duncan got up and walked round the bed to join her. He bent over and spoke quietly into Grace's ear.

'I don't know if you can hear me Mrs Hobson,' he said. 'It's Duncan Harvey. I wanted you to know I'm going to take good care of your daughter.'

A tear trickled down Paula's cheek.

He continued. 'And I'd like to be able to call you mother-in-law.' He glanced at Paula. 'I promise if we have a bunch of kids at least one of them will be called Grace.' He kissed her forehead and straightened up. There was a box of tissues on the bedside table. Duncan took a handful, handed half to Paula and kept the rest for himself.

Nothing more was said between them until the rest of the family re-entered the room. The nature of Grace's breathing changed. They stood. Duncan held Paula's hand and then, as though preordained, Grace Hobson took her final deep breath and slipped into death. Paula hugged her father. She looked over his shoulder, smiled sadly and then mouthed to Duncan. 'Yes, please.'

Lightning Source UK Ltd.
Milton Keynes UK
10 March 2010

151182UK00001B/176/P